CW01497088

Nisha J. Tuli is an internationally bestselling author whose books feature kick-ass heroines, swoony love interests, and slow burns with plenty of heat. When she's not writing or reading, Nisha can be found enjoying travel, food, and camping with her partner, two kids, and their fluffy Samoyed.

Also by Nisha J. Tuli

THE ARTEFACTS OF OURANOS SERIES

THE NIGHTFIRE QUARTET

Not Safe for Work

NISHA J. TULI

PIATKUS

PIATKUS

First published in the US in 2025 by Forever,
An imprint of Grand Central Publishing, a division of Hachette Book Group
Published in Great Britain in 2025 by Piatkus

1 3 5 7 9 10 8 6 4 2

Copyright © 2025 by Nisha J. Tuli

The moral right of the author has been asserted.

*All characters and events in this publication, other than those
clearly in the public domain, are fictitious and any resemblance
to real persons, living or dead, is purely coincidental.*

All rights reserved.
No part of this publication may be reproduced, stored in a
retrieval system, or transmitted in any form or by any means, without
the prior permission in writing of the publisher, nor be otherwise circulated
in any form of binding or cover other than that in which it is published
and without a similar condition including this condition being
imposed on the subsequent purchaser.

A CIP catalogue record for this book
is available from the British Library.

ISBN 978-0-349-44303-4

Printed and bound in Great Britain by Clays Ltd, Elcograf S.p.A.

Papers used by Piatkus are from well-managed forests
and other responsible sources.

Piatkus
An imprint of
Little, Brown Book Group
Carmelite House
50 Victoria Embankment
London EC4Y 0DZ

The authorised representative
in the EEA is
Hachette Ireland
8 Castlecourt Centre
Dublin 15, D15 XTP3, Ireland
(email: info@hbgi.ie)

An Hachette UK Company
www.hachette.co.uk

www.littlebrown.co.uk

Dear Readers,

Not Safe for Work was inspired by the early years of my career when I worked as an engineer in my twenties. Being a biracial woman of color in a male-dominated environment was interesting, to say the least, and a few scenes in this book have some very real-life inspiration.

As a result, this is the most personal book I've ever written. If you ever find yourself thinking, "People wouldn't do or say that," I can assure you they do, and they did.

With that all in mind, I'm listing the content warnings you can expect in this book. There are some serious themes woven into the narrative. You'll find instances of sexism and racial microaggressions, along with nonconsensual touching and an incident involving the sharing of an intimate image from a past relationship. None of these things ever occur between the two main characters.

However, this story is also fun and humorous, as well as spicy hot, and full of angst, because our lives contain multitudes, and ultimately, it's about finding your happiness both in love and your career. If you've ever read one of my books, then you know how much I love a slow, agonizing burn, and this journey will be no different.

This book is a love letter to my past self, who knew within a few years that engineering was never the right choice for me. I took a lot of chances over the years to find myself here, writing this letter to you now.

I hope you love Tris and Rafe's story as much as I enjoyed creating it.

They are my heart, and I hope they'll become yours, too.

Love,
Nisha

To the person I was and the one I became.
It's never too late if you want it enough.

To my fellow engineering girlies, circa 2001–2003.
We always said we'd write a book.

Not Safe for Work

Chapter One

"On a scale of one to ten, how would you rate me?"

My attention snaps to Brian with a blink. He stands with an elbow propped on the wall of my fuzzy grey cubicle, wearing an expectant look.

"What?" I ask, not entirely listening, most of my divided attention reserved for the conversation that is currently distracting me.

"Between one and ten—what do you think?" He sweeps his hands down the length of his body like he's the prize girl in a sequined dress on a game show.

Why is he asking me this? Brian is a sweet guy, but I've never seen him that way.

Even if I did, I maintain an ironclad policy against dating any of the humpbacked trolls who stagger WMC Purcell's halls. Once upon a time, I vowed never to dip into the regressive shallows of a workplace gene pool ever again.

An atomic cloud of male laughter bursts from the office situated kitty-corner to mine. I roll my shoulders, trying to ignore it and focus on Brian. He's white, in his early thirties, and wearing a blue polo and dark, baggy jeans.

My thoughts catch up to the present. Brian was telling me about his date last night, and I missed the part about how it went because I was too focused on what was happening across the hall.

"I'd say you're a ten," he says in earnest, and I cover my mouth as something resembling a laugh-snort muffles my embarrassment. I can always count on Brian for the gentle pets my ego laps up like a newborn kitten. "I'd say I'm a seven. I have a good job, make a mean lasagna, and I know how to treat a woman."

As he's talking, my attention wanders back to Rafe Gallagher's office and the brief snippets of conversation floating across the hall.

"Trishara?"

Again, I look over. With his hands stuffed in his pockets, Brian is staring down at me with his brows furrowed in expectation. I shift as the rough fabric of my desk chair scratches the backs of my thighs.

He just referred to himself as a seven. I probably should respond to that.

"Don't sell yourself short, Brian. You're a great catch."

He flashes me a smile. "I think we'll probably go out again. She said I should call her."

"That's great," I say, meaning it. "Then you should."

Brian's primary goal in life is to settle down with a sweet wife and have lots of kids who play team sports and grow up to find stable jobs and provide a gaggle of grandchildren. And if that's what the future Mrs. Paterson also wants, then all the power to them. It sounds nice.

"You think it's okay? I shouldn't wait three days?"

As more laughter floats from Rafe's office, I offer Brian an absent wave. His gaze remains fixed on me as though I hold every answer to the mysterious ways of women in the palm of my hand.

"If a woman likes you, she wants you to call. Don't fall for that 'rules' garbage."

He considers my words, his expression skeptical.

"Would I lie to you? Trust me. If she likes you, she wants you to call."

His shoulders release, tension dipping out of his frame.

"Thanks, Tris. You're the best."

He scratches the tip of his nose, his gaze turning distant. I'm sure he's already mentally rehearsing what he's planning to say to his potential future bride.

"Have you been out with anyone lately?" he asks a moment later, and my somewhat average mood tumbles down a hillside.

Lately, the only *out* I've been is to the Chinese takeout place at the end of my block. *Out* is then promptly followed by a wardrobe change—flannel adjacent—and a USB-powered date with my Lelo Sona 2.

"Not really," I say, my smile bland, hoping Brian takes the hint I'm spelling out with flashing red strobe lights. I make a show of checking my smartwatch. "Oh, looks like it's almost time for the big announcement."

Brian pushes away from the narrow opening of my cubicle. "Who do you think the lucky two will be?" He rubs his hands together as if this is a mystery worthy of Professor Plum.

"I couldn't *possibly* guess." Somehow, he completely misses my sarcasm as he considers my response, a furrow denting his brow.

My gaze drifts to Rafe's office again, where he sits at his desk conversing with two other men. His is a real office, not this starched, achromatic cube. With walls and windows and a large faux-wood desk and a leather chair in which he is casually tipped, laughing at something Jeremy has just said. They've been discussing whatever male sportsing event is currently in season, not that I'm at all interested in what they've been saying for the past twenty minutes.

Months ago, WMC Purcell's head office announced the launch of a new leadership program to identify the company's most promising future stars.

Every branch across the country would select two up-and-coming engineers to spend three weeks on a training retreat at a mystery destination, where they'd rub elbows with senior executives and be gilded as future WMC royalty.

A year-long executive training program for five lucky winners is also up for grabs.

It's a golden corporate ladder descending from heaven.

Or a noose, depending on how you look at it, I suppose.

But nepotism and favoritism are the foundation on which this company was built.

Thus, the first name on that list will be Rafe's. His uncle manages this branch, but more notably, his father is one of six senior VPs at WMC.

They are the kings, and Rafe is their swaggering crown prince.

"You coming?" Brian asks with a jerk of his thumb.

"You go. I'll come in a minute."

The muffled thunder of footsteps echoes through the building's pebble-carpeted halls as everyone descends on the atrium in a swell of excited chatter, thrilled for an excuse to get away from their desks for an hour.

Also, there are rumors of cake after the announcement.

After Brian leaves, I turn to my computer, minimizing my

LinkedIn page with a discontented sigh. I'm considering applying for a new job with a sustainability consulting firm, but my inertia mimics the consistency of hardened lava.

I've been at WMC Purcell for almost five years, and I've completely stalled out. My future stretches before me, but the road I'm traveling is blank.

A loud thud ricochets from across the hall, and I spin around, curling my lip.

Rory has his face plastered against the narrow half-window, his ruddy cheek rendered into featureless putty. Where did he come from?

"What the hell, man? That hurt," Rory growls as he pushes himself from the glass and whips around to glare at Jeremy and Scott, the two men sitting in Rafe's office. They're laughing so hard, I'm surprised they haven't choked up a lung.

Rory lunges, but Rafe leaps up, snagging him by the arm.

"Relax. It was an accident," Rafe says as Rory shrinks back.

Rafe isn't laughing, though. In fact, he looks pissed.

It's evident from his hunched shoulders that Rory's also furious, but honestly, it's hard to tell the difference from his typical *Homo habilis* posture. He wipes a hand under his nose, glares at Jeremy and Scott, and stalks out of the office with his hands curled into fists.

As Rafe's cousin on his mom's side, the second WMC leadership retreat spot is already earmarked for him. What does it feel like to know you've earned nothing yourself? Maybe they think it's rightfully theirs.

Jeremy and Scott file out after Rory, still laughing about whatever boneheaded man thing caused the window crash. These men are the Khakis—white hetero men of mediocre competence and undeserved confidence who wouldn't know their way to a clitoris if someone strung them over a swamp rife with testicle-eating crocodiles.

And they rule this place from bottom to top.

As I slide on the flats I kicked under my desk earlier, a sensation prickles the back of my neck. I peer over my shoulder to find Rafe watching me through his office window.

If I had to rate *him* on a scale of one to ten, I'd have two very distinct answers.

Considering the question from the objective viewpoint of a completely disinterested bystander with absolutely *no* emotional attachment, I'd give him an eight.

He dresses marginally better than the other Khakis, and there's that curling thing his hair does when he's due for a haircut—okay, maybe a nine.

But he's my Lex Luthor. My gateway to the Dark Side. My nemesis.

And that feeling is mutual.

Maybe a 9.5.

His deep brown eyes burn like caramel, brittle but fiery, definitely leaving layers of scar tissue if you get too close. Maybe a 9.75.

It's casual Friday, and his navy Henley fits him in all the right ways, skimming over broad shoulders, curved biceps, and the tantalizing hint of defined abs.

Fine, a 10.

He turns to grab his phone off his desk, the tendons in his forearms flexing in a way that borders on erotic. Dark jeans cling to the most magnificent ass I've ever seen. He's a sculpture with a discus competing in the Olympics circa 800 BC.

Fine.

Rafe Gallagher is a fucking eleven out of ten.

The catch—and isn't there always one?—is Rafe's personality.

When he opens his mouth, his stock plummets, landing him squarely in the neighborhood of a floundering two. He's overconfident and smug, and we've spent the last several years locked in a battle of professional wills.

He tucks his phone in his back pocket and strides past my cube, throwing me a smirk that conjures up images of fairy tales, villains, and maidens locked in high stone towers.

I frown because despite our offices being so close together, Rafe and I haven't interacted much beyond professional necessity (including several work-related disagreements) for a while. But lately, I've caught him looking at me more than once with an expression I don't understand.

And that smirk.

(Admittedly, there are days when that smirk makes him a twelve.)

"It's cake time, Trishara!"

Again, I'm caught off guard when Molly Ackerman appears around the corner with a huge smile on her face. She's one of my best friends and the only thing that makes this place tolerable. She has pale white skin dusted with freckles. Standing barely five feet tall, she's wearing a denim jumpsuit, bright pink Chucks, and her usual retro cat-eye glasses. Her red hair hangs to her shoulders in a wild mess of curls. She's adorable, and I love her.

With a roll of my eyes, I stand and smooth down the front of my outfit. I'm wearing a vintage-inspired peplum dress in hunter green and a pair of cherry-red ballet flats. I don't believe in things like casual Friday. "Let's get this charade over with. They better have sprung for bakery cake and not that cheap grocery store crap."

"You love the cheap grocery store crap," Molly says, linking her arm through mine.

"I know, but it's the principle."

We join the flow of humans as we coalesce like swarms of locusts infesting the central atrium filled with grey tables and grey plastic chairs. It seems we're two of the last to arrive. A hand waves as we enter, and Brian gestures us over, pointing to the two empty seats he's saved at the front.

Amid the din of chatter, I glance across the row at Rafe sitting at the far end.

Every department in the building is here: procurement, accounting, and human resources.

Clearly, they all heard about the cake, too.

Thanks to these other departments, the gender ratio is a little more balanced. Me, Molly, and a handful of others make up the small but mighty contingent of WMC's non-male engineers. There was a time when the idea of smashing through glass in a male-dominated field was thrilling. But over the years, it's just left me as wrung out as a threadbare dishcloth.

Someone has set up a small stage at the front of the room consisting of large wooden blocks covered in pebbled grey carpet. Grey. Everything is grey. I used to love this color. It represented my future. The color of corporate America. The color of high-rise offices and boardroom tables. Of inked contracts and binding handshakes.

But as the years have passed and I've been skipped over for every promotion I've been more than qualified to fill, grey represents something else. The color of a wheel that spins endlessly, only stopping for a chosen few. Now, it's the color of my faded future.

David Gallagher—Rafe's father—steps onto the stage and clears his throat. He's deigned to visit the peasants today.

Our branch lies sprawled like a concrete octopus in the suburbs, where the parking is ample and the surroundings are sterile. In contrast, WMC's glossy executive team perches at the top of one of the highest skyscrapers in downtown Chicago.

David looks just like his son—only older and more refined. Handsome, painfully so, and I glower at the annoying gift of the Gallagher family genes. He wears a perfectly tailored suit, probably cut from the souls of past WMC employees.

Rafe's uncle Charles joins David on the stage. Charles is also constructed from the Gallaghers' gorgeous DNA blueprint but lacks the swagger to drive the point home.

He's more down-to-earth and prefers to join everyone for 99-cent wings and beer at the Swan and Rooster—the nearby pub favored on Friday afternoons—where we all pretend happy hour with our coworkers is a viable substitute for meaningful relationships.

Charles wears a loose white button-up shirt, baggy medium-wash jeans, and white gym shoes. David eyes his brother with cool detachment, as if he's judging his informal attire.

Apparently, David Gallagher doesn't believe in casual Friday, either.

Charles taps the microphone in his hand, a screech erupting

into a collective flinch as a thousand eardrums rupture. His nervous laughter echoes through the room, and part of me pities his gene's rejection of that Gallagher charisma.

The room has grown warm, the sun beating through the glass ceiling. I fan myself where sweat condenses in the hollow of my throat, shifting as the backs of my thighs stick to the plastic surface. When I glance across the room, my gaze catches Rafe's, who's again peering in my direction. I narrow my eyes, trying to summon my most damning manifestation of resting bitch face.

His response is another evil smirk that's suddenly leaving me conflicted in ways I don't care to examine too closely.

He's Lucifer, wearing the disguise of a Ralph Lauren model.

"Hello, everyone," Charles says timidly into the microphone. The crowd ignores him, too absorbed in their conversations.

David Gallagher arches a dark, judgy eyebrow full of such disdain that I'm surprised Charles doesn't melt into the floor. It's then I notice Rafe watching his father with his jaw clenched and his eyes sparking with what seems like anger. What I suddenly wouldn't give to be a fly on the wall at the Gallagher Thanksgiving dinner.

"Everyone, please!" Charles says louder this time, and an audible hush descends over the crowd. He waits a few more seconds before taking a deep breath and powering on. "I'm very excited to welcome you all here today to announce the candidates representing the Chicago branch at WMC Purcell's first-ever Rising Stars Leadership Retreat. This is a very special opportunity for two of our most promising engineers."

He pauses as if waiting for applause and turns tomato red when it fails to materialize.

We're all just here for the cake.

"Anyway," he squeaks, then drones on for a few minutes about WMC and its corporate mandate. I tune out as I stare around the room for something interesting to occupy my attention.

It's growing warmer, the air stifling as the sun rises higher. A trickle of sweat runs down my back, and I shift as my skin peels off the plastic.

Molly looks equally uncomfortable, her pale skin flushed as she pushes limp curls out of her face.

"I know you've all been wondering where the retreat will be held," Charles says. "I'm pleased to say it will take place at the Naupaka Resort on the beautiful island of Maui."

A collective sound, part groan and part gasp, rushes through the crowd, and I can't help but join them. Three weeks in Hawaii sounds like a dream. I know I'm not going, but I allow myself the briefest fantasy of pink umbrella drinks and crystal-clear water, anyway.

"The first rising star"—Charles takes a dramatic pause—"is Rafe Gallagher."

A polite round of clapping ensues, and I look over at Rafe, expecting a smug smile. Instead, I see a heated look pass between father and son, the senior tipping his chin so slightly I nearly miss it. Rafe blinks slowly, then pushes himself up and strides onto the stage, where he stiffly shakes hands with his uncle and father.

Charles clears his throat, and I watch Rory, sitting a few rows back, his knee bouncing in anticipation. He's the very worst kind of Khaki. Not just drab but outright corrosive. The office lech, he's a repulsive pig who has more than one count of sexual harassment against him, and that's just the tip of his crimes. His very presence makes my skin crawl off my body.

I keep dated notes about him saved in a password-protected folder on my personal cloud drive—just in case. Of what, I'm not sure. But I have to believe that someday, they might prove useful.

I return my attention to the front, where Charles is still talking. He glances nervously at David before they both inexplicably look at me.

Then, in a move I never saw coming, Charles Gallagher draws a wildcard and flings it hard enough to slice an artery.

"Please congratulate our second Rising Star of Tomorrow, Trishara Malik."

Chapter Two

An uncomfortable tension twists in my lungs. My brows squeeze together, and I'm convinced that I've misheard my name. I've blacked out, and I'm going to wake up staring at the glass ceiling.

I'm imagining Rafe standing over me, an eyebrow arched in disdain. Molly trying to revive me as she gently slaps my cheeks. Brian yelling about how he's a seven and asking if he should text his date from last night.

"Tris," Molly hisses. "Tris!" Her fingers dig into my arm as she shakes me loose. "Go! Charles just called your name."

My mouth parts with a surprised breath. "That can't be. That makes no sense."

"Miss Malik," Charles says. "Will you please come to the front?"

Heads are turning, people peering through the crowd, wondering why the second lucky contestant hasn't floated up to accept her tiara.

"Tris," Molly hisses again. "Go!"

"He said my name," I hiss out the side of my mouth, my eyes never leaving the towering forms of David, Charles, and Rafe Gallagher, who study me like a snarling three-headed beast, ready to tear me limb from limb.

"Yes! That's what I'm trying to tell you." Molly shakes me again, placing her hand in the middle of my back, attempting to dislodge my ass from my chair.

"But why?"

Molly is panicking as hundreds of curious stares find me in the crowd. "Go!"

It feels like I've just done something very, very wrong.

"Miss Malik," comes a different voice. This time it's David. He's taken the mic from his brother, and his gaze bores into me like he wants to tear out my spleen and feed it to his pet hyena. I see where his son gets it. "Please. Will you join us at the front?"

Finally. *Finally*, my brain catches up with my body, and I push myself up, wincing at the sting as my thighs tear away from the rough plastic. I place one foot carefully in front of the other. It's a good thing I'm wearing flats today. My legs feel as hollow as plastic straws as I reach the front.

The room is awkwardly silent. They must wonder why I'm acting so strange.

Why *am* I acting so strange?

Because this shouldn't be me.

Because I graduated with a 4.0 GPA, and I was supposed to *do* things. I was supposed to make something of myself. And I tried. I really did.

After finishing college at the top of my class, I snagged a great job at an environmental start-up—one of those cool, hip places with an espresso lounge, unlimited PTO, and a pool table in the middle of the floor. I thought I'd make a difference working directly with large corporations to minimize their adverse environmental impacts.

But that turned out to be a complete disaster, some of it my fault and some of it not.

When an opening at WMC presented itself, I was desperate. The job involved project management and engineering design for clients in the energy and mining sectors. It wasn't what I ever saw myself doing, but it felt like I had no choice.

I was shocked when they offered me the position, and I accepted it on the spot.

So, I tried to put the past behind me and decided this would be my dream instead. I settled in to assemble the next thirty-odd years of my career with my sights set on the corner office and the hairline cracks in the thick glass ceiling over my head.

But I hadn't counted on just how deeply the stagnant stick of sexism remains rooted in the mud—even if they built the engineering building where I finished my degree without a single women's bathroom.

First, I was passed over for a supervisor promotion in favor of a man with less experience and fewer projects under his belt. That was three years ago. Then there was the operations manager job that went to a man less than a year from retirement and a string of reprimands on his employment record. Then there was the department head job that went to a man—nay, a boy—who had arrived fresh from college and whose dad worked alongside David.

Little by little, each of these insults chipped pieces of me away. Battered by the elements, the edges of my ambition slowly eroded into a shapeless, worn surface.

Then, a year ago, an opening came up for team lead of the environmental division.

I'd worked in each of the five departments that formed the

division. My record was impeccable. I'd exceeded all of my KPIs. I'd demonstrated my ability to lead over and over, stepping up to help solve every problem we ran into. I poured my heart and soul into the application. Done all they'd asked of me. And they gave the job to Rafe.

To make matters worse, Rafe then found my presence so objectionable that he asked to have me moved to a different team so I wouldn't be reporting to him. And though I can't really explain it, *that* hurt more than I've ever been able to admit out loud.

It was the final dart straight to the center of my chest. I went into myself for weeks until Molly finally dragged me out. But the fight died in me then. None of it seemed worth it anymore.

Now, I come to work and do what I'm asked, but I've stopped trying to excel. I am no longer one of this company's bright young stars. My shine wore off long ago.

So, what am I doing up here?

Somewhat tentatively, I approach the center of the platform, where Rafe waits with his hands stuffed into the pockets of his designer jeans. Casual Friday suits him—of course it does. Everything looks good on him.

"Excellent," Charles says, gesturing me closer with a hand hovering an inch above my shoulder. He positions me next to Rafe, a foot of space separating us. Charles is saying something else about the retreat, but I've stopped listening, white noise roaring in my ears.

"Let's get a picture," Charles says, gesturing to his executive assistant, Belinda. She's on the floor, perched in a squat, her phone aimed at us like a medieval crossbow.

"Stand together," she orders, waving her hands. I don't move, I can't move, but Rafe shifts an infinitesimal inch.

"Closer!" Her high-pitched screech is so unnerving that I finally do as she asks and move a fraction closer to Rafe.

Belinda sighs and stands up with her hands on her hips.

"What is wrong with you?" She walks towards the platform, lays her hand on my calf, and *shoves*. Surely, this is some kind of HR violation. I stumble, and Rafe's hand catches my waist, steadying me. That simple touch burns through the fabric of my dress as a sharp inhale scrapes the back of my throat. What the hell was that?

Tossing a dark look over my shoulder, I find Rafe looking down at me with a devious smirk. I don't think I've ever stood this close to him—has he always been so tall?

"Careful, Malik," he says.

It's so low it's a whisper, but his voice stamps itself between my shoulder blades, sending the worst kind of shiver down my spine. I narrow my eyes before turning back to Belinda.

"Slide in just behind her," Belinda orders, and Rafe must also feel the pinch of her screech because he concedes.

Now he's standing so close I can feel the warmth of his body. He smells like soap and fresh laundry. No cologne. It's casual day, and this is Rafe's natural smell. Why am I even noticing this? I can't stand Rafe Gallagher. He's a jerk, and I've never met anyone more full of himself. He's eye candy. Nothing more.

To prove my point (solely to myself), I flip a thick lock of my black hair over my shoulder, lashing it against his chest with the ferocity of a lion tamer's whip. I hear him emit a small grunt, but he says nothing in response.

My own smirk is triumphant. Score 1 Trishara.

Belinda returns to her crouch, pointing her camera at us. I feel the curiosity of every eye in the room and applaud my rigid stance on casual Fridays. I look amazing in this dress. It makes my waist look tiny and my butt look high and round. It was worth the hours spent hunting through the racks of my favorite discounted designer shop.

Belinda takes approximately three thousand photos as I breathe through my mouth, trying not to ingest a single stray particle of Rafe's aroma. She stands, nods at her phone, and taps on the screen. "This will be perfect for the company newsletter."

Finally released from her web, Rafe and I break apart. I shake off the lingering effects of my body's traitorous physical reactions. Even if he wasn't the world's biggest asshole, Rafe has a girlfriend, Hannah. I think. Molly and I actually have a theory they've broken up because I overheard him on the phone in his office ages ago discussing rings with what I assumed was a jeweler, but an announcement never came.

I fully expected her to show it off at the office summer barbecue last month, but Rafe attended alone. Maybe she was just busy.

Regardless, she's thin and tanned, with long blond hair and blue eyes. The kind of woman practically every straight man lusts over. Gorgeous and sexy and supermodelish. I've only met her a few times at various company functions, and she sort of treated me like I was beneath her notice. But I also only briefly interacted with her, so who knows? She might have simply been expressing herself because she finds work parties boring. I know I do.

"How about a round of applause for our lucky pair?" Charles says into the microphone, and the room erupts into clapping amid demands to get to the cake. "Please enjoy some refreshments and have a great rest of your day."

At that, the room erupts into chatter as the herd lumbers towards a long table where an army of tidy frosted white cake squares have been set out on tiny paper plates. Giant coolers sit at the end, where lemonade is poured into clear plastic cups.

Molly runs over and hops up on the stage. "This is going to be amazing!" Her eyes shine with zero sums of jealousy. I'm so lucky to have her.

"It doesn't make any sense. Why me?"

"That's a good question." Rory stands on the other side of me now, his shoulders stooped, glowering at me with a pair of dull green eyes. He steps forward, lips twisted into an ugly sneer. "How did you—"

"Don't," Rafe practically snarls, a large hand clamping onto his cousin's shoulder and jerking him back. "Shut up before you say something stupid. As usual."

Rory pins Rafe with a glare. "How did she swing this?" He points an accusing finger as though I'm the one responsible. Molly bristles, her chest puffing up like an angry peacock.

"Just shut up, Rory," Rafe says again, his jaw hard and his eyes flashing. "Go have some cake." His command oozes with authority, and my stomach tightens just a little bit. But why is he defending me?

"Fine. Have *fun* in Hawaii," Rory spits with a stream of venom before turning and heading for the front of the cake line, shoving his way in like the asshole he is.

"Sorry about that," Rafe says, assessing me up and down as though he's also searching for an explanation written on my skin.

"I don't need you speaking for me," I bite out.

Rafe's mouth flattens into a line as Molly tugs on my hand. "C'mon. Let's get some cake too."

I scan the room, looking for David or Charles Gallagher, but they've already escaped.

I turn to Molly. "Get me a piece, will you? I need to do something first."

Without waiting for a response, I toss a glare to Rafe and then hop off the stage, heading towards Charles's office.

"Tris! Where are you going?" Molly calls.

"I just need to talk to them," I shout back as I exit the atrium and beeline for Charles's office.

Belinda's desk sits empty outside the wide double doors. She's probably in the cake line. One door sits slightly ajar, and I hear David and Charles talking. I don't bother to knock as I burst into the room.

Both men turn at my entrance, their eyebrows raised. David Gallagher, in his flawless suit, is so damn intimidating that I clutch my stomach and regret my decision to come storming in. But I gather the shreds of my courage and straighten my shoulders.

"What is it, Miss Malik?" David asks with a chilly gaze.

Miss Malik. Women in this office are always referred to as *miss* like we're all in a regency period drama. Only the men are granted the dignity of their first names. I plant my fists on my hips and adopt my most put-upon look.

"Why was I selected for the leadership retreat?"

A brief pause hangs in the room before David answers. "As one of the company's bright young minds, we felt you earned the opportunity to represent the Chicago branch."

His face is so straight you could hang a fireplace mantel by it.

"Bullshit." The word erupts from my mouth—nearly five years of disappointment launched at him in two acidic syllables. "I've been passed over for every opportunity I've ever applied for at this company. I've barely advanced in the almost five years I've worked here."

At first, I'm unsure if I imagine the guilt crossing David's face.

The two men exchange an uncomfortable look I can't parse.

"We'd like to give this opportunity to someone who represents the future of this company," David says, leaning against Charles's desk as he folds his arms and crosses one ankle over the other. "You are correct that we've been remiss in recognizing your talents and those of many others. WMC is taking the necessary steps to correct that."

The skin on the back of my scalp burns hot. "Excuse me?"

"We understand that WMC is lacking in certain areas, Miss Malik. And we'd like to do something about that, starting by offering you a spot at the retreat."

I blink, unsure about how to feel about this. He isn't wrong. WMC *should* be doing more to encourage a more diversified workforce, and something like the leadership retreat is a perfect way to do that. Attending will open doors left and right.

But something about this conversation feels off.

"Is this for *me* or to make *you* look good?" I ask.

David levels me with a confident look, his eyes the same fathomless brown as Rafe's. The color of deep dark holes drilled into the center of the earth.

"We're sending you because we see a lot of potential in you, Miss Malik."

"So, you admit I should have been awarded at least one of those promotions?"

His expression gives away nothing, and I make a mental note never to agree to a game of poker.

I already know he's the kind of man who votes left every four years because he likes the *idea* of a world built on equality, but he's also never had to consider what that really means beyond his limited worldview.

There's doing the right thing, and there's doing the right thing for the wrong reasons.

"Do you want to go or not?" he asks, clearly deflecting my question.

"Of course I want to go."

I *do* want to go. I do want this chance, but I can't help but feel like this is also some sort of trap.

"Then what is the problem here?"

I'm not sure where to begin. I weigh salient arguments and articulate scathing points in my head, prepared to spear him with my logic and fire his detestable privilege at him like a cannon. I want it to hurt. I want it to *burn*.

Instead, what comes out of my mouth is "I want to fly first class."

This isn't my proudest moment.

David blinks. It's the only chink in his suit of Armani armor.

"Very well."

He glances over his shoulder at Charles, who wears a worried expression, his hands clasped on his desk as if wishing he could hide under it.

"Have Mrs. Hunt book a first-class flight for Miss Malik."

Charles nods slowly.

"And I want a suite," I continue. "On the top floor. A big one with a balcony and a view of the ocean."

"Fine," David says, the cool edge of his tone faltering just the tiniest bit.

I fold my arms and cock my hip. "And new luggage."

I'm on a roll now, and I can't seem to stop myself.

"Put it on your corporate card. Charles will approve the expense."

I try not to let my surprise show at how well this is working. He definitely has something to gain here, too.

"And I want a raise."

"Miss Malik," David says, a warning nestled in his voice. I raise my hands in surrender. Fine, that was one ask too many.

I'll return to this later because I'm sure we're wading into murky legislative waters.

But I also know HR departments exist to protect the companies they work for, not their employees, so today, I'm deciding on the path of least resistance. I don't like it, but maybe this retreat—despite everything—is a chance to start fresh and regain what I lost. One last gasp before I finally concede that this place isn't a part of the future I want for myself.

"Okay, fine. No raise."

"Are we good here?" David tilts his head and pins me with a dark look that rivals his son's. I wonder if they practice together in front of a mirror, out-glaring one another.

I nod. For now, we are.

He dips his chin in response.

"Then have a nice time, Miss Malik."

Chapter Three

Molly's eyes widen when I drag my new suitcases from my closet. She blows out a low whistle as I flop one on the bed and flip it open. After my run-in with David and Charles, I took the afternoon off and headed straight for the nearest Louis Vuitton.

There, I purchased a complete luggage set, including a ridiculously overpriced makeup bag and tote. These gorgeous creations are now the most valuable thing I own. I've been deeply considering the logistics of having myself buried inside the largest one.

"Gallagher is going to flip," she squeals, running a loving hand along the smooth monogrammed leather. "Look at this stitching. And the hardware. It's so *shiny*. I can see myself in it." She crosses her eyes and sticks out her tongue at her reflection.

I scoff. "Let him flip."

She kicks back and leans on the headboard as she watches me pack. Last night, we went out for dinner as a bon voyage before I leave this afternoon. After too many Moscow mules, we stumbled to my apartment, where Molly spent the night curled up on the other half of my bed.

I open my drawer, pulling out a myriad of items with price tags still attached. I've been shopping nonstop for the past week, curating the most ideal *tropical-meets-party-girl-meets-business-casual* wardrobe anyone has ever beheld.

"Maybe you'll meet someone interesting," Molly says as she eyes up the sexy red dress I'm holding. It was much too expensive, but the color is perfect against my light brown skin, and the cut makes my boobs look amazing. I couldn't resist. I'm not sure if I'll need it, but I'm hoping a reason presents itself.

"I'm supposed to be there for work," I say as I carefully roll it into a tight bundle and place it in the suitcase.

Molly rolls her eyes, "Oh yeah, that dress definitely screams 'work.'" We both giggle before her expression turns sly. "That dress has nothing to do with your obsession with Rafe, does it?"

She says it so casually that there isn't anything casual about it.

I pause my packing to shoot laser beams with my eyes. "I'm not obsessed with Rafe."

I'm totally obsessed with Rafe, but not in the way Molly is implying.

No, my obsession was forged in the hellfires of acrimony. My obsession is purely professional, and I operate on the premise of keeping an eye on your enemies. I should embroider that on a pillow or tattoo it on the inside of my thigh. "As soon as we land in Maui, I'm ditching his ass. Rafe Gallagher isn't ruining this trip for me."

"Mm-hmm," Molly says, not looking at me as she flips through a magazine, avoiding my gaze.

"Even if I didn't loathe him, he has a girlfriend."

"Except he doesn't," she says, looking up. "I know you keep trying to convince yourself of that, but there is no way they're still dating."

I know she's probably right, and my stomach responds with this weird spinning thing I don't like.

So, I scoff as I slide open my underwear drawer. "It doesn't matter. You know I don't date at the office."

Molly sighs, and I avoid looking at her, knowing I'm about to be scolded. "Everyone isn't Leo, Tris. Stop projecting what he did on every man you meet."

Finally, I meet her gaze, clutching a fistful of silky thongs.

Leo.

The reason I flamed out at my first job with Sustain—the one I actually wanted.

Two charismatic brothers owned the company—they were both brilliant and gorgeous, and Leo took an interest in me during my first few months. Starry-eyed and flattered by his attention, I leaned into it. He had that whole tortured artist vibe, even if he got his start by puzzling out water quality calculations. He was in his thirties and too old for me, and I already knew he would probably break my heart, so I started dating him.

It lasted a year, though I didn't see him often, considering he split his time between Chicago and LA. But he had a way of making me feel special, and so I fell in love with him, too.

Then I found out he had another girlfriend on the other side of the country. All the signs had been there, but I ignored them, overwhelmed by his focus (when I had it) and an extreme lack of youthful judgment.

When I confronted him, he didn't take it well. He thought I was overreacting, which tells you everything you need to know about him right there. I broke it off, and I was sure he would fire me.

Instead, he did me one better and shared a private photo of me with his brother. Before I knew it, everyone in the office had enjoyed an eyeful of me in my underwear, and I had no choice but to quit, enter the witness protection program, and change my name to Susan.

Molly is the only person outside those days who knows the entire story.

"I . . . know," I say, responding to her comment, though even I hear the lack of conviction in it.

"A vacation fling is exactly what you need," she insists.

We've had this conversation before. Many times.

And I'm grateful that she cares enough to worry.

But she also doesn't get how dark those days were for me.

After I left Sustain, it became clear everyone in the "environment scene" is a hypocritical gossip, and no one else would hire me. Leo knew everyone and essentially had me blacklisted. I'll never forget an interview in which the firm's partners claimed they couldn't hire someone with my image problems—as if wearing underwear is a crime and I wasn't the victim of a gross breach of trust. I could practically see the word *whore* written in speech bubbles hanging over their heads.

"Why do you think I bought the dress?" I ask, hoping to assuage her concerns.

I know she's right, and I do want to move past it, but much like my career, my love life has also gone stale and dry.

"Good," Molly says. "Then make sure you wear it."

Once I'm finished packing, I call my Lyft, and Molly scoots off the bed and goes in search of her coat.

"Have so much fun," she says. "I'll miss you. Work is going to be so boring without you. Text me every day. I want to hear *everything* that happens."

She wraps her arms around me and squeezes tight.

"I'll send you a million pictures," I promise. "It'll be like I never left."

After checking in at the ticket counter and handing off my luggage, I head towards the airport lounge, intent on taking advantage of all the freebies afforded by my first-class ticket.

I'm wearing a sleeveless black jumpsuit and a pair of gold sandals. I can already feel the warm breezes and hear the crash of the ocean. I don't really like sand—I hate how it gets inside everything—and I don't particularly care for swimming, but three weeks with ice-cold drinks sipped in my own private cabana suits me just fine.

The airport lounge stretches into miles of black leather seating arranged around pale wooden tables. I flash my phone at the friendly woman sitting at the front desk, and she waves me through.

My first stop is the bar, where I order a glass of Prosecco. Then, I grab a small plate with a few tiny desserts and find a chair facing the floor-to-ceiling windows. I love watching the planes take off to far-flung destinations. I imagine the passengers heading on adventures to witness their first waterfall or sample their first bite of some new dish they didn't even know existed. I imagine them falling in love with their new favorite place or, best of all, sharing a kiss on top of a mountain at sunset.

I love the endless possibilities of airports and the way anything can happen.

A moment later, my phone buzzes with a text from my dad.

My parents nearly exploded with pride when I told them about the retreat. They have only some idea of how much I've floundered since college. I never told them about Leo because I knew they'd disapprove of our relationship. And it was easy enough to hide since he wasn't around much. When things went off the rails, I couldn't bear to tell them, so I lied and said I left Sustain because it wasn't the right fit.

When I couldn't find work, I was terrified that I'd have to move back home and be forced to explain what happened. They would have been horrified. I love them to death, but they're big on milestones and achievements. They're only impressed if my younger brother and I are accomplishing something. I couldn't bear their disappointment if they ever found out what I'd done to myself.

During my job search, they worried endlessly, calling me every day and inviting me over for dinner to stuff me full of samosas and send me home laden with plastic containers filled with vindaloo and roti.

If they knew about all my missed promotions, their quiet pity would crush me.

Finally, having good news to share about my job was a sigh of relief for all of us.

I slide open my phone.

Dad: You got to the airport? All checked in?

Me: Yep. I'm just waiting to board.

Dad: Do you need anything?

Me: No, I'm good.

Dad: Call your mother when you land. I'm proud
of you.

Me: Thanks. Love you.

I smile at my phone and then place it on the table.

After a few minutes of watching the planes, I pull a book from my monogrammed tote and settle back with a new romantasy series I recently started.

"Is this seat taken?" asks a deep male voice about fifteen minutes later. I scowl up at Rafe Gallagher, who stands with a messenger bag slung over his shoulder. I can't help but notice his hair is just the kind of messy that makes me want to leave him everything in my will.

"What are you doing here?" I ask, striving to look down my nose from a seated position.

"Going to Hawaii." He pulls his bag over his head and sinks into the leather chair beside me.

"I know that. But what are you doing *here*?" I gesture to the room to encompass our surroundings. "Shouldn't you be waiting out there?"

He shrugs his wide shoulders, and I also note how his burgundy button-up clings to the curve of his biceps. The sleeves are rolled to his elbows, and my attention briefly lingers on the flex of his forearms, the light dusting of dark hair, and the veins that pop against his tanned golden skin.

"Belinda said she booked our tickets together," he says, his gaze focused out the window.

Dammit, Belinda. This is *my* blackmail.

I look around the room again. "Where's your dad? Is he on this flight, too?"

Rafe shakes his head. "No, he left yesterday to meet with the other execs before the retreat begins."

He shifts in his seat, his hips thrusting as he tugs on the legs of his jeans and settles back. Someone, *somewhere*, must have turned up the furnace as I stare at his denim-clad thighs, willing my gaze away from anywhere deemed inappropriate by the WMC Purcell HR manual.

Rafe glances at me, giving me a once-over. "A little early to be drinking, isn't it, Trishara?" he asks, eyeing the delicate glass perched in my hand.

Pinning him with a defiant stare, I drain the rest of the contents in one gulp. I might regret that later. "It's five p.m. in London."

"We aren't in London."

I place the glass on the low table between us. "You're almost as smart as everyone pretends you are, Rafe."

A muscle tics in the precise line of his chiseled jaw, and he turns back to gaze out the window. Assuming that ends our conversation, I flip my book open.

"What are you reading?" He tips his head to the side and peers at the cover. I was just getting to the part where the main character was about to give a revenge blowjob to the hot fae prince who kidnapped her, but there's no way I'm telling Rafe that.

"Why are you turning red?" he asks, a light dancing in his eyes.

My nostrils flare. I refuse to be embarrassed. I'm a grown woman, and thanks to my trust issues with the entire male species, it's been almost a year since I've had sex. There's nothing wrong with fulfilling my needs through the pages of a smutty novel. Rafe raises an arrogant eyebrow when I remain silent.

"You can borrow it when I'm done," I answer. "Maybe you'll learn something about how to please a woman."

I don't wait for a response. Instead, I ignore him and return to my reading, finding it impossible to concentrate thanks to his suffocating presence.

A moment later, Rafe stands and snags my empty drink.

"What are you doing?" I ask.

He peers down at me with the delicate glass dangling from one of his large hands.

"Getting you a refill."

"Oh...thanks."

He tips his chin and heads for the bar.

My frown deepens as I wonder why on earth he's being nice to me.

Rafe and I don't *do* nice.

The first time I met him was a few weeks after I'd started at WMC. I was distracted by my phone and nearly crashed into him in the hall. He grabbed me to keep me from falling, and then I looked up into the most beautiful, deep brown eyes I'd ever seen.

We stared at each other for several seconds, and it sounds ridiculous, but it almost felt like a movie. Like that moment when the crowd parts and you see someone across the room and zap—instant attraction.

But I immediately recoiled from it. After what happened with

Leo, I wasn't about to fall for another pretty face. And certainly not one at the office. I froze up, shook him off, and then walked away.

Over the next few months, I did my best to avoid him, though it wasn't always possible due to the nature of our work. He was smart and charismatic, and he reminded me too much of Leo—not physically—but Rafe had the same effortless, confident aura. It scared me. *He* scared me.

It was about a year into my time at WMC when we were assigned to the same project and got into a heated disagreement about how to reroute a pipeline around a protected wetland. His method was cheaper and quicker, but I was positive it would result in an inferior outcome. We argued about it until we reached a begrudging compromise, but neither of us was satisfied.

From that moment on, we couldn't seem to agree on anything. We butted heads at every turn. Slowly, we became something else. Slowly, we became adversaries. Everything became a competition between us. Who could work the fastest. Who could solve problems the most efficiently. Who could produce the best results.

And it's been that way ever since.

A few moments later, Rafe returns with a fresh glass for me and a beer for himself. He's also acquired a small ceramic plate with a few miniature desserts—I already devoured several before he arrived. I watch him pick up a tiny lemon tart and pop it into his mouth before he grimaces.

"Problem?" I ask.

He drops the plate on the table like it's personally offended him and wipes his hands. "Tastes a bit like cardboard."

"Oh," I say because I thought it tasted fine. I didn't realize Rafe Gallagher had such a picky palate. He goes for his beer, taking a long swallow, and I give him a pointed look when he wipes his mouth with the back of his hand.

"Someone told me we're on London time," he responds, and I huff out an unexpected snort. I cover my mouth, my cheeks flushing at the undignified sound. The corner of Rafe's lips twitch, almost like he's clamping down on a smile.

It catches me entirely off guard.

Rafe smiles a lot. He smiles at his friends and his coworkers. He smiles at his girlfriend and his assistant. He smiles at the Khakis and Belinda. At Molly and Brian and Charles. Even at his dad, who I get the sense he doesn't like very much.

But Rafe Gallagher never, *ever* smiles at me.

He's beautiful when he smiles. I can see that. He's got straight white teeth and a dimple that pops in the corner of his cheek. His brown eyes turn bright, like the color of warm sunshine reflecting through syrup. He's the guy who shakes hands and makes everyone feel like the most important person in the room. He's so magnetic, he's the North Pole.

And I could blame it on our combative relationship, but he's that way even with people I'm pretty sure he doesn't like.

That single moment of suppressed amusement might be the closest he's come to smiling at me in a very long time, and it fires a weird, twisty feeling in my stomach that I don't like one bit.

I stare at him for a second too long and then blink, turning away.

While we wait for our plane to board, we don't say much else. Rafe scrolls on his phone while I try to read and pretend he isn't there.

Finally, it's time to leave, and we find ourselves on the plane.

Not only did Belinda book Rafe in first class with me, but she also booked our seats together. She's getting a strongly worded email as soon as I connect my laptop at the hotel.

"I want the window," I demand as Rafe shoves his bag in the overhead bin.

He gives me a one-shouldered shrug as if it doesn't make the slightest difference. It doesn't to me either—I don't care about the window seat—but needling each other is what we've always been good at. With a nod, I slide into the row and plunk down, wiggling my butt deep into the plush leather.

"Comfortable?" Rafe asks as he sits.

"Very," I say, stretching my legs out and crossing my ankles, admiring my toes manicured in Strawberry Margarita. Rafe settles in his spot, his long legs offering him less freedom to move around, even with the added cabin space. What is he? Six-three? Six-four?

"What?" he asks, and apparently, I've been staring. I need to stop this. In theory, anyone would be drawn to Rafe, assuming you're into that whole "looks just like Henry Cavill if he was ten years younger" thing.

A flight attendant with golden blond hair tied into a smooth knot arrives, holding a tray lined with stubby plastic water bottles. We help ourselves as she asks, "Can I get you a drink? Mimosa? Or—"

"Yes, please," I say before she can finish.

"Make it two," Rafe says, flashing her a smile that inexplicably fills my lungs with puffs of green. She gives him an appreciative once-over before she nods and turns away. See? I'm not the only one who finds him attractive.

"Won't you be a little warm dressed like that?" I ask after our drinks have been served, and we wait for the plane to take off. He looks down at himself and then back up at me.

"I'll be fine," he says.

"Not really a flower shirt and shorts kind of guy?"

"Why are you so worried about what I'm wearing?"

"I'm not. You just look hot in that." My cheeks burst into flames as I realize what I've said. "I mean jeans and long sleeves. It's going to be more than eighty degrees in Maui, and with the humidity, it'll be stifling…" I can't stop babbling as I try to cover up my Freudian slip, and Rafe's mouth curls into a smirk.

A smirk. I guess that's the closest to a smile I ever get.

"Oh, never mind." I sit back and fold my arms, staring out the window as the plane starts to move.

"I know you're obsessed with me, but don't worry, Tris, I'll be okay."

I turn to glare, trying to convey the fathomless depth of my desire to see him jump from this plane somewhere over the Pacific. Ideally, without a parachute.

When the overhead announcements come on, the blond flight attendant gives me a look that suggests she'll be keeping an eye on me if I'm not paying attention to the safety procedures.

With a huff, I settle back into my seat, daydreaming about the next three weeks. It's not all bad, even if I'm stuck with my least-favorite person ever. I wish Molly were here—we'd have had such a good time sneaking in some delicious food and going shopping in between whatever the powers that be at WMC have planned for us.

But Google assured me the resort has over six hundred rooms

and like six pools and nine bars and twelve restaurants. Plenty of space to ensure I'll see Rafe as little as possible.

Sure, this is a work trip, but I'm also planning for some R&R. If the only reason I'm here is to make David Gallagher look good, then I'm not wasting this chance to enjoy an all-expenses-paid bit of paradise.

My period just ended, I'm fresh from a Brazilian wax, and I just had my eyebrows rebladed. After four years of casual flings, I swore off men and sex when the last one wanted to get more serious. I wasn't ready for serious. I'm still not.

But what was an act of self-preservation became a certified drought, and at this point, the only person I'm punishing is me. Not only am I working on my tan and reading as many romance novels as I can, but Molly's right, and it's time to find someone hot to make out with. I desperately need to get laid.

But…I also can't help but focus on the actual reason for this trip.

Most of me has given up on my future with WMC, but I can't help but nourish a small kernel of hope. What if I could secure one of those spots in the training program? What if I could turn things around? Or what if I'm just kidding myself?

I did fire off the application for the job I was considering with EnviroTech a few days ago to remind myself that it *is* probably time to move on.

What happened in my past is the past, and I don't have to keep being grateful to a company that doesn't value anything I have to offer just because they gave me a job when no one else would.

But my confidence is also shot, and I don't like my odds.

I sigh as my gaze flicks to Rafe, who's lying with his head back and his eyes closed. I study his annoyingly pretty face for several moments, noticing how his eyelashes are long enough to create shadows over the arcs of his cheekbones.

Then I shake my head, put in my earbuds, and put on some music as I stare out the window.

A few hours later, I'm awakened by the sound of an overhead voice announcing a patch of turbulence. When I open my eyes, I notice Rafe appears to be speaking. My phone lies on the console between us, and he's eyeing it with mistrust.

"Mmm hmmfmd mmf," he says as I blink.

I pull out one of my earbuds. "What?"

"How many times are you going to listen to that song?" He gestures to the screen of my phone where Spotify shows the cover of Taylor Swift's *Folklore*. I've been listening to "Exile" on repeat.

"Why? What difference does it make to you?"

"It's weird. Who listens to the same song for two hours?"

I sit up in my seat, not just annoyed but on the verge of homicidal.

"Um, I do? And it's not weird. Plenty of people do it. Ask anyone."

"I don't know anyone who does that. I don't do that."

I exhale a long-suffering sigh. "Okay, Rafe. If you don't do it, then I guess no one can."

"That's not what I meant."

"Why would this bother you? Am I hurting anyone? I like this song, okay?"

"It doesn't bother me. It seems to bother *you*."

I give him an incredulous look. "You're the one who started this!"

"I don't care if you want to listen to the same song for hours." His tone suggests *I'm* being the unreasonable one, and I wonder what the maximum prison sentence is for causing a violent incident on a trans-Pacific flight.

I stare at him. It's been a while since we've done this.

When things first turned competitive between us, we channeled our desire to one-up each other by subtly and carefully riding the confines of professionalism.

An offhand comment designed to subtly and cleverly undermine one another during a conference call. A change of time or location of a meeting to ensure the other is a few minutes late. Debating over everything.

There was also the time I stole the *e* off his keyboard and snapped the lever on his chair so it was stuck on the highest setting. He's so tall that his knees wouldn't fit under his desk until they could find him a replacement. *Someone* was constantly unplugging my monitor, and I couldn't keep the same stapler for more than a week before it went missing.

But then he started dating Hannah, and the games stopped.

Instead, we resorted to the silent treatment and hundred-yard stares beamed across the conference table in our continued battle of wills. It's been a while since we've experienced this sort of forced proximity, and it feels like we're falling into an abandoned but familiar pattern, bickering like we used to.

"Can I just enjoy the rest of the flight in peace?" I ask, picking up where we left off two years ago, ignoring how the familiarity of our fighting almost feels like snuggling into a warm blanket.

He raises his hands in supplication. "Okay, okay, I'm sorry."

"Good." I go to put the bud back in my ear.

"It's just weird," he says, and I throw him a look dark enough to summon an eclipse.

This is going to be a very long three weeks.

Chapter Four

Rafe doesn't comment on my music again for the rest of the flight, though I'm pretty sure I catch him reading over my shoulder during one of the spicier scenes in my book. I glare at him, annoyed that he's interrupting my daydreams about a broody fae prince.

Rafe's knee keeps bumping mine throughout the flight despite the ample space in the cabin. I chalk it up to his very long legs and am proud of myself for withholding a comment on his extravagant manspreading. I can be mature about things.

We both reach for our glasses on the console between our armrests, and as his hand brushes mine for the eleven-hundredth time, I stuff down the little swoop in my stomach. I keep having to breathe through my mouth, so I don't accidentally inhale the essence of Rafe. Just another hour or so before we make it to the hotel, and I can pretend he doesn't exist for the next three weeks.

We're now soaring over the islands, circling in for our landing, and I'm glad I insisted on the window. The water is breathtaking—the most clear, vivid blue I've ever seen.

Rafe leans over to see out the window. I flatten myself to the seat, attempting to give him a clearer view. His response is to eye me with suspicion. Why *am* I being agreeable? There's no need to fight about everything, I reason. Soon, he'll be a very tall and very distant memory. I can let him have this.

He leans in farther, and I slip and accidentally breathe through my nose, inhaling a whiff of the same smell I remember from our photo together. Clean and fresh, like the guy bathing in a waterfall in a soap commercial. His breath is warm as it skates across the exposed skin of my collarbone. My skin erupts into gooseflesh, and I clamp my eyes shut, holding my breath as I curse my body for being such a horny, traitorous bitch.

Finally, he sits back up and I let out a long hiss, my head swimming from a lack of oxygen. Mercifully, he stays in place as we coast to the earth, landing with a soft bump.

Once on the ground, we collect our suitcases and head for the ride-share pickup. Rafe swipes the screen on his phone a few times and stuffs it back in his pocket. "Our Uber should be here in a minute."

"Great," I say, inhaling a deep breath and rolling my shoulders.

We're surrounded by tourists and exhaust fumes, but the air has an entirely different quality from the one we left behind. It's warm and humid and makes my limbs soft. I can already picture myself standing on my balcony, enjoying the ocean breeze.

Rafe gestures to my monogrammed suitcases. "Those are some fancy bags, Malik. My father really approved those?"

I glance down at the luggage in question and give one a little twirl—they really are so beautiful. "He told you about that?"

Rafe shrugs. "He mentioned you had a few travel requests, but he's not usually big on generous acts unless it gets him something he wants." His eyes narrow the slightest bit. "What did you do to earn such favors?"

My eyebrow arches, and my head tips. "He didn't tell you why?"

Rafe's eyes darken to the shade of an autumn storm. "No, why?"

"You should really ask *him*," I reply with a shrug as Rafe's brows draw together with confusion.

Thankfully, I'm saved from further explanation by our car's arrival. I have zero desire to relive that exchange in Charles's office with anyone ever again, least of all Rafe.

We load our suitcases into the trunk, and I take a seat in the back. Rafe pauses outside the opposite door and then opens the front.

"Mind if I join you?" he asks.

The driver waves him in. "Not at all."

I watch Rafe drop into the front seat and try not to be offended. This is weird, right? Who sits in the front of an Uber? Was he so over sitting next to me that he literally couldn't stand it for the duration of this ride?

The driver pulls away from the curb, and immediately, Rafe strikes up a conversation, asking questions about the area, the man himself—who's native to the island—and the problems plaguing Hawaii's oversaturated tourism industry.

They laugh and joke like they're old friends, and I hate how jealous I am that Rafe has such an easy rapport with this stranger. Maybe I'm envious of his gift that puts everyone at ease, or maybe I'm annoyed that he seems to have that effortless camaraderie with everyone but me.

Instead, he uses my name like it's a swear word.

By the time we arrive at the hotel, they're practically braiding each other's hair while I'm stewing in annoyance. However, most of my ire melts away as we pull up into the circle in front of the sprawling white building.

Everything is gorgeous—even better than the photos. Massive fountains spray in graceful arcs, and tall marble columns stand sentinel on either side of massive glass doors. It's stunning. It's breathtaking.

A giddy smile spreads across my face, picturing three weeks of cocktails with paper umbrellas and the sea and the surf and all the fresh seafood I can eat.

After exiting the car, we roll our luggage along marble tiles through the ostentatious lobby. The soaring ceiling ends in a massive stained-glass dome that filters warm Hawaiian sun into prisms of colored light that dance across the floor.

We wait at the reception desk, and a smiling woman gestures us over.

Rafe and I step forward simultaneously, nearly colliding, and then grind to a halt.

"You go," I say with a wave. "From this moment on, I don't want to see you, hear you, or even remember you exist. Have a delightful time."

Rafe presses his lips together, and I notice they're rather plush and full, and I wonder what it would be like to—*No. Stop.* I don't wonder anything.

"Ladies first," he replies.

"That is so sexist."

"Then I'll go first."

"No, you won't."

He makes an exasperated sound, and at this point, I don't care who goes first, I just want to see how far I can push before he ends up rocking himself in a corner.

With one last glare tossed in his direction, I head for the desk and give the woman my name. Kalena (according to her nametag) taps away on her computer, the smile never leaving her face.

"Ah, we have you here for three weeks with WMC Purcell, Ms. Trishara Malik and Mr. Rafe Gallagher." She looks up from her screen and gives me an owlish blink. "Will you be needing two keys?"

"Excuse me?" I ask, not sure what she's getting at.

"Two keys? Usually, each guest likes to have one. I'm happy to create as many as you need."

"There is only one guest," I say, my pulse kicking up.

"We have you in the Orchid Suite for the duration of your stay for two people. You'll love it. It has the best views in the hotel." She pauses, indecision seeping into her expression as she watches me slowly dissolve into a pile of horrified silt. "I'll get you two keys. You can always get more if you need them."

My heart throbs in my throat.

Why does she keep talking about keys?

Why would I need so many keys?

"No, there's been a mistake," I finally gasp.

I notice Rafe standing a few feet away with another desk clerk also tapping at his keyboard, a line drawn between his brows.

The clerk looks up and makes his way over to Kalena before their heads bend together in a universal gesture of *something is up*. The two confer quietly for a moment, and then the man gestures Rafe towards our end of the counter.

"There is a mistake," I say again. "It's supposed to be two rooms. One for each of us. A suite for me. Check again. *Please.*"

Kalena resumes tapping at her computer, her steady smile dipping at the corners. I feel Rafe approaching, his big body stopping just behind me as we manifest a set of pleading stares directed at the hotel clerk who now holds the fate of our entire world in her hands.

This can't be happening.

Kalena finally looks up. "I'm so sorry, Ms. Malik, Mr. Gallagher, but we only have one room booked under your names."

"Okay, he'll take another room then," I say, pointing to Rafe with a bit more flourish than necessary. When my knuckles accidentally connect with his stomach, he grunts and glares at me as I offer him an apologetic look over my shoulder. Geez, his stomach is hard. My hand is throbbing. Is he wearing a steel undershirt?

Kalena leans over the counter and lowers her voice, clearly worried I'm about to make a scene. "I'm sorry, but we are completely booked up. There are no more rooms."

My eyes dart around the sprawling lobby. "There has to be. This hotel is massive. You must keep some on reserve for emergencies."

She nods, and I breathe a sigh of relief.

"Normally we do, yes, but it's an extremely busy week, and even those are gone."

"How can that be?"

"We have several weddings and conferences booked," she says in a way that suggests it should explain everything.

"He'll take anything." I gesture to Rafe again, this time being sure to avoid his knuckle-bruising abs of iron.

"Excuse me? I will not," Rafe interjects, stepping up to the desk.

I attempt to silence him with a look, but he rests an elbow on the counter and flashes that hundred-watt smile he saves for everyone else.

But wait, this is good. No one with a beating heart could fail to be moved by that smile.

"There must be something else?" he says, smoother than the velvet lining of a jewelry case.

Kalena starts in on her keyboard again, her fingers flying.

"I'm really sorry," she says after another minute, and I sympathize because she seems genuinely distraught about disappointing him.

"A broom closet. A sofa in the lobby. A towel on the beach. Anything," I beg as Rafe gives me increasingly incredulous looks I choose to ignore. I'm starting to lose it. Rafe's standing too close. His scent and his heat are confusing me as I try to find a way around this. I'm hot and dizzy, and why does everything smell like Irish Spring?

Kalena hits a few more keys and then crisply slides two small cardboard envelopes across the desk with definite purpose. "I'm sorry. This is all we have. I can call around, but every hotel in the vicinity is booked."

She nudges the white rectangles again with a finality that suggests she's done with me, and I stare at them numbly.

"Don't look at me like that," I snap when I catch Rafe's glare. "This isn't my fault. You're the one ruining *my* vacation."

"This isn't a vacation, and you think I want this?"

He swipes the keys from the counter and then takes off towards the bank of elevators, rolling his suitcase. I hesitate, but now he has both keys, so I reluctantly chase after him.

We stand side by side as we wait for the elevator.

"Just stay away from me," I say.

"No problem. You're the one obsessed with me. Not the other way around."

"Shut up. I'm not obsessed with you. God, your ego is the size of Canada."

The elevator pings, and we lurch for the entrance, our suitcases bumping and our bodies colliding. Rafe steps back and gestures inside.

"Ladies first," he says, his previous glower replaced with a smirk that would make Satan look like a cinnamon roll. I *know* he's saying it just to piss me off.

Refusing to give him the satisfaction, I sidle past and turn around, not looking his way. He saunters inside, presses the button, and we silently ride up. The doors open again, and I hold out my hand.

"My key."

He places the small cardboard rectangle in my hand, his fingers brushing mine as a jolt of electricity zings straight to my navel. Ignoring it, I step off the elevator and march down the hall, swiping the key against the electronic pad and throwing open the door.

Despite everything, I can barely contain my awe.

The vast space is covered in white tile, punctuated with pale blue, turquoise, and hot pink accents. Straight ahead is an entire row of floor-to-ceiling windows overlooking the bright blue sea.

Kalena said it was the best view in the hotel, and my anger with Belinda and her inability to make even the most basic travel plans shifts down a notch.

As I pass through the suite, a kitchen with gleaming white cabinets and countertops sits to my right. A nest of sleek white sofas is angled to look out the windows, where a large, curved balcony supports a hot tub and two loungers. There's also a large glass dining table surrounded by fabric-covered chairs, along with a desk in the corner.

Rafe lets out a low whistle, and though I agree this is a whistle-worthy room, the sound lodges into the middle of my back.

"I cannot believe this," I say, dragging my suitcases farther into the suite.

After leaving them standing in the middle of the room to go exploring, I find two massive bathrooms—one with a huge walk-in shower with multiple heads and another with a deep, large soaker tub.

I enter a room with the biggest bed I've ever seen. Pushed up against the far wall, it's covered in crisp white sheets and blue and pink pillows, the headboard carved of deep mahogany wood. More windows look out to the sea, and a glass door exits to the other end of the balcony.

I do another circle of the suite, frowning. Something isn't adding up.

Rafe's head is in the refrigerator, stocked with wine, beer, and a mountain of snacks. He pulls out a bottle of lager with a hipster label and pops off the top.

"This could be worse," he says, taking a deep gulp. I turn away, distracted by the bob of his Adam's apple and the bit of stubble covering his jaw.

"Do you notice something?" I spin back to look at him, hands planted on my hips.

"What?" He lowers the bottle and looks around.

"There's only one bed."

"That can't be possible. This suite is huge."

"Well, unless it's hidden in a secret dimension, I only find one bedroom and one bed."

He gives me a skeptical look before he proceeds through the suite. I stand in the kitchen, tapping my foot as I wait for him to discover what I've already discovered. A moment later, he pops back into the main room.

"You're right."

"Did you think I was hard of counting bedrooms?"

He ignores my comment. "How can a suite this size have only one bedroom?"

It's then I notice a glossy brochure sitting on the kitchen counter, proudly welcoming us to the Orchid Honeymoon Suite.

Rafe is reading over my shoulder as I let out a groan.

"I. Will. Kill. Belinda," I snarl, crumpling the brochure between my hands and grinding my teeth. "I will slash her tires. I'll…"

"Put laxative in her coffee," Rafe adds.

I look at him, startled by the support.

He seems equally horrified, but that might be because it's the first time we've ever agreed on anything.

"Yeah," I say weakly.

"Should we wrestle for who gets the bed?" he asks, and maybe it's the long travel day and the stress of sharing a room with *Rafe Gallagher*, but I nearly burst into laughter at the unexpected quip. He never jokes with me. Is he trying to be…charming?

I cram the urge back into my throat, exhaling an undignified snort that I'll be revisiting with horror in my head again and again. It will be a cold day in hell before I laugh at one of Rafe Gallagher's jokes.

"This is my room, so I get the bed," I say.

"How is this your room any more than it's mine?"

"Belinda booked the suite for *me*."

He gives me a side-eye, and I have to hand it to him—the man's side-eye is so flawlessly executed that I've never felt more side-eyed in my entire life. "Yeah, I'm still not entirely sure why my father agreed to that. This must be costing the company a fortune."

"Your father," I say with renewed hope, wondering why this hadn't already occurred to me. "You can stay with him!"

Rafe's eyes narrow. "I'm *not* staying with him."

The menace in his voice is so...final that I resist the urge to argue.

I blink at him and he blinks at me.

"Then I'm definitely taking the bed." I cross the suite to grab one of my suitcases. I deliver it to my room and then march back out for the second as Rafe tracks my every movement.

This would have been so much more dramatic with just one.

With my shoulders thrown back, I wheel the rest of my luggage behind me.

"Fine, I'll take the sofa," Rafe says. "But you owe me a big, massive, epic favor, Malik. It's going to be some—"

I slam the door, cutting off whatever he was planning to say next.

Chapter Five

After I call my parents to let them know that I've arrived safely, I immediately text Molly.

Me: Belinda screwed up and booked us ONE room. And there is only one bed.

Molly: Us who?

Me: Rafe!

Molly: OMG. Where are you sleeping?

Me: He's taking the couch.

Molly: Try not to kill him, okay? I can't bail you out from Chicago.

Me: I promise nothing.

Molly: I'll come visit when you're in prison. At least orange is hot on you.

Me: Thanks, you're a good friend.

Molly: Go have fun! Remember, you're finding someone gorgeous to have a vacation fling with. 😉

Me: It's not a vacation. 🙄

Molly: You know what I mean.

I click away from our text thread and into the Official WMC Purcell Leadership Retreat app. An entire app seems a little excessive, but at least the schedule for the next three weeks is very conveniently laid at my fingertips. I can look forward to a mixture of rah-rah inspirational talks and workshops, team-building exercises, and the requisite "downtime" to prove WMC is all about that work-life balance.

I swipe through a few screens and discover that tonight is the welcome mixer at the Oceanside Bar.

Me: Fine. There's a party tonight. I gotta get ready.

Molly: Message me tomorrow. I want every detail.

Me: Love you.

Molly: Love you, too.

With an hour to prepare before the party, I unpack my clothes, hang them in the closet, and attempt to smooth out the wrinkles in my dresses with my travel steamer.

A click of the suite's front door catches my attention. I tiptoe over and peek my head out to discover Rafe has left. I breathe out a sigh of relief. We can do this. We'll just stay away from each other. He wants to be as far from me as I want to be from him.

I shoot off an email to Belinda demanding she fix this mess. I've always suspected she hated me, and this only confirms my theory. The *honeymoon* suite.

Either Belinda has a better sense of humor than I've given her credit for, or she's still mad about that time I accidentally spilled an entire glass of red wine on her during an office mixer. Someone knocked into me, and it wasn't my fault, but she was wearing cream linen, and it was a massacre.

A short while later, I'm dressed in a sleeveless pink dress with a bordering-on-daring neckline and a ruffled skirt that stops mid-thigh, all paired with my shiny gold sandals. I untie my ponytail and let my black hair settle around my shoulders. The barely there waves have absorbed the humidity, turning my tresses into a waterfall of thick curls.

I massage the bridge of my nose as I feel the stirrings of a mild headache. Feels like a level 2 or 3. Sometimes, I can push through one of this intensity, but I don't want anything ruining my evening. Digging into my tote, I take out my supply of painkillers and pop a couple into my mouth. After swallowing them with a gulp of water, I stuff my lipstick, phone, pill case, and key card into a little gold handbag and sling it across my body.

I head downstairs and back through the sprawling lobby to locate the Oceanside Bar.

The space is filled with pale wooden tables and chairs, with one wall entirely open to a swath of beach and the crashing sea beyond. The sun is setting over the water, painting the surface in glittering streaks of pink and orange. I inhale a deep breath of fresh, salty air.

This is pretty much heaven.

Rafe sits on a bench just beyond the entrance with his phone pressed to one ear. He runs a hand through his hair, rumpling it to annoying perfection. He's changed into a pair of white shorts and a pale blue T-shirt that stretches over the bunched muscles of his shoulders and back like a second skin.

"Hannah," I hear him say in a tone bleeding with exasperation.

I go still at the sound of her name.

"We've already talked about this," Rafe sighs with obvious frustration, and I really should keep walking, but at this moment, it feels like it's now my sworn duty to gather intelligence.

Molly and I were sure they'd broken up, but they're clearly still talking. (Though he doesn't sound that happy about it.)

What's going on?

I don't care. I just want to know.

He's distracted and doesn't notice as I pull out my phone, pretending to check something on the screen. I'm an espionage pro. He sits back and leans on the wall, his head falling against it. His eyes drift shut as if begging for strength.

"Look, I have to go. There's a thing." A pause. "Fine. Goodbye."

He disconnects the call and stares at his screen for several long seconds, a muscle feathering in his jaw. He's shaved since I last saw him, clearing away the day's five o'clock shadow to leave behind smooth, lightly tanned skin.

"Trouble in paradise?" I ask, unable to help myself.

He looks over at me, his evil stare burning straight through the center of my soul.

"No," he says, pushing up and disappearing through the crowd.

Okay, I deserved that. Obviously, he's upset. I weave through the throng and spot him with his elbows propped on the bar. The bartender sets down a glass of scotch, which Rafe snatches up before taking a long sip.

"Sorry," I say. "That was none of my business."

He peers down at me from his impressive height. I hate that he can probably see the top of my head. I should have worn heels. Hannah is nearly six feet tall, and kissing someone close to your size is probably nice and mitigates the chance of neck cramps.

Not that I'm short—I'm average—but he's Thor, and I really need to stop thinking about kissing.

"You want to talk about it?" I ask.

I understand that's what I'm *supposed* to say as a caring member of humanity, though the last thing I want to discuss is Rafe and Hannah's relationship problems.

His nostrils flare as he takes another sip of his drink.

"No, I don't."

Then he burns me with another scathing look before he walks away. He rolls his neck and shakes his shoulders like he's the star quarterback giving himself a pep talk before the big game. A moment later, someone approaches, and he holds out a hand, giving it a firm shake. I watch as the storm clouds dissipate over his head to reveal his neon smile.

"Fine," I mutter under my breath and order myself a mocktail so bright pink it's bordering on obnoxious.

"Hi," comes a voice next to me. An East Asian woman about my age with chin-length, wavy black hair and dark brown eyes gives me a friendly smile. She wears a simple red A-line dress and a pair of black ballet flats.

"I thought I'd come and introduce myself. I'm Lan."

"Trishara," I say, giving her a bright smile. "Nice to meet you."

"Which office are you from?"

"Chicago. You?"

"Seattle," she says while scanning the room. "I'm glad there are at least a *few* other women in this sea of men."

WMC has fifty-three offices across the country, making our numbers here a cozy one hundred and six. I'd estimate that at least ninety percent of them are men. Most of them white.

"Did they pick you to fill your branch's diversity quota too?" I ask, and Lan snorts, covering her face with the back of her hand and nearly choking on her wine.

"I wouldn't put it past them. Though we held a contest, and I won."

"You did? What kind of contest?"

"We had to build a fully functioning remote control car and race it," she says. "I won by two point six seconds."

"Well done," I say, honestly impressed. I wouldn't have any idea where to start building a car, remote-controlled or otherwise.

"How did you get chosen?" she asks as the bartender delivers my drink, placing it on top of a coaster. I take a tentative sip from the bright green straw and press my lips together. It tastes as loud as it looks. Even for me, this is sweet.

"Well, for one, the boss chose his son," I answer, and Lan wrinkles her nose. "And second, WMC has apparently realized they're living in the past? So they sent me here to prove they aren't." I wave a hand around the room. "Not sure how well that's working."

Lan's eyes grow wide, and she covers her mouth as she snorts again. "What a bunch of assholes."

"It's not all bad. I managed to extract a few perks."

She breaks into a grin. "I think we're going to get along quite well, Trishara."

I laugh and take another sip of my mouth-puckering drink. Giving up, I place it back on the bar and ask for a glass of sparkling water with lime.

"Call me Tris," I tell Lan. At least this trip won't be a total bust if I make one new friend out of it.

The bartender brings me a fresh drink, and we clink glasses as we drift into the middle of the room, where everyone is chatting and introducing themselves. I recognize some faces from past events and meetings, but most are new to me.

As we mingle, I glimpse Rafe outside on the beach. I'm surprised to see him alone at a table, sipping his scotch and staring at the water as if it personally wronged him.

For the briefest of seconds, I consider walking over to check if he's okay. But then I recall how he dismissed me earlier and decide to keep my distance.

Someone is speaking into a microphone, anyway.

An elegant woman stands at the front of the room wearing a crisp green sheath dress. Her blond hair is stylishly cut above her shoulders, and she wears a thick gold necklace that oozes money. Diane Hart. She's tough as nails, a total legend, and the author of *The Glass Ceiling*, a bestselling book about climbing the corporate ladder as a woman in a male-dominated field.

She became my beacon of hope when I joined WMC, and I've read her book at least four times.

My dormant sense of ambition stirs in my chest. Her presence reminds me of the person I wanted to be before first Leo and then WMC squished all sense of hope under their heels.

She stands with the six other heads of WMC Purcell—all white men wearing various hues of beige and cream, including Rafe's father, David Gallagher. With her classically beautiful features, Diane is a sparkling emerald nestled among colorless rocks.

She holds the mic and pauses with her focused attention sweeping over the room. Slowly, everyone silences under the weight of the queen's stare.

"Welcome to WMC Purcell's first annual Rising Stars Leadership Retreat," she says in a voice that is both cool and commanding. "We're thrilled to have you here and hope this will be a chance for you to get to know your peers from across the country while learning some new skills and tactics to help inspire greatness in those around you. We're honored to welcome you as our inaugural class, and I'm sure the time you spend here will see you all on your way to the brightest of futures at WMC.

"Of course, this will also be an opportunity for our executive team to get to know you all and identify the *best* of WMC. At the end of our time together, we'll select five people to join our one-year executive training program at our New York office. All expenses paid, including your Manhattan apartment, spending allowance, gym membership, and the best training and mentorship money can buy."

A collective murmur circles around the room at Diane's announcement, reminding everyone of why these places are so coveted. Sure, the retreat is a nice perk, but securing a spot will set the recipients on a diamond-encrusted merry-go-round for life.

Lan crosses her arms and cocks a hip. "I'm winning one of those, so help me," she says, laser-focused on Diane like she's trying to send her brain signals from across the room.

"How many times have you read *The Glass Ceiling*?" I ask.

"At least six," she replies, and I grin as we share a conspiring look.

Bruce Woodward, the CEO of WMC, steps forward. Diane hands him the mic with a glare, her lips pursed in distaste. Part of me wonders if they made her conduct the intro as the only woman on the executive team.

As Bruce speaks, I study the faces in this room. A small, anxious part of me wonders if I stand even the barest chance of securing one of those spots.

My gaze drifts to the beach, where Rafe is still sitting alone, facing out to the water. When I turn back, I see David notice his son, and the depth of his dark glare makes Rafe's look like child's play.

I remember Rafe's body language when he refused my suggestion to stay with his dad. It must say something about their relationship if Rafe chose *me* as a roommate over David.

Each member of the executive team then graces us with their piece about upholding company values and the importance of our presence. The presentation ends, and we disperse into small groups to speculate about the internship and discuss the upcoming events. Tomorrow, the first workshops begin and so, too, will the real test.

The reality of the training program sparks a fire I haven't felt in years, stirring up a competitive spirit that has never really died—it just took a break. This is the kind of thing I used to excel at. The kind of thing I would stop at nothing to win.

Rafe has abandoned his solitary position and is now moving through the room, smiling and shaking hands. He's a lion finding his pride—a natural-born leader. My stomach twists as he bestows his bright smile on a group of people, who all turn his way. Why do I care that he's that person for everyone else?

Then he finds me in the crowd, his gaze burning into me. I hold my ground as our eyes lock across the room, his pupils dilating into bottomless pits. He's the King of Hearts, demanding my head. My stomach drops, and my skin breaks out in a sheen of sweat that has nothing to do with the humidity.

"Who's that?" Lan asks, sucking on the end of her straw. "Does he belong here? He's gorgeous."

A low growl rumbles in my throat. "That would be the aforementioned son of David Gallagher and my mortal enemy."

Lan's eyebrows rise as she hits the bottom of her drink, making a loud noise with her straw that feels like a slurp of judgment.

"What?" I ask.

With her fingers still pinching her straw, she looks up with an innocent expression. "Enemy?"

I run my hand down my face and adjust my neckline as Rafe turns away, displaying the broad expanse of his back. "We've been working together for years, and let's just say we don't really get along."

Lan digs through her ice cubes, searching out the last dregs of her cocktail, avoiding my gaze like she *knows* something.

"What? Why do you keep making that face?" I ask.

She looks up with a devilish gleam in her eyes. "I mean, I know

I've just met you, but I've never seen someone make such intense *fuck me* eyes from clear across the room. But okay, you are *enemies*." She adds one-handed air quotes around the last word, and I narrow my gaze.

"Stop that. He is not. We can't stand each other."

Lan waves a hand and smirks. "Yeah, okay. Sure. I *totally* believe you."

Chapter Six

*A*fter the mixer, Lan and I head to one of the resort's many restaurants to continue our evening. We end up at the Taproom, paneled with dark wood and filled with plush velvet chairs. The menu specializes in locally made charcuterie and Prohibition-style cocktails.

After we find seats, more WMC rising stars join us, pushing tables together.

Gossip is the lifeblood of any corporation, and tonight, it receives an infusion while everyone scoops up heaping teaspoons of dirt on each executive member. Thanks to WMC's fondness for nepotism, we're regaled with transgressions committed at Thanksgiving dinners and family weddings delivered by silver-tongued nephews, dropping judgments like princes holding court.

I try to be interested, but the entire thing feels like a waste of my fleeting youth. I'll get wrinkles just listening to this drivel. I wonder where Rafe ended up and try not to examine that thought too closely.

On my left sits Andy. He's from Sacramento, and he's kind of cute. Maybe more than just kind of, with nice grey eyes and wavy brown hair and a little more fashion sense than the average Khaki. We've been chatting for a while, but I'm out of practice. My vagina's so dark and dusty it's layered with cobwebs, but I think he's into me.

"So, what made you choose engineering?" he asks, leaning in closer than is strictly necessary. Yeah, he's definitely flirting, but this is typical for these events, where the ratio of straight men to women is as lopsided as the wage gap. In a field of dead grass, we become wildflowers attracting bees.

Still, he's not entirely uninteresting, so I allow it.

Maybe Molly is right, and I need to loosen up on my strict no-work dating policy. What happened years ago has no bearing on the present. Besides, it's just flirting, and it doesn't have to mean anything. I just hope he has a flashlight.

Of course, he's just asked the most boring question in the history of questions, but I answer it with good nature. "I really wanted to do something that makes a difference," I say, earning me a curious blink. "I'd hoped to work in the environmental sector on projects that would bring clean water to people who needed it. Stuff like that."

It's partly the truth. In a way, I sort of fell into this. I was good at math and science in high school, and my teachers encouraged me to consider engineering.

My parents never pressured me to choose any particular career path, but I knew how happy they were when I opted for something sensible and stable with good pay and good benefits.

When my dad immigrated to the US decades ago, he struggled. He spent over a year searching for a job despite his electrical engineering degree. He met my mom a few years later after he was more settled, but those early days never left him. He did everything he could so my brother and I could have a comfortable life.

That's all both my parents ever wanted for me, and I'm trying desperately not to disappoint them.

Andy runs a finger under his collar. What I've just described is the very antithesis of what WMC stands for. In fact, WMC doesn't create or protect anything. We're simply contracted out by other corporations when they want to upgrade or build a new plant, and it makes more sense to work with us than to hire entire new design and construction teams. While WMC *does* have an environment division (the one I wanted to lead), it often feels like that work is only for show.

"You?" I ask.

Something nudges my arm, and a chair is shoved into the too-small space on my other side. Rafe plops onto it, his eyeteeth elongating into fangs.

"What the—"

"Hey, Tris," he says, staking me with his Count Dracula stare before it swivels to Andy. "Hey, man."

The air around us becomes weirdly tense, and I lean back.

"Hey?" I reply.

"Rafe," Andy says, sitting up straighter as he attempts to match Rafe's patented Dark Lord glare. But in comparison, Andy's a fluffy duckling waddling behind his mother. I should probably find that sweet. "Nice to see you again."

I frown at them both. "You know each other?" I ask.

The way they're looking at each other suggests there's some history here.

"We met at the team lead meeting in Spokane in the spring," Andy says, and I press my lips together. The team lead meeting that *I* should have attended.

"Rafe and I work together in the Chicago office," I say, feeling the need to explain his sudden and overbearing presence.

"That's cool," Andy replies, still looking at Rafe like he wants to challenge him to a duel in the middle of the bar. I think about Rafe suggesting we wrestle for the bed, and an unbidden smile comes to my face. No, that wasn't funny. Or cute. Or charming in the slightest.

"Anyway," I say. "Andy, you were telling me why you got into all this." I make a pointed effort to angle myself away from Rafe, hoping he'll take a hint and find someone else's blood to drink.

"Yeah," Andy says, returning his attention to me. "As I was saying…" Andy continues talking as I zone out, catching snippets that predictably include something about Lego and dismantling radios with his father.

It's not that Andy isn't captivating (maybe he is, I'm not sure); it's that in my attempt to turn *away* from Rafe, I'm now pressed *against* his arm. Thanks to the inexplicable way he's wedged himself in between me and Lan, all I can feel is a line of heat burning down the middle of my back. I hear him chatting with her while he shifts, his scent collaring me around the throat.

Against my better judgment, I inhale deeply, filtering the smell of babbling brooks down through my lungs, where it settles just beneath my navel.

Rafe shifts again, draping his arm over the back of my chair as he leans forward to speak with a guy across the table. His actions seem reflexive because he's ignoring me entirely. While it frees up a few inches of space, the side-effect is that I'm now pressed along the shape of his ribs with my shoulder cradled in the nook under his arm.

Our previous position was a cool arctic breeze compared to

how I'm currently boiling under my skin. Andy is still talking, and eventually, he has to notice I'm not really listening.

Suddenly, I wonder what it would be like to just sink entirely against Rafe? To lay my head on the swell of his shoulder? To slide my palm flat against his—I go rigid, banishing my thoughts into an iron box sealed with titanium chains.

Andy has finally gone silent, drawing my attention to where he's staring at Rafe's hand, casually dangling over my chair. I witness the scene from his perspective. To a casual observer, it might seem like Rafe is staking a claim, and a bead of sweat meanders down the length of my spine. But Andy has this all wrong.

"You need another drink?" Rafe asks, his mouth so close to my ear that I leap an inch from my chair.

"What?" I'm not entirely in control of myself right now.

"A drink? Yours is empty."

I look down at my glass, and sure enough, my mocktail is gone. I barely remember drinking it. The ache in my temple has returned, and I massage the corners of my forehead with my thumb and forefinger. I need to lie down.

"I think I'm okay," I say carefully, studying him closely with a skeptical eye.

"You look a little flushed," Andy says. "Do you want to go for a walk? Get some air? It's a really nice evening." He says it pointedly to Rafe in a challenge that he bats away. At least there's one other person in this room Rafe refuses to smile at.

A shooting pain climbs over my scalp, and I try to stand, but I'm nailed to my chair. It's Rafe's arm. His scalding muscular arm has snaked its way around my waist, pressing an inferno of heated flesh against my back.

"Why don't you stay?" he asks, still speaking into my ear, his breath pulling up gooseflesh across my skin. What's happening? Why is he doing this?

I turn my head to find his mouth so close to mine that his exhale ghosts against my lips. I *know* he feels the shiver that works through every crevice of my soul because his eyes darken to the shade of hundred-year-old bourbon.

"Because I want to leave," I say.

"Okay," he says. "But have a glass of water first. You look like you're about to faint."

Sure. No. Why is he being so bossy? I want to lie down, but I can feel Rafe's thigh touching mine, and my synapses have short-circuited.

"Run along, Andy," he continues.

My hand moves of its own accord, gripping Rafe's forearm. This is my kryptonite. My silver bullet. My stake through the heart. His arm flexes, and it takes a moment to settle the flutter between my thighs.

But then my mind clears, and I wonder who the fuck he thinks he is. It's clear Rafe doesn't care for Andy, but I don't belong to him. I'll do what I want with who I want.

I shove him off, leaping to stand up.

"Let's go," I say to Andy, ensuring my purse is secured across my body.

Andy stands, but Rafe grabs my wrist. "Tris. Don't leave."

I inhale a shuddering breath, exasperation swelling in my chest, threatening to crack a rib.

"Can I speak with you for a moment?" I gesture to Rafe, pointing to the corner like a schoolteacher who's over everyone's shit.

Then I march away, spinning around and folding my arms over my chest while he jogs over.

"What?" he asks, running his hand through his hair, blasting through all my defenses. It's like he *knows* exactly what that does to me. He stands so close that I have to look up.

Dark lashes frame deep brown eyes flecked with the tiniest golden sparks.

"What are you doing? We agreed to stay away from one another. Why are you interfering?"

He steps even closer, his hand gently circling my bicep, and my heart does an erratic leap in my chest. "Andy isn't a good guy. Don't go anywhere with him."

I blink through a tangled nest of thoughts and emotions that straddle many lines between confused and annoyed. "I don't know what your problem with him is, but I can handle myself."

His expression collapses into some hidden version of Rafe I've never seen before. It's vulnerable and imploring. "Just trust me."

"What are you trying to say?"

"Nothing."

My eyes grow so wide that I feel the edges of my eyelids scrape at my patience.

"Oh, that's very helpful. *Why* are you being even more annoying than usual tonight?"

The Rafe of a moment ago vanishes. He dons his cape and twirls his mustache, resuming his starring role as the villain in my story.

I take a step back, hitting the wall behind me and pressing a finger to his chest. His very hard and very sculpted chest. *Focus.*

"Look, we may be stuck here for the next three weeks, and we might have to share a room, but I want you to stay out of my way. I don't know what you're doing, but I want no part of your dick-waving contest. Leave me alone. Is that understood?"

Rafe's fists ball at his sides as he looms over me like a very sexy but very angry tower. For some reason, I think of a tarot card reading I once did and how the woman with her fake plastic jewelry told me the Tower represents chaos and destruction.

I don't wait for an answer as I slip around him and return to the table, where Andy is still waiting. But Rafe spoiled any possibility of a good mood, and my headache has reached decibel ten. "Sorry. I'm going to have to take a rain check on that walk. Maybe some other time," I say.

"Sure," Andy says. "Do you need help getting to your room?"

I pause, wondering if he's being chivalrous, but Rafe's warning about Andy has taken up rent in my mind. Can I trust him? Rafe is making me doubt my judgment. And that, more than anything, is the icing on tonight's layer cake of annoying.

Regardless, I've had enough of men in general tonight.

"I'm good, thanks. See you tomorrow."

I catch Lan's eye and wave goodbye, but not before delivering one last withering look at Rafe. He's standing in the corner watching me with a satisfied twist to his mouth.

I know it's childish, but I mouth the words *I hate you* as I exit the bar and return to my room.

Chapter Seven

The next morning, I lie in bed, listening for evidence of Rafe on the other side of the door. He returned shortly after I did last night, and I opted for the mature response—locking myself in the bedroom and calling down to the front desk, begging for another suite.

I tried to explain to the nice people at the Naupaka Resort that they don't want a murder investigation tainting their property. Apparently, they didn't take my threat seriously because here I still am.

Meanwhile, *Belinda* is ignoring all of my many emails and phone calls, so I'm stuck.

I shower and dress in a pale pink sleeveless button-up, grey pencil skirt, and my favorite black heels. When I'm sure Rafe has vacated the suite, I head downstairs for breakfast. As I wait for my order, I scroll through my phone, and Molly's name pops up on FaceTime. I stuff in my earbuds and answer.

"Morning," she chirps. "How are you?"

I blow out my cheeks. "Give me a minute."

I fill up my plate from the buffet and find a secluded table in the corner, propping my phone against the saltshaker. Then, I recount every gory detail from last night. When I'm done, she's wearing a grin so wide I can see every one of her teeth.

"What are you smiling about?"

"I'm just happy you and Rafe are getting along so well."

I snort and take a bite of my eggs. "I wanted to strangle him."

She nods solemnly, but her smile can barely be contained.

"What is up with you?" I ask. "You're trying not to say something."

"Nothing. Interesting news about Hannah, though."

I wave a hand. "Yeah, I'm sure they're just having a rough patch and will figure it out."

"Tris," Molly replies. "It's been at least several months, according to my notes. They aren't getting back together."

I snort a laugh. "Stop it. You don't have notes."

Molly's smile is wide. "Okay, well, I'm glad you haven't killed him. This Andy guy sounds nice."

"Yeah, maybe."

That earns me an impatient sigh. "Tris, I don't care who it's with, but it's been over a year since your last date. That's not normal at your age. You have to let the past go and allow someone in." She peers into the screen, giving me a somber blink of her eyes.

I huff out a laugh. "Shut up. I'm not *abnormal*."

"Your virginity is growing back at this rate. You'll be a religious miracle. Disciples will make pilgrimages to wash your feet." I snort and roll my eyes, glad I thought to put in my headphones. Still, I dart a cautious glance around the room, but I'm safely distanced from eavesdroppers.

"It's not that bad," I protest. I know she's right, and I'm met with a wall of judgy silence. I roll my eyes. "What would I do without you to worry about me?"

"I have no idea."

"I gotta go," I say, checking my phone. "I need to be upstairs in ten minutes."

"I'm expecting hot sex stories," she says, and I huff.

"I'll talk to you later."

We say our goodbyes, and I head out of the dining room, checking the WMC event app as I walk. My schedule includes a half-day session called "Leadership I: Inspiring the Change You Want to See in the World" and then everyone is invited to a boat cruise departing midafternoon. Pushing all thoughts of Rafe to the side, I focus on the positive. A boat ride sounds amazing, and maybe I'll learn something this morning.

I enter the conference room to find a nondescript square with grey walls and scratchy carpet filled with tables arranged in large *U* shapes. Half the attendees were assigned to this room and the rest to another. Lan waves me over, gesturing to an empty seat between her and ... Rafe.

Why did I think I'd spend the next three weeks avoiding him?

I hesitate, scanning the room for other options, but it's hardly fair that he gets to chase me away from my new friend. As I make my way over, I feel the tactile rake of his gaze. It drags up from the tips of my toes, and I can't be sure, but I swear he pauses on my mouth before finding my eyes. My lips tingle, and I roll them together.

Dark circles shadow his eyes, suggesting the couch probably isn't that comfortable. His hair is artfully disheveled in that way where it looks like he wasn't trying, but he probably was. He's wearing dark grey pants and a pale pink dress shirt. His sleeves are rolled up to his elbows, and I'm convinced he must be testing me. His muscles give a sexy little flex as he squeezes his pen.

Not sexy. Just... regular.

It's a totally platonic and uninteresting flex. It's not affecting me at all.

What's really weird is that we kind of match in our pink button-ups and grey bottoms.

As I drop into my seat, his gaze tracks over me again, and the corner of his mouth ticks up while the barest crinkle hugs the corner of one eye.

My breath flutters, and my heart skips.

That wasn't a smile, not exactly, but it wasn't nothing.

"Tris, meet Gabrielle," Lan says, pulling my attention from Rafe.

Gabrielle smiles and reaches out a hand. "Nice to meet you." She's a Black woman with deep brown skin, high cheekbones, and short curly hair. She's super stylish in a yellow short-sleeved sweater and cropped black pants.

"Tris," I reply. "Great to meet you, too."

"What happened to you last night?" Lan asks. "You were talking to that cute guy one moment, and the next, you were gone."

"Yeah," I say, conscious of Rafe leaning towards us. He's not even pretending he isn't listening. "I suddenly developed this giant pain in my ass, and I wasn't really in the mood for conversation anymore."

Lan and Gabrielle both frown, and I hear Rafe snort. My fists ball in my lap.

"Are you okay now?" Lan asks in a tone of equal concern and confusion.

"Yeah, I'm fine. Hopefully, whatever it was got the message and learned to piss off."

Gabrielle and Lan exchange a wary look.

I'm saved from having to answer any further questions when today's instructor calls for our attention. She starts handing out papers for our first team-building exercise, and we're assigned to groups of four: me, Gabrielle, some guy named Pete, and, of course, because the entire universe is conspiring against me, Rafe.

Our task is to construct a fully working Ferris wheel from a collection of household objects and a partially assembled motor. The exercise itself shouldn't be hard, but apparently, this will demonstrate how some people are leaders and some are followers. I wonder at the point of sharing all this beforehand, but I guess they know what they're doing.

Sitting before us is a box of dried linguine, a few cans of Play-Doh, a small motor, bamboo skewers, a pile of rubber bands, paper, pens, paper clips, and a pile of thumbtacks. Each group huddles around their tables as we all set to work.

"Okay, so we use the linguine for the spokes and Play-Doh to hold it together. The skewers as pivots to make it spin," I say.

"That should work," Gabrielle says. "I can set up the motor."

"Hmm," Rafe says, rubbing his chin with his other hand on his hip. He hasn't shaved this morning, leaving a shadow on his cheeks and along the precise line of his jaw. The rough sound of his fingers against the grain causes a tickle below my navel. "I think we should use the skewers. The pasta won't be strong enough."

Immediately, the tickle dissipates, irritated at his questioning.

"Sure it will," I counter. "It's thick pasta. We'll use the rubber bands to secure a few pieces together to strengthen them."

"That's just extra work when we could just use the skewers. We'd be done faster."

"I wasn't aware we were so short on time."

Rafe taps his temple, and a nonzero percentage of me wants to bend his finger back until it snaps. "Time is money, Trishara. One day, you'll learn that."

"Is that supposed to be some kind of dig? Why don't we take the time to do it right? Ensure there are no accidents and delays due to poor construction?"

We continue firing questions, and we both know neither of us is talking about the Ferris wheel anymore. I know we're remembering the first argument we ever had, along with a similar one last year about a reactor design that both our teams were working on. Gabrielle and Pete watch us with guarded expressions as Rafe and I continue to lob carefully veiled digs, swimming in the murky deep end of appropriate office behavior.

"Should we take a vote?" Pete ventures. "Pasta or skewers? They could both work."

"Shut up, Pete," I say, not taking my eyes from Rafe.

"Don't tell him to shut up," Rafe says to me as if Pete isn't there.

"Fine, then you shut up."

"This is why I got the team lead position," Rafe says. "You aren't a team player."

Red. All I see is red.

Crimson explosions of blood and cinnamon hearts dripping sugary scarlet juice down my chin. Fiery and hot and raging. I'll lob Rafe into the sun.

"I didn't get it because I'm not the boss's son. *Everyone* knows that."

Whoa. I know it. He knows it. We all know it, but I can't believe I just said it out loud.

Tension crackles like an electric storm. Rage simmers in his gaze as I imagine him tossing me in the back of his trunk and spiriting me away to his secret lair carved deep inside a mountain.

That tingle returns. What is wrong with me?

Our voices have risen, and everyone in the room is watching us, including, to my utter dismay, Diane Hart, vice president, superwoman, and bestselling author. She must have slipped in to observe, and I'm arguing with Rafe like a lunatic.

"Is there a problem?" the instructor asks, clearly irritable at being upstaged by our outburst.

Rafe and I stare at each other with so much heat that I'm surprised the carpet doesn't catch fire.

"Not at all," he grinds out.

"Then focus on your task. You're distracting everyone."

"Fine," I say. "Use the skewers."

"Use the pasta," he says, and I let out a sigh dramatic enough to garner me a Daytime Emmy.

"Are you kidding me? Do you just live to irritate me?"

Again, there's that smile that isn't quite a smile, his eyes burning with an intensity I'm sure the devil himself would covet. The fist he makes causes the veins on his arms to stand out, and I trace them with my gaze, traveling up to his face where he's watching me like a jaguar stalking prey across the Sahara.

My stomach flips and then crashes so hard it makes my knees go rubbery.

I'm a masochist. I need therapy.

Gabrielle, bless her heart, attempts to dispel the tension by grabbing the pasta and gathering it into small bundles.

"You finish these," she says to Pete as she darts uncertain glances between us.

"Tris, you assemble them." She hands me the Play-Doh, probably to distract me like one might with a toddler. I set to work under the weight of Rafe's stare.

"You help her." Gabrielle points to Rafe, and he nods.

We say nothing as we construct our wheel, one segment at a time, molding pieces of Play-Doh to hold it in place. The room is crowded, and our elbows and hips and thighs keep bumping. With each brush of his body against mine, I go weak and fluttery and absolutely stupid.

As it turns out, Gabrielle is the best leader in our group because she gets us focused, issuing orders and instructions, and before long, we have a perfectly working Ferris wheel that spins merrily on its bamboo skewer pivot.

Gabrielle claps her hands and gives a little hop as it whirrs into motion. Pete grins, and I'm guessing he's just relieved we've finished without becoming our scapegoat again.

"Sorry I told you to shut up," I say, feeling like an asshole. "I wasn't in my right mind."

"It's cool." Pete skirts a glance over me and then to Rafe with an expression that says *this is none of my business.*

I'm furious with Rafe for getting under my skin. How am I supposed to stay away from him when we share the same room and fate is conspiring to throw us together?

"Good suggestions," Gabrielle says to me. "It works great."

"Great job with the motor," I respond, and she smiles proudly.

The class instructor walks over to observe our work, noting something on her clipboard.

Diane is still seated in the room's corner, her legs crossed and her arms folded as she studies us like rats in a lab. She's wearing another sheath dress, this time in cream, with a chunky statement necklace.

What a fool I made of myself. Maybe I can talk to her one-on-one later and explain what happened. Surely she understands what it's like to be passed over for a promotion simply for being a woman?

Eventually, everyone in the room completes their projects. Some work better than others, and one falls apart completely when they switch on their motor. I cringe, thankful ours remained in one piece, even if our group was a disaster.

"Thank you," the instructor says. "I hope this was an informative exercise in leadership and how teams naturally find their rhythm." The look she directs at Rafe and me is so sharp that it nearly draws blood. We share a glance, and I know we're both dreaming up spectacular ways to make the other one suffer.

"Now that the work part of the day is over, it's time for some fun. We'll meet at the hotel marina in one hour to embark on our afternoon boat tour. A late lunch will be served. Bring your swimsuits. You're dismissed."

A general swell of excited chatter ripples through the room as everyone gathers their things and heads upstairs to change.

"Meet me in the lobby, and we'll all go together?" I ask Lan and Gabrielle as they pack their bags.

"Give me your phone," Lan says, and she enters her number into my contacts.

I head for the elevator, and while I'm waiting, Rafe arrives to stand next to me, his hands stuffed in his pockets. He ignores me and stares at the doors like he's trying to burn a hole through the metal. I consider telling him to take a different elevator, but we're going to the same place, and I don't have the energy.

(And maybe we've antagonized each other enough for one day.)

The elevator dings, and we ride in silence as it slowly climbs to the top floor. Just as the doors slide open, Rafe's phone rings. He pulls it out of his pocket, hanging back as I head down the hall.

"Hey," I hear him say as he follows several paces behind. "What's up?"

There is a weariness in his voice that makes me look back.

"Hold on just a minute." He presses his phone to his chest as we enter the suite. He kicks off his shoes and dumps his bag on the sofa before stepping onto the balcony and firmly sliding the door behind him.

He paces for a minute, running his hand through his hair before facing the balcony, leaning on the ledge with an elbow, his head dropping forward. It's a posture of defeat.

An unfamiliar knot of worry twists in my stomach. I've spent the better part of five years consciously and unconsciously aware of every move Rafe Gallagher makes. Our close proximity is concentrating that awareness, calcifying it into something I'm not sure how to name. It sits lodged in my stomach like I've swallowed a chess piece.

Turning away, I enter the bedroom, close the door, and walk to the dresser to pull out my swimsuit. It's then I notice the balcony door at this end has been left open, possibly by the cleaners. The gauzy white curtains billow into the room like ghosts as I catch snippets of Rafe's voice drifting from the far end of the balcony.

I should close the door. This is none of my business.

"Hannah," I hear him say in an exasperated voice that I thought he mainly reserved for me. This is an egregious violation of his privacy, and I'm a terrible, horrible person who will roast in the flames of hell. But I also move closer to the door. "Can you please stop?"

I hold very, very still, worried he might hear me if I so much as blink. My hand grips the handle as I will myself to close it. But my curiosity is as hungry as a shark scenting blood.

I lean forward ever so slightly, wishing the ocean would shut up and stop muffling his words.

"I know that," he's saying now. "Look, the next few weeks are going to be really intense. I won't have much time to talk. We'll discuss this when I get home, okay?"

I frown. Sure, we're busy, but they're also giving us plenty of free time. Even after checking emails from the office, he should have time to address whatever seems so important. It definitely sounds like something's wrong, though.

Rafe has gone silent, and I wonder if he's hung up when he speaks again. "Hannah, I gotta go." I can hear the strain in his voice. Like he's doing everything in his power to remain patient. "There's a thing I have to get to."

Then he goes silent, and I hear the balcony door open as he reenters the suite. I resume changing, listening as Rafe bangs around in the kitchen, slamming the cupboards and muttering to himself.

This is none of my business. Rafe isn't my friend, and his problems aren't my responsibility. But he *almost* smiled at me today, and our fight about the Ferris wheel was so ridiculous that I find myself opening the door. Wearing my high-waisted red polka-dot bikini, I pad into the kitchen in my bare feet.

"You okay?" I ask, regretting the words the instant they're out of my mouth. Why am I getting involved?

He runs a hand down his face and then through his hair, causing it to stand on end. He's undone the top buttons of his shirt, and I catch a fleeting slice of an exquisite collarbone attached to a smooth, hard chest.

"Not really," he admits, bracing his hands against the counter. He's opened a beer and is staring intently at it as if it might break into song.

"Do you want to talk about it?" His gaze flicks to me, and for once, there is no menace in it. No dark, brooding glare. His supervillain is dormant.

If anything, he looks anguished and vulnerable, and something about that unlocks a door somewhere deep in my soul. I see several things cross his face. Distrust. Fair enough—why am I being nice to him? Frustration. But for once, it's not directed at me. And finally, weariness. But I have no idea what that's about.

He shakes his head, and I'm not sure if I'm disappointed or relieved when he says, "No, I don't want to talk about it. You should go get ready."

I open my mouth to reply, but there's a dismissal in his tone, so I refrain. I don't take it personally. Whatever this is, he needs a moment, and it isn't my place to push him. *This* has nothing to do with me.

"Okay, if you change your mind, you know where I'm staying," I joke as I gesture to the bedroom.

Though his face doesn't change, something else happens. It's not a smile, but it's not that twisted smirk, either. It's a flicker in his eyes, so subtle that I'm sure anyone else would miss it. But I see it because I've logged five years studying Rafe's every gesture and silent look.

Amusement. The tiniest spark of laughter lights up his eyes like faceted shards of topaz. It squeezes my lungs like a fist.

"Sure," he says. "Thank you. I appreciate that."

I nod and then return to the bedroom to finish getting ready.

No, it wasn't a smile, but it was...something.

Chapter Eight

The "boat" turns out to be a four-hundred-foot yacht large enough to accommodate all of us, including WMC's executives, who are here to "mingle."

So far, the only mingling they're doing is from the top deck perched over us like stone gargoyles. With their sunglasses shielding their faces, it's hard to tell if they're watching or actually sleeping. I'm caught between wanting to hunt down Diane to explain the scene she witnessed earlier and hoping that if I never bring it up, she'll forget it ever happened. I'm a mess viewed from every angle, proven by the fact that I also can't stop wondering about Rafe.

Lan and I lounge on one of a dozen deep white sofas that line the polished wooden decks, sipping on drinks and munching on canapes. When I see how much money WMC is spending on this, I realize I should definitely have held out for that raise. When I get home, I'll go straight to David and demand it. Clearly, they can afford it.

Andy finds us shortly after the boat sets sail, accompanied by a man named Frank, also from Sacramento. They settle on either side of us, Andy on my left and Frank on Lan's right.

Andy's light brown hair is messy from the breeze, and he's

wearing a blue-and-white striped T-shirt along with a pair of navy shorts. He's handsome in a nonthreatening way, and with him, I never want for smiles. He offers them freely, showering them on me like confetti as I luxuriate in the sunlit glow of a generously given grin.

As I sip my wine, I scan the deck, definitely not looking for Rafe. He probably stayed behind to chalk pentagrams on the floor of our suite and summon his closest friends from the ninth circle of hell.

"Having fun?" Andy asks. "How was your session this morning?"

My nose flares at the memory of Rafe and me firing verbal crossbows like mercenaries with nothing left to lose.

"It was fine," I say, summoning a tight smile.

His eyes tilt over me in an obvious attempt to check me out, and my stomach dips. I feel good in my favorite swimsuit—the bright red material perfectly contrasts with my skin and hair. I don't usually burn, but I've layered on sunscreen in a war against time and skin damage.

Andy's friend Frank is chuckling about something with Lan, whose expression suggests she's been dipped in acid. I scoot closer to rescue her from his unwanted attention.

"And *I* said we should implement a short skirt Friday in our office," Frank says.

My lip curls as Lan and I stare at him, unblinking. Did he really just say that? Oblivious to our horror, he goes on snickering to himself.

"Maybe we should do that here," he adds as if this is an idea worthy of the Nobel committee.

"Sure," I say, giving him a bland smile. "You go first."

His face crumples into a glare. "Ha. Ha."

I roll my eyes. "Seriously, what is wrong with you?"

"Stop it, Frank," Andy adds, perhaps a moment too late.

"I think I'll go for a walk," Lan says, pushing herself up.

I catch her hand. "Do you want me to come?"

"No, you stay here. Have fun." She winks before turning to Frank and waving in a shooing motion. "You go away. Bother someone else and think before you open your big dumb mouth next time."

Frank's bottom lip droops into an undignified pout, but he does as he's told, slinking off with his tail tucked into his shorts. Lan flips me a wave and bounds off through the crowd.

"Sorry about him," Andy says, stretching his arms along the back of the sofa and crossing an ankle over his knee. "He's harmless but isn't house-trained yet."

"Yeah, we have a few of those in our office, too," I say, thinking of Rory. "Sometimes it's amazing how numbed to all this bullshit you're forced to become."

"Not all men are like that. On behalf of the entire gender of male pigs, I apologize."

He gives me a crooked smile, and I try to pretend he didn't just "not all men" me.

Despite that, Andy's smile is charming, and my stomach swoops again.

We chat for a while as the boat cuts over the water. It's a perfect day with the sun high and the breeze tosses my hair. As we keep talking, Andy is definitely getting cuter. He moves closer, his hip brushing my thigh, and I lean into it.

This is nice. This is easy.

I'm conscious of the need to release my fears and stop letting the past define the potential of my future. If I don't want to die alone, I have to get over myself.

But I can't seem to settle into this. If I abandon my firmly established rules, then that person would need to be worth the risk. Does that person exist? Or maybe I'll just stay single. I've heard enough stories to suggest many women are much happier that way.

"Do you want to go for a swim?" Andy asks. "They're stopping the boat so people can get off and go snorkeling. It's supposed to be spectacular down in this cove."

I shake my head. "Oh, I don't really swim, but I'll come and watch."

We both stand, and Andy grabs my hand as we head for the main deck. I allow him to tow me through the crowd, unsure of how I feel about this.

When we reach the bottom level, I peer over the railing, where about a dozen people float in the water, wearing snorkeling masks and basking in inflatable tubes, splashing one another.

"You sure?" Andy asks.

"Yeah, have fun." He releases my hand and tugs off his shirt, tossing it onto a lounger. I surreptitiously check him out and can't complain about what I see.

He runs to the end of the boat, tucking himself into a cannonball before he plunges off the edge.

Lan and Gabrielle wave up at me from the water, and I stand and watch the fun for a few minutes. Eventually, I wander back to my seat and dig out my phone. I fire off a series of texts.

First, to my dad to let him know how things are going (minus the fact that I'm sharing a room with my male coworker—I might be almost thirty, but certain things are just easier to keep to myself).

Then to Molly about my disastrous morning and the conversation I overheard with Rafe and Hannah.

Molly: I wonder what's going on. Did you ask him?

Me: I can't ask him that.

Molly: I think you should ask him.

Me: Don't be crazy. He'll rip my head off and eat it like a praying mantis. He'll think I'm prying.

Molly: But you are. (And it's the females who do that)

Me: I know, but not for the reasons he thinks.

Molly: . . . what reasons, Tris?

Me: Nothing. Never mind.

Molly: 😉

I pause, studying our words. What *do* I mean by that?

Rafe would assume I'd be digging for gossip and something to lord over him. And maybe he'd be right if we were talking about the Tris of a week ago. But the one sitting here now . . .

A shadow falls over me, obliterating the sun and sending an inexplicable shiver down my spine.

"What's so interesting?" Rafe asks.

My head snaps up, and I stuff my phone into my purse, my eyes narrowing in suspicion.

"You came," I say.

"Why wouldn't I?"

I shrug as he lowers himself onto the sofa. He's close enough that our elbows touch, and that tiny, meaningless fragment of contact sends a heated wave of sensation straight to my toes.

In comparison, Andy's touch feels almost clinical.

Stop. I shouldn't be comparing them.

"You seemed pretty upset when I left. I thought you might like some time alone," I answer.

Rafe gestures to one of the waitstaff and orders a beer while I order a glass of Prosecco. He exhales a loud sigh as he falls against the sofa, his long legs stretching out and his eyes closing. I enjoy a slow perusal, noting the way his black T-shirt has ridden up, exposing a tanned sliver of toned stomach. He's wearing white shorts and leather flip-flops, and even his feet are nice.

"Are you sure you don't want to talk about it?" I ask.

I *am* prying because I'm a giant snoop, but he looks so distraught that I have a weird, unfamiliar desire to ease his burden.

"You won't care" is his reply, and I frown.

"Why would you say that?"

He peers over at me, raising an eyebrow in a way that hooks me right through my stomach. I shift, pressing my thighs together. His eyes drop to my bare legs as I attempt to put some distance between us. But he's screwing with me because he shifts in the same direction, as if he, too, is just getting more comfortable. When all our maneuvering is said and done, we're still touching, and I'm still much too aware of it.

"Do you care what happens in my life, Malik?"

I open and close my mouth. I care. I've cared all along, but I've done such a good job of ensuring I never admit that to myself.

He snorts and scans the horizon, his eyebrows drawing together.

"Hannah and I broke up," he says.

The words flow in a rush, like a raging storm, as if he couldn't wait to set them free. My breath stops as his shoulders lift like he's just released a thousand-pound weight. Yes, we already suspected it, but hearing it confirmed shifts something on its axis.

I think about the early years we spent antagonizing each other. For a while, I even wondered if, in my attempts to keep Rafe at a distance, we had actually gone full circle and started flirting in a weird, competitive way that I kind of respected. I'd never have let it amount to anything, of course, but there was something layered in the silent corners of our charged encounters.

Then he started dating Hannah, and I realized that whatever attraction I'd imagined had been entirely one-sided all along. Talk about humbling. But that was fine because I wanted nothing from him or anyone. I worked very hard to convert that initial spark I refused to embrace into fire and loathing, and that's the way I liked it.

But suddenly, every innocuous word and touch and look of the past two days takes on an entirely different meaning. I think? His arm around me the other night. Begging me not to leave with Andy. The way he keeps touching me.

It hasn't been just the last few days, though—it's been the last few months. Something shifted—something *he* initiated that forced me to notice him beyond our professional interactions. I'd erected an inflatable bouncy castle between us—crossable but not without some difficulty—but a firing line has just blown it full of holes, leaving it flattened on the ground.

Rafe is single. Rafe is no longer in a relationship.

Why does it feel like everything just changed?

He gives me a questioning look, and I realize it's been several seconds, and I haven't responded.

"Oh, I'm so sorry."

Why does that sound so insincere?

"Then...why does she keep calling you?"

He cuts me a sharp look. "How do you know that?"

Oops. I press my lips together and wrinkle my nose.

"Sorry, the door to the balcony was open in the bedroom earlier, and I heard you say her name. I didn't hear anything else, though, I swear."

It's at that moment our drinks arrive, and I accept mine, taking a big sip to cover my embarrassment.

He closes his eyes and tips his face to the sky. "Whatever. It hardly matters what anyone hears. It happened about six months ago."

Six months.

More than enough time for the body to grow cold.

He peers over at me. "She keeps calling because she wants to get back together."

"Oh" is the only thing I can come up with. Should I be more

encouraging? Should I tell him he should work things out? I'm not his therapist, and I might not be a totally impartial bystander. "And you don't?"

He throws me a wry look, and I wince. Stupid question.

"No, we've been—" He stops. Chews on the corner of his lip. "Never mind. It doesn't matter."

He lets out a deep breath and leans his elbows onto his thighs, the beer bottle clasped between his hands. He picks at the paper label as he watches the water. His knee is still touching me, and if I was cognizant of his presence before, the last thirty seconds have just shifted me into hyper-awareness.

Rafe is single. Rafe is available. Why does this matter?

I study his leg pressed against mine, and now this means *something*. I think.

"Okay," I say, wondering if he also feels the weird tension stretching between us. "If you change your mind, I'm happy to listen."

That wins me another sharp look as he seems to weigh my words in his head. But I mean them sincerely and not because I'm looking for a way to destroy him. He must see that in my face because his own expression softens. It's not a smile, but this, too, is . . . something.

"Thanks," he replies, returning his stare to the water, where dozens of people frolic, shouting and screaming in the waves.

He gestures to the water. "Why aren't you down there?"

I pull a face. "I don't like swimming."

"What kind of person doesn't like swimming?"

"This kind of person," I say. "What difference does it make to you?"

I guess that's it. One moment of quiet civility has already evaporated, and we're back to our usual patterns.

"It's strange," he adds, and I narrow my eyes.

"You can be a real jerk, you know that, Gallagher?"

Something like shame flashes across his face, catching me off guard. That's not how this works. We share our insults like jellybeans, never regretting their casual dispersion. There are always more where they came from. He's not allowed to change the rules and feel guilty.

"That was great!" Andy interrupts, walking up to us and toweling off his wet hair. Lan and Gabrielle follow closely behind, hands clasped and smiling.

Rafe and Andy stare at each other like this is *West Side Story*, and they're about to break out into a knife fight. Or a song. But probably a knife fight.

Andy drops into the space on my other side, his wet hip brushing against mine. I shift, disliking the feeling of the cold material against my skin. It puts me even closer to Rafe, who is warm and dry, and so many other things I don't have the courage to name.

I give a pointed look to the mile of empty space on his other side, but Rafe doesn't move.

"You gotta come in next time, Tris. I promise it's awesome," Andy says, drying his face.

"She doesn't like swimming," Rafe says, a thread of irritation in his voice.

I frown. Wasn't *he* just making fun of me?

Andy's scowl matches my own. "Okay, man. It was just a suggestion. Calm down."

"Don't tell me to calm down," Rafe says.

I share a look with Gabrielle and Lan, who watch their exchange intently.

The ease of Andy's disposition slides away, and I drop my head in my hands. He leans across me, and I'm forced to sit back.

"Dude, what is your problem? First, you scared her away from me yesterday, and now you're acting like I've morally offended the lady's honor because I suggested she go for a swim. Are you two a thing or something?"

"No!" I say, maybe a little too forcefully, and four sets of eyes find me, each weighing and judging with varying degrees of suspicion. I clear my throat, willing my voice to a normal volume. "No, I mean, we're just colleagues. Rafe, stop being weird."

But it's too late, and they're both standing, fists balled at their sides. I rub my face with my hands and groan. Why are men?

"Then what is your problem?" Andy asks, their chests just inches apart. Rafe is taller and bigger and there's that rip-open-the-sky expression on his face I'm so familiar with. Andy stands his ground, but I can sense his understandable wobble of concern.

"Boys. What is going on here?" An icy voice slithers through the tension.

David Gallagher stands a few feet away, wearing a white short-sleeve button-up shirt and khaki shorts, his hand stuffed casually into a pocket like he's just stepped from the page of a Burberry catalog. He's the picture of old money and distinguished elegance.

He swirls the glass of whisky in his hand before taking a sip, his cold eyes never leaving his son. "Is this how a Gallagher behaves? I thought I raised you better than that."

Immediately, Rafe's entire demeanor transforms, and he retreats into himself. This is his defense mode, I realize. He did the same thing this afternoon when speaking with Hannah.

This is a vulnerable Rafe. This is a Rafe that makes my stomach twist in a foreign way.

Andy backs off, thunder clouding his expression.

David Gallagher sweeps an arrogant glance over both men, who've been reduced to scolded little boys. He swirls his glass again, the clink of ice barely audible over the din of the boat.

"Sorry, sir," Rafe says, and Andy echoes the apology before throwing Rafe a scathing look and stalking off.

We all stare at one another, and I consider tossing myself overboard just to escape this awkwardness.

Then it's Rafe's turn to walk away.

I stare at his back until he disappears, and that's the last I see of him for the rest of the night.

Chapter Nine

$\mathcal{E}$arly the next morning, I wave my swipe card against the glass door of the hotel gym.

It beeps merrily, and I haul it open. Inside, the ceiling stretches high overhead, and a polished row of treadmills lines a wall of windows offering a view of the beach.

After the incident with Rafe and his father on the boat, I hung out with Lan and Gabrielle while keeping my distance from Andy, no longer in the mood for any type of male attention.

The problem with a party boat is that you're trapped. Thankfully, it started raining, and we were forced to return early.

When we docked back at the hotel, I went straight to my bedroom and locked the door before I called down to the front desk, begging them to find us another room. Still no luck. They also politely (but sternly) requested that I stop contacting them until they call me with an update. Next, I tried Belinda since she still hasn't answered any of my emails, but I'm pretty sure she's blocked my number.

Rafe was already gone when I emerged this morning. I've considered asking again if he can bunk with his dad, but now I'm not sure after witnessing their interaction on the boat last night.

Today, the sky is grey, and it's still raining.

On my way down, I overheard some hotel staff telling a group of tourists to expect some unusual weather over the next few days—including possible thunder and lightning—which is apparently rare around here. It's just my luck that it might happen when I'm visiting because storms have made me nervous since I was a kid.

Hopefully it will blow over.

My gym shoes squish against the rubber floor as I head towards the free-weight area. Coming to a halt, I let out a dramatic sigh because, *obviously*, Rafe is standing in front of the mirror with a giant dumbbell clutched in each hand. Is there nowhere I can hide?

I stand momentarily fossilized as I watch him work.

One. Two. Three.

He's Hercules, biceps swelling, the veins in his neck straining, and the curl resting on his forehead practically waving at me with coy fingers. Of course he's here. A man doesn't look like that without some serious hours logged in the gym.

At first, he doesn't notice me, which is surprising because it *feels* like the sound of my panting fills every corner of the room. My mouth has become sandpaper, and I hate that I intend to replay this moment in my daydreams until it disintegrates from use.

His fitted black tank reveals the caps of his rounded shoulders, the dips in his back, and the pronounced swoop of his collarbones. The thin material of his shorts clings to his ass and his thighs and his . . . *oookaaay*.

And that's it—the very last stone has just been turned in the winding corridors of my filthy imagination.

This isn't good. Despite that initial spark I felt, I've never considered Rafe an option for me. Sure, I always found him attractive, but that's it. He works at WMC, and I *cannot* go down that road again. But now I'm experiencing all these strange thoughts and feelings, and they're hurtling towards me at the speed of light, streaking across my vision in a blur.

I've been standing still for too long, and finally, he notices me, my phone clutched in my hands and my lips slightly parted.

"Tris," he says, as if I've just shocked him with a defibrillator. "What are you doing here?"

My mouth snaps shut, and I plant a hand on a hip, trying to pretend I wasn't just imagining him naked on a chaise as I feed him grapes with my teeth. "The same thing as you, Rafe. I exercise too, you know."

Now *he's* the one staring. I freeze as his gaze travels up the length of my body: my shins, my thighs, the hem of my shorts, the dip of my navel, the scoop of my sports bra, the strap curving over my shoulder.

With each beat, my heart pounds in my chest until it's thrumming so hard I grow lightheaded. These are the same clothes I always wear to the gym, but when examined under the weight of Rafe's careful scrutiny, it feels like I'm stark naked.

"Then, by all means," he says, gesturing to the weight rack. "Don't let me distract you."

"Thank you for the permission," I reply with as much sarcasm as I can rally. I move past him and select my dumbbells after putting in my earbuds and cranking up my music to drown out his presence.

I'm not the lithe gym type, but I like food and wine and the only way I can reasonably consume either of those at a rate I find acceptable is to work out at least four or five times a week. I'm not naturally muscular, tending towards softness, but I am healthy and fit and could lift a lot of weight if necessary.

As I work, the music does nothing to distract me, and my gaze keeps wandering back to Rafe. I get lost in the flex and bunch and flex of his arms and his back and his stomach, and who turned up the temperature in here? It would be a shame if his shirt suddenly melted off his back.

This is insane. I need to leave. Rafe might be single, but he is still bona fide WMC stock, and I refuse to do this to myself again. Rafe is still Rafe. He's arrogant and full of himself, and we hate each other. I'm literally the one person in the world he refuses to smile at.

He was so turned off by the idea of working with me that he kicked me off his team.

Shaking myself off, I move through my routine: shoulder presses, upright rows, flys, and lateral raises. I try to tame my eyes. To get them to cooperate, but they're drawn to Rafe like flowers to sunshine.

More than once, I catch him staring, too. At the moment, he's looking at me like he's trying to see straight to the very essence of my soul. My stomach loops on a roller coaster, the air in the room thinning.

He said he broke up with Hannah, but she wants to reconcile. They'll probably get back together, and then I can stuff these feelings into a tidy compartment where I can keep them secured forever.

I picture Rafe and Hannah in their perfect little house in one of

Chicago's most elite gated neighborhoods, raising their attractive children, who attend private school in miniature navy blazers as Rafe follows in his father's footsteps.

Why does that image make my stomach hurt?

After I'm done with my weights, I cast one more look at him. I'm becoming messy and unwound, spiraling like threads at the end of the spool, and I don't like it at all.

I hop on the treadmill, hoping to sweat this anxiety out through my pores. I watch the ocean churning through the bank of windows, but I am aware. I am *so* aware of the man I'm trying to forget behind me.

At the end of my run, I jump off the treadmill and grab a chilled bottle of water from the mini fridge in the corner. Rafe approaches, wiping his forehead with the hem of his shirt, revealing a set of carved abs and a trail of dark hair that disappears into the waistband of his shorts.

Suddenly, I can't breathe. I wonder what it would be like to run my tongue along those tight lines and grooves. Then I give my head a vigorous shake as if anything could dislodge that image. I hope he attributes the flush on my skin to my run.

"You heading back upstairs?" Rafe asks, and I nod, replacing my now empty water bottle with a fresh one. "How was your workout?"

"It was fine," I say in a clipped tone, annoyed with myself for being a fool and annoyed with him for existing at all.

"About last night," he says, rubbing the back of his neck. "I'm sorry. I didn't mean to go all caveman on you like that."

I take a long gulp of my water and wipe my mouth with the

back of my hand. "So why did you? Why are you so opposed to Andy?"

His gaze hardens, a muscle feathering along his jawline. "I'm not."

"Really? Because your behavior would suggest otherwise. What do you have against him?"

"You just deserve better than an asshole like that."

I raise an eyebrow. "I do?"

He blinks as if surprised by my question. "Of course you do."

"You hate me, Rafe. Why do you care who deserves me?"

The corner of his mouth trends north. And it's not exactly a smile, but it's something that might exist close to one. I take a step back, overwhelmed by the force of the dimple that imprints on his cheek and the way his shirt stretches over his chest like it's grateful to have been chosen from his suitcase this morning. He lifts the hem to wipe away a line of sweat, exposing a swath of golden skin, and I'm so close to passing out it's pathetic.

Rafe moves closer, and even after a workout, he smells so good that I kind of want to lick him like a chocolate-dipped cone. Another step and my back hits the wall with an audible *oof.*

With his eyes shining like polished copper pennies, Rafe moves so close that nothing but atoms vibrate between us. I suck in a breath, my breasts ghosting against his chest with the barest brush. He plants his elbows on either side of my head, leaning so close it compresses the space in my windpipe until I'm breathing lead.

His head dips, his mouth a phantom against the shell of my ear. "I do hate you, Tris. I hate you *very* much."

My mouth parts. My thoughts are coated in mud. His head

pulls back, and then he does it again. That lift of his lips that borders on the edge of . . . something.

After giving me a prolonged once-over that would corrupt a demon, he walks away, disappearing into the changing room.

My knees have become water, and I slide partway to the floor. With my heart galloping in my chest, I press my hand against it, knowing only one thing for sure: Rafe Gallagher is giving me some very mixed signals.

Chapter Ten

*O*nce I've gathered the shreds of my tattered libido, I return to our room, relieved to find it empty. After an icy cold shower, I change into fresh workout clothes, donning a black tank top and shorts. The app says we're focusing on team building today—oh joy—and will be heading to Blue Lagoon Adventure Park.

An hour later, I find myself bumping along in the vinyl seat of a yellow school bus that pulls into the parking lot. There, I spy a giant outdoor obstacle course made up of ropes and ladders, wooden walls, giant tires, muddy ponds, and bridges swinging from trees.

After hopping off the bus, I huddle with Gabrielle and Lan under the cool drops of the continuing drizzle. I can't help but notice that my friends are standing a little closer than might be typical for a professional environment. I think of Rafe towering over me in the gym, our bodies so close I almost drowned in his heat.

Gabrielle turns away to speak with someone, and when Lan catches me watching them, she leans over and whispers in my ear. "The internship is still my priority, but nothing is saying I can't have a little fun on the side, is there?"

"Obviously not," I agree, willing myself not to look for Rafe in the crowd.

Most of WMC's rising stars are in their late twenties and early thirties. I turned twenty-nine a few months ago, and the eternal question of *what's next* is creeping up louder and louder. I've spent so many years focused on my career and avoiding long-term relationships, indulging in casual flings that are only about physical release, but how much longer can I keep this up?

What do I want? Marriage? Kids? That would mean I'd have to learn to trust someone with my heart again.

The executive team is also here, sitting under a large white tent, black sunglasses shielding their eyes and coffee mugs clutched in their hands. I assume they're full of vodka.

From reading her book, I know Diane never married or had children, and I wonder why she made those choices. Does she regret any of it? Or is that question simply a product of my own internalized expectations?

Marriage might be nice—I like the idea of having a partner as my constant. Children have never been high on my list of priorities, but I suppose if I met the right person who I could see myself having kids with, I wouldn't be opposed to the idea.

The instructor starts yelling out orders, dragging me from my thoughts. She tells us to convene in groups of four for today's challenge.

While a mad scramble ensues, I notice Rafe across the parking lot. Our eyes meet, and something hot and jagged flares in my chest. I'm still reeling from this morning, and my thoughts are having trouble catching up.

Lan tugs me towards Gabrielle, who's standing with Andy. We become a foursome, and I watch Rafe join a group with two men and one woman whose names I don't know yet.

Andy presses a hand against the small of my back. He seems to be over the incident on the boat and clearly isn't allowing Rafe to scare him off.

"Glad we'll be working together," he says with an uncomplicated and sincere grin, but I'm not sure how I feel about this anymore. The initial spark has dimmed, and it has absolutely nothing to do with Rafe.

Sure, okay. Let's go with that.

My gaze drifts back to Rafe. Is he thinking about this morning, too? His thin grey T-shirt stretches against the lines of his chest and his shoulders, and I lick my lips without meaning to.

The instructor begins to explain today's rules. We're being judged on our teamwork, how we support our teammates and strategize, and, of course, how we keep up. Being a successful leader is about more than just mental stamina; it requires physical stamina, too.

The winning group will be awarded a private dinner with the executive team this evening. It's a chance to impress and help secure a training spot at the end of the retreat. Lan is practically salivating at the notion, whispering strategies under her breath as she squints at the obstacles and then assesses each of us with a critical eye.

I'm not worried. I'm good at things like this. I crave physical activity as long as no one tries to make me dribble a basketball or spike a volleyball. My teammates all seem fit enough, and I like our odds.

As we gather in our assigned places, my gaze finds Rafe again. He glares and cracks his knuckles, and I point at him and then to a spot on the ground before grinding my toe into the dirt. His eyes darken to the hue of cinnamon swirled in chocolate, and the barest curve forms ever so slowly on his lips.

It's not a smile...I don't know what it is.

I turn away, but I feel his gaze burning a hole in my back. I resist the urge to turn around, but my resolve crumbles, and I peer over my shoulder to find him watching me with a hungry intensity that sets my pulse galloping.

A whistle shrieks, shocking me back into focus before my team discusses our plans.

We work well together under a shower of light rain, clearing the first few rounds as we strategize through every obstacle, climbing over angled walls and sliding down ropes. If Andy's hands seem to end up on me a little more than is strictly necessary, I tell myself I don't mind.

After several hours and many nail-biting rounds, our team is soggy but still standing and prepared to head into the final round. Predictably, the second team left is Rafe's. We're going head-to-head for that coveted dinner.

"You should probably just give up now," Andy taunts.

Rafe grinds his jaw, and Andy gives him a bland smile, clearly getting under his skin. Andy moves closer to me, placing a hand on the small of my back, and Rafe's eyes go dark.

"If you're scared, just say so," Rafe taunts. "It's obvious who's going to win this."

I roll my eyes. "Can we stop with the barbarian chest beating? Everyone play nice. Especially you, Gallagher." I point my finger at Rafe, and after giving me a *Who me?* look, he has the grace to look at least a little abashed. But then he pins me with that smile that isn't a smile, and my skin erupts into a field of goose bumps that have nothing to do with being cold.

"Everyone!" Our leader claps her hands and blasts a shrill tweet on her whistle. I swear I'm going to shove that thing down her throat. "Our final two teams will now repeat the entire course, front to back. The team that captures the red pennant first wins. You can arrange yourselves however you wish. There are no rules other than you cannot interfere with the other team in any way, or I will immediately disqualify you. Do I make myself clear?" She directs her question to me and Rafe, obviously remembering us from the Ferris wheel challenge.

The eight of us nod sagely, and Rafe and I exchange a glance that burns like lava through my veins.

"You take the tires." Lan is pointing to Gabrielle. "You were fastest on those. Andy, the rope wall. I'll take the tightropes and the swing rope, and Tris, you're on the monkey bar rings. I've never known a woman with such freakish upper body strength."

I smile, preening at the compliment, whether she intended it that way or not.

Gabrielle is the first to go, and we all stand behind her at the start line. A moment later, Whistle Mouth emits a screech, and everyone is off. As Gabrielle tackles her obstacles, we head for our respective stations, getting into position.

I'll be the last to go right before the finish line. I climb onto a wooden platform standing about five feet above the ground. Two long ropes stretch over a pool of muddy water, each with about a dozen wooden rings dangling in a row.

My hands are raw, and my shoulders are tired from having done this several times already, but I rub my wet palms on my legs and focus. It'll take less than a minute to cross.

When a familiar head of dark brown hair climbs up the ladder, my determination solidifies into iron. Rafe jumps on the platform and strides over, puffed up like a rooster.

"Gallagher," I say, forging my voice with a challenge. "I'm going to kick your ass."

"Big talk for a small girl, Malik." I see we're into using last names. This feels appropriate and gives me the distance I need right now.

A round of cheers rises in the distance, and we both peer through the trees as Rafe's teammate Joe and Lan clear the tightrope strung between two thick trees. It's the last obstacle before they tag off with us.

Lan and Joe jump down from the circular platform attached to the trunk, sprinting through the bushes to where Rafe and I are waiting. They're neck and neck, and this is going to be tight.

As Lan and Joe ascend the top of the ladder, they run for me and Rafe, both of us hunched in ready stances. The distance between us is about ten feet, and just as they're about to reach us, several things happen at once.

Someone trips. I'm not sure who because everything becomes a tangle of limbs as Lan and Joe morph into a human squid. Lan's shoulder thumps into my chest as she tumbles. I step back, my foot meeting nothing but air. Arms windmilling, I attempt to recover my balance, reaching for something to stop my plummet off the edge.

Unfortunately, that thing is Rafe. My fingers snag on the fabric of his shirt, my hand fisting into the material. But momentum propels me over the side, throwing off his balance.

Rafe careens towards me, and I scream as I begin to fall. His broad frame crashes into mine, his arms wrapping around me as we tumble. Time slows to a drip as we descend, air whooshing in my ears until, all at once, I'm engulfed by a tide of mud, driven under the surface by two hundred pounds of bone and muscle.

Mud fills my eyes and my nose and my mouth, and this is how I die.

My lungs burn as I fight for air. I feel Rafe moving on top of me, his hands touching me everywhere. Limbs flailing, I kick and punch for what feels like forever, when finally, his weight shifts, and a pair of strong hands lift me out of the muddy water. As my face breaks the surface, I gasp, choking and coughing as I clutch my chest. My lungs ache, and my vision drips with murky rivulets. We're both on our knees, the water coming up to my chest.

My head spins, and I collapse against Rafe, his solid form saving me from another brush with death.

"Tris, I'm sorry. Are you okay?"

He's rubbing my back. He almost killed me, so I guess we're back to first names.

"Rafe!" I half shout and half gasp, my face pressed into his chest. I'm not sure why. This isn't his fault, but my life just flashed before my eyes, and I can't catch my breath. He folds me against him, arms wrapping tightly around me, and my capacity to examine this gesture is limited right now.

"Tris, I'm so sorry," Lan calls. She stands with Gabrielle on the platform, shouting down at us. "I tripped! Are you okay?"

I shake my head, trying to dislodge the mud wedged in my ears and my nostrils and my eyes. I push back a ropey strand of mud-caked hair. This is going to be a nightmare to get out.

Rafe helps me stand, and then the shrill sound of a whistle breaks through a wall of shocked silence.

Skreeeeee.

"You!" Whistle Mouth points to me. "You're disqualified for interference."

"What? That was an accident!"

She brandishes her accusing finger like someone died and made her the Lord of Blue Lagoon Adventure Park. "I saw you grab him and pull him in the mud!"

"It was clearly an accident," Rafe says. "Let's just start from the rings. We would have been even, anyway."

I throw him a suspicious look. Why is he defending me? His team wins by default if I'm disqualified.

"I said she's out," Whistle Mouth replies.

"That's not fair!" I argue.

"It's really not," Rafe counters. "I want to win properly, not by default."

Thus, his motives become clear. He's not being nice; he just wants to make sure everyone sees when he beats me.

"And now you're disqualified for arguing with the referee!" Whistle Mouth says. "Both teams are done!"

The crowd's collective groan mingles with cries of protest and outrage. Whistle Mouth blows so hard that her entire head turns into a roasted beet.

"My decision is final! Teams three and four will compete for the top spot instead."

Rafe and I open our mouths to complain again, but Whistle Mouth silences us with another bleat. "If you want to argue further, I'll disqualify you from this entire exercise, and you can both return home on the next flight out of here."

Well, that does it. Our mouths snap shut, and Whistle Mouth fires another screech in our direction, punctuating her threat with a shrill exclamation point. She then walks off, gesturing for teams three and four to make their way to the start of the course.

Rafe's jaw tics as he watches her back, and I open my mouth to apologize for grabbing him. He cuts his glittering gaze in my direction, and my apology dies on my tongue.

"Don't look at me like that," I say. "This isn't my fault!"

"Well, it's not mine, either."

"Whatever, Rafe. Why do you even care? You can have dinner with the executive team any time you want. Don't pretend you haven't spent summers at their sprawling beach houses sipping cognac and harrumphing confidently at each other as you disdain the rest of us plebeians."

But I've really said the wrong thing because his expression becomes a shard of obsidian dipped in ink.

He opens his mouth but then must think better of what he was about to say because he closes it so hard I'm surprised his skull doesn't shatter.

After assailing me one last time with the heat of his fury, he splashes out of the mud pit and storms away.

Chapter Eleven

Rafe and I are forced to ride on the bus back to the hotel together. Covered head to toe in mud, we smell weird, and everyone politely declines to sit with either of us. Maybe it's not only the stench but the scene we made and the inescapable aura of drama that's following us. It feels like we're causing issues wherever we go.

As the bus rumbles and lurches back to the hotel, we don't converse with words, instead using a series of carefully architectured glares to express the infinite chasms of our mutual irritation.

I'm not even sure who I'm mad at right now.

Other than Whistle Mouth.

My hatred for her spans the widest, deepest sea.

I shake out my hair, raining flakes of mud onto the rubberized floor. I'm sure my gym shoes are ruined, and I hope that I can salvage my clothing.

By the time we arrive at our suite, I feel like I've been dipped in glue. A trail of grime streaks the pristine tiled floors, and I make a mental note to tip the cleaning staff extra tomorrow.

"Can I use the shower?" Rafe asks, finally breaking our stalemate. "The tub isn't ideal for getting this off, and I'm not really a bath guy."

"Sure," I reply because it's a reasonable request, and I'm not a monster. "You might as well go first. This is going to take me a while." I gesture to the stygian mass of mud-caked hair plastered to my head. I'll need an entire bottle of shampoo to get this out.

"You sure?" he asks, clearly doubtful of my uncharacteristic graciousness.

I blink at him. "Just don't use all the hot water."

He rolls his eyes and disappears into the bathroom, crumbs of mud littering a path in his wake like he's luring small children to his gingerbread house. A few moments later, I hear the water start.

It would be a dick move to sully any of this pristine white furniture with a muddy ass print, so I grab a can of sparkling water from the fridge and head outside to wait on the balcony. The rain has momentarily cleared as clouds hang in the sky, but at least I can watch the sun inching towards the horizon. Today's winning team will be sitting down to dinner soon, enjoying a spread of high-end cuisine and the singularly unique flavor of success.

Before we left the Blue Lagoon Adventure Park, I noticed Rafe in a heated discussion with his father. I couldn't make out what they were saying, but I assumed it was about the contest. Why does David care? Surely, Rafe's future at WMC is already secured?

My phone buzzes, and I fish it out of my waistband pocket, wiping a smear of mud off the screen. It's a text from Molly.

Molly: How was your day? How's Andy?

After we were all disqualified, Andy played it off like he wasn't bothered, but I could tell he was irritated with me and Lan. My instinct was to apologize, but I reined in the urge. We did nothing wrong. It was an accident, and Whistle Mouth was out of line.

Me: Eh, I don't know about him.

Molly: Why?

Me: Because

I pause and stare at the screen, unsure of why I'm hesitating to tell her this.

Me: Rafe and Hannah broke up. That's what they're fighting about.

Molly: I WAS RIGHT

Me: But she wants to get back together, and she keeps calling him.

Molly: Oh . . . that's . . . interesting?

Me: Is it?

Molly: I'm not sure.

Rafe calls to me from inside the suite. "I'm done. Shower's all yours."

The door to the second bathroom slams, and I stare at my blank screen. I'll text Molly later to dissect every angle of this development. First, I desperately need to get this mud off.

It takes several shampoos and an entire bottle of body wash until I'm finally clean. When I'm done, I pull on my silk robe and emerge into the living area, toweling off my hair.

I spy Rafe sitting on the balcony, wearing nothing but a pair of grey sweatpants. Good grief, is he trying to kill me? I nibble the inside of my lip in hesitation, decide I'm being a drama queen, and head outside.

"Hey," I say, suddenly and painfully aware of the single layer of silk standing between Rafe and my naked body. He taps on his phone for a second and then tosses it on the table beside him, exhaling a sigh. Tucking his hands behind his head, he leans back and tilts his face to the setting sun.

"Hey," he replies, and while it absolutely shouldn't, that single casual syllable spreads over my skin like warm honey.

"I'm sorry," I venture. "I didn't mean for things to happen that way. I wanted to beat you fair and square, too."

He opens his eyes and looks up, his gaze finding mine. It's bronze and molten, gilded by evening sunlight. "Don't sweat it, Tris. It was an accident."

The way he says my name at that moment feels so intimate, almost like he's never said it before. I've always understood how we fit together. In our own dysfunctional way, we've always made sense. But the ground is shifting, and I can feel him erasing all of my carefully drawn lines.

Then, something happens I wasn't expecting.

Rafe's face breaks into a slow, steady grin, hitting me with the heat of a thousand suns. It twists a potent spike of radiance, multiplying until I'm forced to step back. The dimple and the teeth and the curve of his full and perfect lips. The burnished light flaring in his dark brown eyes. The crinkle in the corners.

For the first time since I've met Rafe Gallagher, that *smile* is directed at me, and my entire world wobbles and goes sideways.

"The look on your face when Lan ran into you—"

He laughs, oblivious to my turmoil, throwing his head back with abandon. I'm not imagining it when a single ray of benevolent light beams from the sky and illuminates him like the angel in a Renaissance painting.

It takes a moment to return to my body. My outer shell shatters, and then...I laugh, too.

Rafe and I are laughing together.

"Your face when I grabbed you," I add, and he laughs even harder.

"Can you believe Whistle Mouth had the *nerve* to kick us out?"

"That's what I call her too!" I practically scream, and before long, my sides ache from laughing so hard.

He shakes his head, wiping the corner of his eye. "We should break into her room and put plastic wrap over her toilet seat," he says. "Or hide a dead fish in her closet."

"That's so immature," I say. "But we totally should."

He smiles again, and I'm so flustered that my neck goes hot.

"Why are you looking at me like that?" he asks, and I realize I've been staring like a psycho.

"Thanks for sticking up for me," I reply, finding my tongue.

It isn't the first time. He did it with Rory when I was picked for this. And there was that time some asshole in a meeting talked down to me like I was a six-year-old, and Rafe made him apologize. I overheard him once telling someone off for hitting on me and clearly making me uncomfortable.

His smile dims, and his expression becomes inscrutable.

"No problem," he replies and leans back on the lounger, closing his eyes and releasing me from the power of his attention. The band around my chest eases, my body sagging in relief. I need a moment to sort through what that smile just set free.

It offers the bonus of allowing me to admire him. Golden light reflects off the dips and curves of his torso, highlighting the cinder blocks of his chest and the bricks of his stomach. My tongue runs over my lips, begging for a taste. I want to bury my nose in his throat. Trace my fingers along the taper of angled muscle framing his hips.

Squeezing my hands, I force myself to look into the sun's blinding light. Maybe if I fry my retinas, Rafe won't be such a distraction.

"I was planning to order room service," I finally say, trying to make my voice sound normal. "Do you want anything?"

With his eyes still closed, he replies, "Yeah, I'll have a burger and fries, thanks."

Before I return to the suite, I give myself another moment to ogle him.

"Stop gawking, Tris."

I jump a hundred feet.

Fuck. He can't see me—how did he do that?

"As if you didn't come out here dressed like that on purpose," I say and hear him chuckling as I duck into the room.

After I order, I change into a pair of shorts and a tank top.

A knock sounds at the door, and a man wearing a black vest wheels a cart into the room.

"Where would you like it, miss?"

"Out there, please." I gesture to the balcony and fetch two glasses and a bottle of white wine from the fridge. Once the man returns to the room, he tips his head and leaves, closing the door as I step onto the balcony.

Rafe is standing at the cart, lifting the silver covers off our plates.

"Could you put on a shirt?" I ask. It comes out more as a demand than a question, but I can barely think right now. My mouth is operating with a set of unapproved directions.

"Why?" He gives me an innocent look, and I summon a glare.

"Because we're about to eat, and it's...unsanitary." I gesture vaguely in his direction as if to demonstrate how his nakedness is contaminating my food. Who am I kidding? I kind of want his nakedness contaminating my...everything.

He sets the metal covers on the cart's lower shelf and smirks as he passes me, entering the suite and disappearing into the second bathroom. With no bedroom of his own, he's turned it into a makeshift closet-slash-dressing room.

A flash of guilt nibbles in my stomach, and I consider offering him space in my closet and then dismiss the idea. I don't need him any closer to my orbit. Instead, I make it up to him by pouring him a glass of wine and setting his food on a small table between the two loungers. I settle on the left one with my knees straddled on either side of the table.

A moment later, Rafe emerges wearing a white T-shirt that molds to him so perfectly that I'm not actually sure this is any better.

"Happy?" he asks.

I suck in a calming breath. I have to stop this.

As he sits down across from me, I pretend I'm assessing his attire—but I make it look like I'm not enjoying it. I hope.

"Yes, now I can stomach my food."

He points at my half-eaten burger. "Oh good, because it looks like you're nearly done."

"I had one bite."

He arches a dark eyebrow as he picks up his burger. It looks so tiny in his large hands. He leans forward to take a bite, and his knees brush mine. I almost flinch at the shock that zips straight to my navel.

He takes another bite, shifting so my legs are sandwiched between his. When his calf presses mine, I try not to react. Was that deliberate? I'm reading far too much into this innocent move-ment. It's just been ages since a man has properly touched me. That's all this is. I think of my electronic friend that I packed and haven't had the opportunity to use. I just need a little me time, and these wholly inappropriate urges will go away.

Our eyes meet across the tiny table. I want that smile again. I want his dimple and the light in his eyes. I want him to look at me the way he looks at everyone else. This is bad. A dimple isn't supposed to be sexual, and I can hardly blame my drought on this. Tension settles around us, but it isn't unpleasant. It's alive and electric.

I need to break out of this moment, and thankfully, Rafe doesn't disappoint me.

"What kind of maniac dips their fries in mayo *and* ketchup?" he asks before taking another bite of his burger. The way his mouth closes over the bun makes me wish I was—never mind. That's even too sad for me to admit. His leg presses harder against mine as I narrow my eyes.

"It's good. Since when is condiment selection related to one's mental stability?"

Rafe snorts, snatches a fry from *my* plate, and dips it in *my* mayo and *my* ketchup. I make an affronted sound that he ignores as he puts it in his mouth, and *now* I wish were a—*stop it*.

A tiny blob lingers in the corner of his mouth, and I bite my lip as his tongue reaches out to catch it.

"Not bad," he says, oblivious to the riot of sensation he's inciting in the needy place between my thighs.

He smiles. *Again.* And I have to look away. This is too much.

We eat a while longer in companionable silence. When I'm done, I scoot back on my chair and fold my hands over my stomach.

"I wish I'd ordered dessert, too." I stare forlornly at my empty plate, hoping something sugary will materialize by the sheer force of my pout.

Rafe finishes his food and wipes his hands on a napkin.

"Hold on," he says, standing up and entering the suite. A moment later, he returns with a glossy white box tied with an elaborate gold ribbon.

"You can have these."

"Ooh, what is it?" I perk up, swinging my legs to the ground. Rafe resumes his position in the lounger across from mine.

"Something I bought the other day."

He shrugs, but the movement is tight as he stares at the box in his hands. I reach out and flip up the shiny tag. Macarons. Fancy ones with little pictures describing each flavor.

"You bought a box of French macarons to keep in the bathroom?"

"Well, I have nowhere else to keep them, Trishara." He gives me a meaningful look, but I completely brush past the point because he smiled at me, and now, he's offering me treats. What am I supposed to do with myself?

He runs a hand down his face.

"Who did you buy these for, Rafe?"

I take the package, stroking the stiff golden ribbon between my fingers.

"I guess…" He stops, grimacing at the box like it's a grenade. "I guess I bought them for Hannah."

"Oh," I reply as something crumples in my chest. I'm so stupid. His half-naked body. His leg against mine. *The smile*. I'm searching for signs that don't exist.

It's fine. I need them to reconcile. It's for the best. As soon as Rafe is back with Hannah, all these pointless feelings will take a hike and leave me the hell alone. Everything will return to the orderly places they belong, and I can keep him at a distance where it's safest.

"I can't eat these."

I place the box on the lounger next to Rafe's hip. I *should* eat them because they'll go stale long before he gets them back to Chicago, and why is it so adorable that he doesn't know that? Macarons are my favorite, and I really, really want to eat them, but there's a symbolism in eating a present he meant for his currently-ex-but-maybe-soon-to-be-current girlfriend.

"I'll just call down for more room service."

I stand, but Rafe wraps a hand around the back of my knee, stilling me. *Killing* me.

"No," he says, his touch lingering for an extra beat. He clears his throat and pulls his hand away. "You can eat them."

He picks up the box and unties the ribbon. "It was stupid. I don't know why I bought them. I think it's supposed to be an apology."

He peels off the gold sticker sealing the box and holds it open.

"An apology?" I ask because I'm deep into this now, I guess.

At first, he doesn't look at me. His gaze is focused like he's contemplating drowning himself in the shallow depths of a cardboard box. When he looks up, his eyes are filled with conflict.

"I just never felt a spark," he says.

"Oh," I say again, and that earlier crumpling loosens like an unfurling paper ball.

"Our parents are friends," he continues. "They've basically been inseparable since they were in college, and when they both had kids around the same time, they planned our entire future. I resisted it for a long time. We would have been married years ago if they'd had their way, but I wanted to see some of the world first. Do some stuff."

"Do some other women?" I joke, and he rolls his eyes.

"I'm opening up here, Tris. Do you mind?"

"Sorry," I say and bite my bottom lip. "But really?"

He gives me a cautious smile, and I'm amazed at how easy this is. Like this is how it's always been. It's still making my heart stop every single time. "Okay, yes. I didn't want to marry the only woman I'd ever been with. Does that make me an asshole?"

I shake my head. "Honestly, it doesn't. I wouldn't want that either."

"Thanks," he says and there's warmth in that word, better than all the flannel scarves and vanilla lattes in the entire galaxy.

"Anyway"—I gesture to him—"you were saying."

"Hannah had always been into us trying things out, and we've always had fun as friends. She's gorgeous, I was about to turn thirty, and..." He breaks off and gives me a strange look as though he was about to say something he shouldn't before adding, "And what was I resisting for?"

I purse my lips but say nothing.

"So we started dating, and it was fine. She's sweet and doesn't take anything too seriously. She's uncomplicated and has lots of friends and people who love her. She's always busy and trying something new."

I lean my chin on a fist and look up at him. "I'm waiting for you to get to the part where any of this makes sense. Does she have a third nipple somewhere? A perpetual rash in an inconvenient place? Is she secretly into whipping you with licorice and calling you Daddy?"

"What?" he asks, his eyebrows drawing together. "That is so weirdly specific."

I shrug. "I read a lot of interesting books."

Amusement dances in his eyes, and this is so addicting.

"Yes, she's all those good things, and she'll be the perfect wife for a million guys. Just not for me."

I sit up, pressing my palms to my knees, suddenly liking this story much better. I am a terrible person. Despite what I just said about needing them back together, I shouldn't be rooting for their demise. I shouldn't care this much.

"Why not?" I have to know. I am dying of curiosity. I need to know why this perfect woman isn't enough for Rafe Gallagher.

"I don't know," he says. "It's not something I can put into words. All I know is that it doesn't feel quite right." He levels me with a look I can't interpret. "I want someone who makes me feel a little like I'm . . . burning in the best kind of way."

He stops, his chest heaving as if admitting this out loud has cost him something. As if this is the first time he really let himself acknowledge these words.

"But how do you explain that? I don't want to hurt her. I don't want our friendship to end. We've known each other since we were babies. And our families . . . I don't want to blow everything up. This will kill my mom. I *know* I should have broken it off a long time ago, but . . . I felt pressured to make it work. She deserves better than that, and I can't give her what she wants."

He's still holding the box of macarons, one hand cupped around each end. I take it from him and place it on the chair next to me as he braces his elbows on his knees and looks down at his feet.

"How have you kept it from your parents for so long?" I ask.

He shakes his head and looks up. "My dad is always working, and I've had to deflect with my mom. Thankfully, she's been pretty busy lately, too. I hate deceiving her, and I think she suspects something is up."

"Is this why you didn't want to share a room with your dad?"

He rolls his shoulders. "Partly."

There's more he isn't saying, but when he doesn't elaborate, I continue. "That's a lot. But surely your family understands if things don't work out? They had to know it wasn't a given just because they're all friends?"

He lets out a dry laugh. "You'd think, wouldn't you? They're all smart, successful people who have every moment of their lives planned. I don't think they ever considered it. This just fits into their vision."

The waves crash below as we sit in silence. I'm not sure what to say. I'm a little surprised he's being so raw and honest in my presence.

"I know there are people in the world with far worse problems, and I must sound like such a privileged asshole right now," he says.

"Rafe," I interrupt. "It's okay. I mean, yeah, there are people who have it worse, but you're allowed to have misgivings about the circumstances of your life, regardless of how they might seem to others."

He gives me a grateful look that unlocks some rusty, buried cavern in my heart.

"I bought a ring in some kind of last-ditch attempt to convince myself this was what I wanted, but the minute I held it, I knew I could never propose. But she found out and thinks I'm just having cold feet right now. She thinks I'm going to change my mind." He glances at his phone lying on the chair like it's a poisoned viper. "She won't take no for an answer and still shows up at my apartment all the time. I was honestly so relieved to come here just to put some physical distance between us. I told her we'd talk when I get back."

"And tell her what?"

"I'm not sure," he says. "I guess the ugly truth, as harsh as it might sound."

I tilt my head, pick up the box, and hold it out to him. He plucks a macaron and pops it into his mouth, and I gasp.

"What?" he asks.

"You can't just blindly choose one. That's sacrilege! You need to consult the piece of paper! What if you just ate caramel, and you don't like caramel?"

"It wasn't caramel."

"What was it?"

He frowns as he chews. "I'm not sure. Something fruity."

"You see what I mean? Now you've thrown off the whole balance of the box."

He snatches it from my hand and closes his eyes, picking another one and stuffing it in his mouth with a grin. He chews slowly, clearly enjoying my distress. I grab the box, clutching it to my chest like a precious baby lamb.

"*That* one was caramel," he says, and I huff out a laugh.

"Please tell me there's a lemon one you didn't recklessly eat." Peering into the box, I spy a yellow macaron and rescue it, sinking my teeth into the chewy crust.

"Lemon?" he asks, giving me a once-over. "I would have pegged you for a chocolate girl."

That brings me up short. Why has Rafe ever considered my flavor preference?

"I love both," I reply, and he nods.

"Good to know." Then his gaze meets mine. "Thanks for listening. You're actually easy to talk to."

I roll my eyes. "Don't seem so surprised. I'm not a total bitch despite what you think."

"I've never thought that," he says, and it sounds sincere, but I can't tell if he's being honest. "What about you?"

"What about me?"

"Are you seeing anyone?"

"Oh. No, I'm not. It's been a while."

"How long is a while?"

I think about my answer, worried about revealing my past, but Rafe just opened up, and I'm enjoying this truce too much to let it end.

"A year-ish," I say tentatively.

"That's a long time," he says. He almost looks relieved, but I must be reading that wrong. "Did you swear off men or something?"

I snort. "Not on purpose."

That earns me a wry smile, and I let out a drawn-out breath. "I went through a bad breakup years ago that sort of scared me off all relationships. He broke my trust in the worst possible way. I tried to start dating again, but I admit I'm having difficulty putting my faith in anyone. I guess I'm looking for someone that makes me feel...safe."

I blink because it's like a light just came on. I don't think I understood that's what I wanted until I just voiced it out loud.

He focuses his intense gaze on me. "I'm sorry that happened. You deserve to be with someone you trust implicitly."

This, too, is uttered with such sincerity that some fundamental part of me shifts.

We're both quiet for a minute until he tips his head and grins.

"Don't be mad about the macarons, Tris. Would it help if I took my shirt off again?"

I make an offended noise as I pick a macaron from the box and throw it at him.

It bounces off the center of his chest as his laughter, his smile, the brightness in his eyes all begin to chip away at the wall I so carefully and purposefully built around myself.

Chapter Twelve

The next morning, I enter my bathroom to find a half-naked Rafe wearing nothing but a towel slung low on his hips. I scream. It's not dignified. It's the kind of scream where clueless girls in cut-offs wander into abandoned houses and are surprised when a masked man jumps out wielding a chef's knife.

"Rafe!" I press my hand to my chest, my breath heaving in tatters. "What are you doing? You scared me half to death!"

He doesn't react to my glass-shattering shriek, simply turning to me with his brows raised. Dark brown eyes regard me with the calm composure of a leopard.

"Using the shower. I liked it last night and have decided it hardly seems fair you've been hogging it."

"This is *my* bathroom." I point to the floor to illustrate my point. That wins me a derisive snort.

"It's not yours any more than it's mine. My back has been sore since we got here from sleeping on that stupid couch. The least you could do is share the good bathroom with me."

He has a point, but I'm not about to admit it. After we talked about Hannah last night, it started raining again and we moved into the living room, where we stayed up late chatting while sharing another bottle of wine.

We told silly childhood stories, and he shared more about his mom and being an only child and how he played hockey in college until he hurt his knee. I tell him about my parents and my brother who works way too hard as a hedge fund manager.

It was far from the worst night I've ever spent with a man.

But he's still Rafe, and he isn't taking my bathroom.

He lifts his arm, and my entire body goes numb as I register what's gripped in his hand.

"What is this thing?" He peers curiously at curved pink plastic adorned with shiny gold accents, all fitting far too neatly in the cradle of his large palm.

"Rafe! What is wrong with you?" I snatch my Lelo Sona 2 from his hand and hide it behind my back. "That is private. Why are you going through my things?"

"I wasn't. It was just lying there. *Almost* like you used it last night." He crosses his arms, biceps bulging as he leans a hip on the counter. My embarrassment deepens to a violent shade of crimson. "What does it do, Tris?"

That smile that knocked me senseless last night is so wide I'm surprised it can fit in the room. I should really be more careful about what I wish for.

I inhale a cleansing breath. I have nothing to be embarrassed about. I'm a grown woman, and last night, I needed to take the edge off. However, finding Rafe wearing nothing but a towel has negated every bit of that effort.

"It simulates oral sex," I say, willing my voice to remain even.

Rafe's arms and stomach tighten, veins popping and muscles straining. His jaw tics, and he rolls his shoulders ever so slightly.

"Is that so?" His eyes drop to my hips for a fraction of a second, but I feel it straight through my soul. "How was it?"

Holy crap. Are we really talking about this? My skin bursts into fire.

"Better than any man I've been with," I say, and shit, did I just insult him or myself?

His eyes sparkle with a gleam. "Maybe you've just been with the wrong men."

I cock my hip and place a hand on it while looking him up and down.

"Maybe men are simply incapable of competing with a little machine," I fire back.

Rafe's smirk becomes the most devious, the most evil, the most *Rafe* I've ever seen. He drops his arms and steps forward, looking down at me from his lofty height.

"Is that a challenge, Trishara?" His voice is low and dangerous as his eyes rake over me, and my traitorous nipples harden into weapons-grade carbon.

I cross my arms, hoping he won't notice, but I'm glass, and he sees right through it.

Eyes darkening, he steps closer, and my inner thighs tighten. He's still glistening and wet, and a single drop of water is making its magnificent way down the center of his chest. All my coherent thoughts become a distant memory.

"Don't pretend you mind me using your shower, Malik. I saw the way you were ogling me last night. Now you get to see me without my shirt again." He flicks the tip of my nose with his thumb and forefinger, and I drop my arms with a sound of indignation.

"How dare you?" Now that he's broken the smile threshold, it seems he can't get enough. This one is half-cocked, and why does that make my stomach flip? He brushes past me, and I spin around, momentarily stunned by the wide span of his back and the top curve of his ass, just barely covered by the towel.

"I was staring because I couldn't believe you weren't burning to a crisp in the sun! Isn't that what your kind does in the light of day?"

I'm rewarded with a glance over his shoulder, his devilish smirk hooking into my sternum. He chuckles darkly before disappearing into the second bathroom and slamming the door.

An hour later, I make my way down to the conference rooms for today's session. According to the app, we're discovering our personality types through a series of tests to determine our best avenues for communication, individual motivation, and learning. Then, we'll divide into groups of contrasting types to solve problems using everyone's strengths and weaknesses.

The rain has picked up, and a boom of supposedly rare Hawaiian thunder sets me on edge, meaning I'm already irritable when I arrive. I really hate storms.

We sit at long tables with our chairs lined up on one side, Lan to my left and, inexplicably, Rafe to my right. My plan is to pretend this morning's conversation about my sex toy never happened, even if I can't stop thinking about it. I just hope he plays along.

I also can't stop replaying his question through my head.

Is that a challenge, Trishara?

However, it's also distracting me from a flash of lightning streaking across the sky, so maybe I should be thanking him.

Whistle Mouth is back, and that shrill, piercing echo is even worse when it's delivered indoors. I suspect it's because of me and Rafe that she's hanging on to her whistle at all times. I grind my teeth, still angry at how we were so unjustly disqualified. Rafe must harbor similar thoughts because I catch him staring at her like he wants to peel off her skin. I'm just glad his Terminator stare is turned on someone else for a change.

"Aren't there some beings who live under a bridge you could sit with?" I ask as some guys that Rafe appears friendly with filter in. One of them calls his name, and Rafe tips his chin. "Ah, there they are now. In all their troll-like glory."

Rafe's eyebrow arches. "And your friends are the pinnacle of anti-trollness?"

I lean back and peek at Lan talking to Gabrielle.

"Of course, look at them. They're adorable. We all are."

Rafe smirks and then gives me one of those head-to-toe looks that does things I don't want. "Yes, you are," he says so low I almost don't hear it before he turns to talk to one of the troll beings sitting on his other side.

I don't possess the wherewithal to dwell on that statement before Whistle Mouth *blows*, destroying everyone's eardrums and sending a collective flinch across the room.

"When is someone going to melt that thing down and choke her with it?" Lan whispers as Whistle Mouth hands out test papers.

"As soon as I get my hands on it," I reply, and Lan covers her mouth to hold in her laugh.

Whistle Mouth cuts a sharp glance my way. Wow, she hates me. "Eyes on your own paper. This isn't a test you can pass or fail. It's simply meant to determine your learning type and what teamwork methods suit you best."

She can claim this isn't really a test, but everyone in the room knows this isn't true. They're looking for specific answers. Specific personalities to fill their hallowed corner office halls. Two members of the executive team sit in the corner, thumbs tapping on their phones. Two white men nearing retirement, here searching for their replacements.

Whistle Mouth blows again, and how is this compliant with health and safety standards? "You have one hour," she says before a flurry of pencils begin scratching against paper backdropped by the increasing sounds of wind and rain outside.

My nerves twist as I stare out the window, but I tune it out, focusing on the task at hand.

Throughout the day, I learn a few things about myself, though most of it isn't a surprise. I'm driven by my sense of competitiveness, enjoy strategizing for the future, and am an introvert. I study my assessment as I pick at my bottom lip. That last one makes sense. I'm comfortable when I'm with a group of people I know, but generally, I'm happy with my own company.

Seeing my competition score strikes a chord deep within my repressed psyche. I *was* competitive, and I still am, but my years at WMC have dulled that edge. I came here intent on enjoying a free holiday, but I can't deny the stirring in my chest that still wants to win.

"You're an introvert?" Rafe asks, leaning over and peering at my page. There is a high degree of skepticism in his voice.

"Yes. Why?"

"Because you're ... you." He waves a hand in my direction as if to encompass just how *me* I apparently am. I frown.

"What is that supposed to mean? What are you?"

"I'm an introvert," he says, showing me his paper. "But a real one."

"Excuse me, are you saying I lied on my test?"

"No, I'm just saying maybe you don't know yourself as well as you think you do."

My jaw drops. "And I suppose you do?"

He shrugs his wide shoulders, and all those changing feelings I tucked away last night are chewed up and swallowed as I fantasize about dangling him over shark-infested waters. I wonder when our next boat trip is. Maybe I could arrange for an "accident."

"I'm just saying you're not exactly ... subtle."

"At least I don't have the personality of a wet paper bag," I snap.

Whistle Mouth strikes again, and I gasp as Rafe and I bestow her with twin dark looks. She points to the far end of the room, sending us to our respective groups. We're each handed a problem we need to solve, taking into account everyone's unique personality type and preferred communication and analysis style.

I'm matched with three white guys: Adam, Evan, and Steve. I recognize Evan as Rafe's troll friend from earlier. Rafe's group sits a few tables away, and I pointedly ignore him, angry and definitely hurt by his comments. Every time I think we're moving in another direction, something comes in to sweep it all away.

We all gather around our designated table, and Evan sits across from me, straddling his chair backward. He gives me a look, and I already sense that I'll hate whatever comes out of his mouth. Sure enough, he scoots the notepad and pen sitting in the middle of the table towards me. "You can be the notetaker," he says confidently.

I open my mouth to protest, knowing he's chosen me because I'm the only woman in the group. But I bite my tongue because sometimes, causing a scene isn't worth the effort.

A boom of thunder practically shakes the walls, and I grip the pen tightly enough to snap it in two. Instead of abating, this storm only seems to be growing stronger.

We spend the next hour debating and discussing. Evan cuts me off at least half a dozen times and takes credit for three of my suggestions. The other two don't even flinch.

After we confirm our solution, we're to write the highest-level points on an easel with a large notepad. We all stare at it until Evan finally looks at me.

"Well?" he asks.

I know exactly what he's getting at, but I refuse to give him the satisfaction. "Well, what?"

"Aren't you going to write our ideas down?"

Now, I'm pissed. I shove the notepad towards him with perhaps a bit more force than necessary. It slides over the smooth surface with a hiss and bumps into his elbow.

"Why don't you do it?"

Evan scratches his chin because I'm not giving him the reaction he wants. "You're the one who wrote the notes."

I offer up a sweet smile that burns with acid. "Right, so it's someone else's turn."

"But you're better at it."

My blood simmers, my cheeks flushing. This idiot can't take a hint.

I grip the sides of my chair, my knuckles turning white. "Why am I better at it, Evan?"

He's utterly confused now, and I shove my chair back and stand.

"Asshole," I mutter under my breath, and Evan looks like I've slapped him.

"Hey, what's your problem?" he demands.

His forehead scrunches, and his beady little eyes turn dim with incomprehension.

I shake my head and storm out of the room.

My heels echo against the hard tile as I take out my frustration on the floor. It's not the worst thing that could happen. It's not the worst thing that *has* happened, but my nerves are fraying for a thousand different reasons, and it's getting to me today. I'm used to this, and nine times out of ten, I let it roll over me like I'm supposed to.

"Tris!" Rafe jogs up behind me. "Are you okay? What happened?"

I offer him a glare and continue walking.

"It's fine," I say over my shoulder. "Just forget it."

But Rafe doesn't listen. He grabs my hand and tugs me back. Something warm and electric shoots up my arm, stealing my breath.

"Please tell me," he says.

"You wouldn't understand."

His shoulders drop. "I'd like to try."

"Why?"

He shrugs and seems to weigh his words before he replies. "Because."

"I don't want to talk about it, okay? I just need some space."

"But the training program," he says.

I pinch the bridge of my nose and lean against the wall. "I don't care, Rafe. I'm not getting it, anyway. I'm not sure why I keep deluding myself into thinking it might happen."

He watches me, running a hand through his hair as he lets out a long, slow breath. I can tell he has no idea how to respond.

"Just go back and finish the exercise," I say. "One of us should win. It might as well be you."

With that, I push off the wall and walk away.

Chapter Thirteen

I wander through the hotel in search of self-medication with my vices of choice: food and wine. I stumble upon a semi-deserted bar overlooking the lobby with windows running along one side.

Finding a table near the edge, I sit and watch a wedding party posing around the central fountain for photos. They're full of smiles, the bride's the biggest. Something twists in my chest as she kisses her groom with googly hearts sparkling in her eyes.

"Can I get you a drink?" a server asks, appearing at my side.

"Several." His smile stretches with a knowing look. "I'll have a glass of wine." I point to something on the menu, and he walks away.

Rain lashes the windows, where I can see the blowing trees and the dark, churning ocean. My mouth turns dry as a massive crack of lightning flashes across the horizon.

"Is this seat taken?"

I turn to find Rafe with his hands braced on the back of the chair beside mine.

"Shouldn't you be overachieving somewhere?"

Rafe ignores my question and sits down as the server returns with my wine. He orders something as I pick up my glass and drain half of it in one gulp.

"You may as well bring another one now," I tell the server, and he nods.

"You hungry?" Rafe asks, picking up the narrow laminated cardboard menu from the table. I give him a wry look. "Right. Silly question. What do you want?"

I eye the storm and the clouds tumbling over one another. "Whatever. Something decadent."

I don't hear anything as he places an order with the server, who's returned with his beer and my second glass. A ball of anxiety is forming in my stomach as I continue to watch outside.

"You okay?" Rafe asks, concern in his gaze. "I'm sorry about what that idiot said."

My gaze snaps to him. "How do you know what he said?"

"I asked him what happened, and then I told him off."

I frown. "Why are you apologizing for him? You should apologize for what *you* said. Are you sure you want to be seen with me, given I'm not *subtle*?"

Shame flashes across his expression. "Yes, I'm sorry for that, too. I seem to be apologizing a lot lately." He leans forward and stretches out a hand but pulls it back, balling it into a fist. "I said that wrong. What I meant was it's hard to believe you're an introvert because you shine in every room you enter."

My mouth parts with a breath of surprise. I forget every last word in the English language, but Rafe's not quite done tying me into knots.

"There's nothing unmissable about you. That's all I meant. That there isn't anywhere you could go where everyone wouldn't notice you."

This is what he thinks?

"And I'm apologizing for every idiot who has ever treated you that way."

There are too many things occurring at once.

"You really think that? About me?"

"Yes," he says, penetrating me with his gaze. "I do."

My chest tightens and loosens at the same time.

There's a lot to unpack here, but I can't seem to get it out right now. "You're one to talk. You claim you're a real introvert, but you walk around schmoozing everyone like you're running for Senate."

Everyone but me, I don't add.

He smiles. It's been only a day since this has become my reality, but I already know the brilliance of that smile will never diminish. That every single time will feel like the first one over and over. I'm so far in over my head that I'm standing at the bottom of the sea.

Rafe stares out the window as another brilliant flash of lightning forks across the sky.

"They think a pretty severe tropical storm might be gathering."

"What?" My stomach drops. "Shouldn't we evacuate? Why are we just sitting here?" Panic claws up my throat as the water swells and the wind picks up, tugging at the palm trees fighting against its strength.

"It's okay," Rafe says, scrutinizing me. "They almost never hit the mainland here—it's more than likely to stay over the water. There's no reason to worry."

I nod, trying to calm the racing in my heart and the tingling at the tips of my fingers and toes.

That's when a giant seafood platter arrives with steaming mountains of lobster and shrimp and an awkwardly angled pile of crab legs. A tub of melted butter is nestled in the forest of shells, and on any other day, a pack of wild wolves wouldn't stop me from inhaling every bite. But my stomach roils as apprehension saws on my nerves.

"I'm not hungry anymore," I whisper.

"But you're always hungry," he jokes, and it *almost* makes me smile.

Hotel staff are scrambling across the beach, gathering lounge chairs and umbrellas, securing everything with ropes, and stuffing them into storage bins. I take a large swig from the glass of water Rafe just ordered and wipe my mouth with my forearm.

"Tris, are you okay?" A hand settles on my back for the briefest flutter before it pulls away. He rubs his palms on the fabric of his dress pants, and I'm not sure what to read into that.

"Rafe," I say quietly as my emotions swing.

"Attention all hotel guests," comes a disembodied voice over a PA system. "We're expecting some strong winds over the next few hours. Please move to the ballroom level and away from the windows. All hotel guests should take cover. Please move in a calm and organized manner." The tinny voice is calm and detached as it repeats the missive again.

Blood drains from my limbs. I can't let go of the chair arms, my knuckles white and my hands aching from the effort. The surrounding diners rise from their seats, moving together in a flow like a school of minnows.

"Tris? What's wrong?" The concern in Rafe's voice almost makes me break as I inhale a jagged breath.

"I don't like storms," I whisper, prepared for him to mock me. To take this and use it against me.

His response, though, is a solemn nod. "You're white as a ghost. Let's go. It'll be okay. This hotel is made of concrete and safety glass. It'll withstand this weather. It's built for this."

Logically, I know this. There are building codes and standards that must be followed. They would have accounted for the worst case scenario. But fear isn't logical.

With a tenderness I would never have expected, Rafe wraps an arm around my shoulders and guides me through the restaurant, uttering assurances that everything is fine.

Organized chaos unfolds before us as we migrate to the ball-room level, where they've requisitioned each massive room as makeshift shelters. I'm amazed at how quickly they put this all together, but I guess they've known the weather was off for the past few days.

Rafe is holding my hand, and he leads me into the largest of the rooms, where we find Lan and Gabrielle seated with a group of other WMC employees. I'm so freaked out that I barely have the capacity to register: *Rafe is holding my hand.*

He pushes me against the wall and presses gently on my shoulders. I sink to the ground while he crouches before me.

"Wait here, okay?" He looks at Gabrielle. "Watch her. She doesn't like storms. I'll be right back."

"Of course," Gabrielle says, scooting closer and linking her elbow with mine. My skin feels like ice, further exacerbated by arctic blasts of industrial-strength air-conditioning.

"What's wrong?" she asks as she rubs my arm. Her voice is soft and soothing.

"I don't have a pleasant history with weather like this."

"Okay," she says, smoothing back my hair. "I guess you're not used to this, huh? In Florida, this is a weekly occurrence."

"Remind me to never go to Florida."

She laughs and squeezes my arm tighter. "Then I'll come visit you instead."

"The cold might kill you," I reply, closing my eyes while a headache builds in my temples. I scramble for my purse, worried that I've lost it, only to find it slung across my body. I dig for my pills, shake two out, and cradle them in my hand.

Gabrielle laughs again. "That's true. You'll have to teach me how to dress."

I smile at her and lean my head on her shoulder.

"I've been through this kind of thing a thousand times. Don't worry—I got you." Gabrielle then whispers in my ear, "Or maybe it's someone else who has you."

A shadow falls over us, and I open my eyes to find Rafe laden with blankets, a pillow, water bottles, and brown paper lunch bags. He's the Mount Doom of hospitality. He places everything on the floor as I pop my painkillers in my mouth and swallow them down.

Rafe gets to work setting up camp, laying out the blanket and gesturing for me to get on top. He passes around water bottles and snacks to Lan, me, and Gabrielle.

"Thanks," I say as he hands me the pillow, touched but also wildly confused by his behavior.

As more people stream into the room, WMC takes up a large quadrant of the space. The mood is boisterous and lively. To everyone else, this is a party as visitors travel between blanket islands like we're having a giant picnic.

The WMC executives have also found their way down and have somehow secured a set of wide leather chairs they've arranged in a circle facing one another. They pay little attention to their surroundings as they talk and plot what I assume is world domination. Maybe I can get Diane on her own in this mess, but I'm far too jittery to move right now.

Thunder booms outside again, and I imagine the walls shaking.

"Are you okay?" Rafe asks, leaning on the wall beside me, his long legs stretched out and crossed at the ankle. "You must be cold."

Rafe pulls up the second blanket and drapes it over my lower half.

"Thanks," I say. "You...don't need to do all this."

Why *is* he doing all this?

He shrugs and closes his eyes in what *feels* like a transparent attempt to appear casual.

"How long do you think we'll be in here?" I ask to the muffled sound of thunder as I latch onto his arm with a firm grip. He covers my hand with his, and something about his warm skin settles my pulse.

He holds up his phone and shows me his screen with his other hand. "I just looked it up, and only a tiny handful of tropical storms have ever made landfall. I promise we'll be fine. They're just being cautious."

I stare at the page he's showing me and then point to a line at the bottom, reading it out loud. "Climate change has resulted in an increase of extreme weather incidents in recent years."

I glance up at him with a dubious look.

"We'll be fine," he repeats before he clicks the button, darkening the screen. "Is there a reason this bothers you so much? Did something happen?"

My gaze swings to him, impressed at his perceptiveness.

"I was in a cyclone once," I say. "My family was vacationing in India and we were spending a day at the beach. The wind picked up. It felt very sudden, and my dad was out in the water, and he—"

My chest constricts. I was eight years old, but I still vividly remember that day. We were lounging on the beach, having a wonderful afternoon. My brother was six at the time, and we were building sandcastles when someone started shouting for my father to come in from the water. It was like a switch had gone off. One moment, everything was calm, and the next, it was like the world was ending.

The wind swelled, and the waves were rolling, and I still remember my father going under, disappearing beneath the waves. My mother was screaming his name over and over. It was the longest few minutes of my life. I don't know how long he was missing, but somehow, he surfaced and came out of the sea, collapsing on the beach. I remember people helping us, trying to revive him as the rain pelted us like stones.

We ran for cover and then had to hunker down as the storm raged for two days. The sounds of the wind and water and the buildings groaning and collapsing are still stamped on my memories. My mother held me and my brother the entire time, but it was the most terrifying thing I can remember.

"I was so scared," I say to Rafe as he listens intently to every word. "It's not like I'm paralyzed with fear—I just get nervous." My tone is sharp, daring him to make fun of me, but he shakes his head.

"I didn't think anything scared you, Malik."

My eyebrows draw together. "Everyone fears something."

"I suppose, but you're always so confident."

I test the words in my head, searching for a barbed meaning woven into the syllables. But I detect nothing. Still, I'm suspicious. "What's that supposed to mean?"

"Nothing. It's a compliment."

Another one. Why is he doing this? He's trying to lure me into complacency. To let down my guard, and when I'm at my weakest, when I'm a wounded dragonfly plastered to his windshield, he'll flick the switch and smear me against the glass.

"Me? I've literally never met anyone who thinks as much of himself as you do."

That doesn't offend him at all. In fact, he grins, and I have to look away as I'm mortally wounded by that dimple. "I can see why it might seem that way when you're as obsessed with me as you are."

My mouth opens. "I am not obsessed with you. I cannot stand you."

As the words leave my mouth, I feel them for the lie they are. A few days ago, it was the incontrovertible truth—well, the second part, anyway—but today, I'm less confident about where I stand on the matter.

"That's why you used to pass by my desk a hundred times a day?"

I blink. He noticed that? It was years ago when we worked in different areas of the building, back when we used to bicker and needle each other with harmless pranks. "How could you possibly have known that? You'd need to look away from the mirror for more than ten seconds."

"So you don't deny it?" he counters.

"Your office was on the way to the bathroom. Get over yourself."

Strictly speaking, I could easily have avoided passing by his office if I wanted to, but I'll die right here before I admit that.

"Did you ever see a specialist?" Rafe asks. "No one should pee that many times a day."

"I hate you," I say, and he laughs.

After that, we both fall silent as we sit side by side, observing the chaos.

"Plenty of things scare me," I say after a while.

"Yeah? Like what?"

"Honestly. Literally everything sometimes." I hesitate, wondering if I should reveal this much of myself. But Rafe is looking at me with trust in his expression, and I allow my truth to fall. "Never being good enough. Never figuring out what I'm going to do with the rest of my life. Knowing that what I'm doing here isn't the right path for me."

"Why do you say that?"

"Because I've stagnated. How many promotions can I be passed over for before I finally give up? I'm doing the same job and making almost the same salary as I was the day I started five years ago."

Rafe's lips press together. "You don't really think that? You know you're smart and capable and talented at what you do. They picked you for this, so they see it too."

I scoff. "Your father picked me in some misguided attempt to even out the field." I cast a hand over the crowd.

"So? That's what he should have done all along. It doesn't make you any less deserving. As you said, I'm only here because of who my father is. It's not because I'm better at my job."

I open my mouth and then close it, shocked to hear him admit any of this.

"I thought it was because you're a better team player?" I ask, referring to his comment from the Ferris wheel challenge.

He rubs his face and shakes his head. "I'm sorry. I don't know why I said that—I didn't mean it at all. But..."

"But we're good at pissing each other off," I finish, and he offers me a rueful smile.

Rafe leans in closer. "Between you and me, the entire exec team got their hands slapped by the new board chair. She's not happy with WMC's hiring and succession planning, and all their asses are on the line if they don't make some big changes."

I arch an eyebrow. That explains why David was so amenable to my travel requests. "But they still chose you and the other nepo babies?"

He shrugs. "Old habits die hard, I guess. And I only agreed to come here to keep the peace with my dad. If I'd refused, it would have caused so much shit between us, and my mom always gets caught in the middle trying to be the peacemaker. I didn't want to cause her any more stress than I already do."

There's something he's not saying buried in the layers between those syllables.

"Do you cause your mom a lot of stress?"

His jaw hardens and he gives a small shake of his head. "Sometimes."

Then, his gaze shifts to his father sitting across the room, where he swirls a glass of whisky in his hand. Rafe opens his mouth and then closes it, clearly changing his mind about whatever he planned to say next.

"Rafe!" someone shouts.

I recognize one of the men from our session earlier. "They're opening a bar in the next room. Come have a drink with us."

"Wanna go?" he asks, and I hold back my surprise that he's including me.

I slouch against the wall. "No, thank you." The last thing I want is to be surrounded by bros and their male self-satisfaction.

"I'm good," Rafe replies, raising a hand.

"You can go," I say. "I don't need you to stay here with me."

"What if I want to stay here with you?"

"Do you?"

"Do you want me to?"

I glare. "Stop it."

He snickers and waves them off.

As they walk away, a huge crash jolts me from my skin, and my hand clamps onto Rafe's bicep with an iron grip.

"Shit," I breathe as my heart races, and I press a hand to my throat. "That was loud."

Rafe shuffles closer, and that does absolutely nothing to calm my nerves. He takes my hand, folding it in his large, warm fingers, and this isn't good. I mean it's *good*. But it's not good.

I tell myself over and over that I hate this. That this is a bad idea, and I don't want him touching me. I should tell him to stop. But I scoot in closer so our bodies are fused at the sides. His hip is against mine, and his thigh leans on my leg, and I almost forget the storm along with my name.

"You sure you don't want a drink?" he asks, giving me a crooked smile that I mentally catalog into the list of Rafe's smiles I'm currently building. The half smile. The full smile. The snarky smile. The genuine one that lights up his face. I need to take pictures. "Might help calm those nerves."

I shake my head. My pills aren't working, and my temples are still pounding. "No, I don't think that will help tonight. But seriously, if you want to go, I'll be fine. I have Gabrielle and Lan." I turn to look at them, but at some point, they abandoned their blanket island and are now across the room chatting with another group of people. "Well, they'll be back."

Rafe smiles again—this is his baseline smile—though there is absolutely nothing ordinary about it. "I'm good. I'd rather stay here, if that's okay?"

Once again, I search for some alternative motive or meaning, but it isn't there unless Rafe is a really good actor.

"Okay. This is kind of freaking me out."

I'm not sure if I'm talking about the storm.

With that settled, we sit back, our arms and shoulders pressed together, and our fingers still twined. Now it truly registers: *Rafe is holding my hand.* I casually implode.

As the night wears on, the ballroom lights flicker, and I swallow the lump in my throat. At another loud crash, they go dark. An arm comes around my shoulders, and I move closer to Rafe, torn between fear and . . . something else.

I think about what I confessed to him last night—that I was looking for someone who made me feel safe. Why did I never realize that until now?

A mouth ghosts against my ear. "The generator probably was

hit by lightning. A hotel this size will have a backup. Might just take a minute for it to fire."

His breath warms the exposed skin on my throat as he pulls me a little closer, still whispering assurances.

Dim lights flare in the ballroom, casting everyone in an orangey glow. Hotel staff pass through the crowd, handing out more food and water, reminding us that everything will be fine. As the hours wear on, a hush falls over the room as people doze off.

My head is pounding. I grunt as I dig my fingers into the base of my skull, trying to relieve the pressure.

"What's wrong?" Rafe asks.

"It's my head. I get headaches. It's kind of my thing."

"Do you want me to..." He trails off as his warm hand rests on top of mine where I'm massaging my nape. I look up at him, noting the crescents of amber light reflecting in his eyes.

"Sure," I say, my voice soft. "That would be nice. Along the outside of my spine."

I show him the spot, and his strong fingers dig into the tendons. A shiver spreads like tree roots over my skin. He kneads the muscle for a minute as I tip my head back.

"Sit here," he says, spreading his legs and patting the ground. The look on his face is unreadable, his jaw tight. I lift myself up and settle between his thighs, taking care to leave a small space between my butt and his...Not thinking about that.

His hands find my neck again, and he digs his thumbs into the tense meat of my traps and shoulders. My eyes roll to the back of my head because he's a goddamn magician.

A moan escapes my lips as he finds a spot that releases ninety-nine percent of my tension. He works away as I make encouraging sounds of appreciation. I'm so caught up that I don't even have the presence of mind to be embarrassed.

Again, I feel the brush of his breath against my ear.

"Are those your sex noises, Tris?" he teases, and I'm sure he's messing with me. He's trying to take my mind off the storm and my pain, but two can play this game.

"No way. I'm much louder during sex." His fingers seem to miss a beat as his breath stutters like a needle skipping across a record. He clears his throat and resumes the massage, saying nothing. I think I might have actually stunned Rafe Gallagher into silence.

"You're really good at this," I say after a few more minutes. He's abandoned my neck and is working his way down my back, and I don't mind this one bit.

"Not too rough?"

I give my head a tiny shake. "I like it hard."

I realize what he's just said and what *I've* just said. Why does everything sound dirty right now? But I've hopped on this train and want to keep blowing the whistle. Crap. Even my internal thoughts are rife with filthy euphemisms.

"I didn't expect you to be so good with your hands," I groan as he presses his thumbs into the ridge on either side of my spine with his fingers braced against my rib cage. It's exquisite.

But I'm also very aware that the tips of his fingers are *so* close to brushing the sides of my breasts, and I'm grateful it's too dark for anyone to witness my expression. We've crept over the line I'd so carefully drawn between us.

"Better than that battery-operated friend of yours," he says, his voice rough.

We're into the weeds with flashlights and fishing nets now. "Gosh, you think a lot of yourself," I quip, and I feel the exhale of his dark laugh against the nape of my neck. His hands drop lower, working the tender flesh at the bottom of my spine, fingers digging into my hips to give him leverage. It. Feels. Amazing.

His thumbs trend downward, and as he touches the top swell of my butt, my entire body tightens.

"How's your head feeling?" he asks.

My head. Right. That's what started this.

I shift to relieve the stiffness in my legs, and my butt brushes between his thighs. The touch is so brief that I can't be certain, but I'm pretty sure he's enjoying this, too. Knowing this might be turning him on sends a shower of heat rushing to my stomach.

"A lot better," I breathe, trying to regulate my voice. "Thank you." A yawn stretches from my throat. "These pills always make me so tired."

I'm not sure who makes the decision. If it's Rafe, or if it's me, or some divine benevolent hand controlling the universe, but a few moments later, I'm lying against him. My cheek is pressed to his chest, and his hand rests on my thigh while the other continues working circles at the base of my skull.

My hand lies against his heart, and I fight the urge to explore the planes of his torso, settling on rubbing the material of his shirt between my thumb and forefinger. I'm lying on a hard floor in a drafty ballroom, but this might be the most comfortable I've been in my entire life.

I inhale deeply, taking in gulps of his fresh, clean scent layered with something smokier and richer, like moonlight and campfires.

"You smell so good." The words fall from my mouth on a slip-stream of drowsiness as I feel Rafe's chin drop to the top of my head.

I don't know what this is. I don't know what to name this.

So, I try not to analyze it too closely.

His arm pulls me in tighter, and the last thing I remember is the scruff on his neck gently scratching my forehead before I drift off to sleep.

Chapter Fourteen

*W*hen I wake up, I am both comfortable and uncomfortable. My hip is sore, and my entire right leg is tingling from a lack of blood flow. The rest of me, though, is pressed up against a wall of male muscle that smells like sunshine. My face is buried into a crook of warm skin with strong arms wrapped around me and a large hand pressing to the small of my back.

My thoughts take a moment to catch up.

Thighs touching, hips adjacent, breasts crushed.

Mentally, I leap back a thousand feet.

Physically, I stay absolutely still, peering up at Rafe through my eyelashes to behold the gloriousness of sleep-tousled hair and the face of the devil cloaked in the costume of a sleeping angel.

"The storm passed," Gabrielle says from somewhere above us. My gaze flicks up to find her folding a blanket. "Everyone can return to their rooms." She then gathers an armful of pillows and hoists them against her chest. "They want us to put all the blankets and stuff in the bins outside. And they canceled sessions today so we can get some rest."

Still keeping entirely motionless, I blink in acknowledgment. Her lips press together like she's trying to contain a smile before turning and heading for the exit.

My focus returns to Rafe, his head resting on the pillow we shared last night. A moment later, his eyes slowly open. They connect with mine. A static charge sizzles in the space between our pupils as we fossilize into stone. It takes approximately one entire century before I finally come to my senses and my body catches up with my brain.

Here in the cold light of day, with the storm passed and all of us safe, the words we exchanged, the touches we shared in the dark take on a different shade.

My cheeks flush as I realize I was practically throwing myself at him. This is mortifying. Did I seriously tell him I make a lot of noise during sex?

"Get off me," I snap, drowning in the shallows of shame.

That releases the tension.

Rafe's arms spring open, ejecting me into outer space, before he sits up with a glare.

"You get off me. You're the one who fell asleep on top of me."

"I did not!"

I totally did, and it was... fantastic.

"You were practically in my lap, Trishara. Was it good for you?"

The way he says my full name, not with fury but with a smolder. The way he's looking at me like he wants to take a bite. The way it was *so* good for me sends a ricochet down my spine.

To cover it up, I snarl and back away. I grab my purse, scoop up my blankets, and spin on my heel. I feel the burn of his gaze on my back like he's trying to dissect me into pieces.

Kidney. Brains. Heart. Slice. Cut. Dice.

I dump my linens into a large grey bin stationed outside. I catch a few snippets of conversation, confirming the wind caused some minor damage to a few buildings, and that's it. We probably would have been fine in our rooms, but I'll be forever grateful they took precautions to keep us as safe as possible.

I scurry through the hotel and find a set of glass doors that open to the beach.

Outside, the air is so thick and humid that it clings to my skin like cobwebs. I inhale an unsatisfying breath that congeals in my lungs.

I shouldn't have snapped at Rafe, but it's so easy to fall into a familiar pattern.

Last night was so beyond the sphere of our usual encounters that I feel like I've tumbled into a void. What started as a joke became something else, I think. The way he cared for me last night rattles the padlock I've kept firmly shut against feeling *anything*.

As I stride onto the wet sand, I kick off my shoes, dangling them from my fingertips.

Hotel staff are busy cleaning up leaves and debris littering the beach, raking the sand into neat, orderly furrows before carrying out the lounge chairs and umbrellas they stowed away last night.

The pale grey sky is streaked with thin wisps of clouds, and the water churns softly with a whoosh. I look over the horizon, reminding myself that everything's okay. Whatever Rafe's motives, he made the night bearable, even pleasurable, if I'm being brutally honest with myself.

Still, I don't like owing him anything.

Exhausted, I sway on my feet, my eyelids heavy and scratchy. I offer a thank-you to the sky for not killing us and head back to the suite.

After I let myself in, I find Rafe on the sofa, his hair damp and curling at the temples from a shower. He's drinking a glass of water, wearing only those infernal grey sweatpants. I take a deep breath, steeling myself and focusing on a point beyond his head.

"Hi," he says, lowering it to the table.

"Hi. Are you done with the bathroom?"

I'm trying not to make this weird. Not very successfully. He nods.

"Thanks." I disappear into my room and wash off the odor of hundreds of bodies and a night spent on the floor. I watch the water circle the drain, realizing it also washes away the smell of Rafe. I am pathetic.

When I'm finished, I change into a pair of shorts and a tank top and retrieve a can of sparkling water from the kitchen. Rafe is scrolling on his phone, lying on the too-small chaise with an arm tucked behind his head and his long legs dangling off the end.

I worry my bottom lip as a wave of guilt needles my stomach.

"Rafe." He looks over at me with a question in his gaze. He's still shirtless, and I steel myself against the heat-stirring force of his six-pack.

Actually, I think it's an eight-pack. Fuck.

"Yeah?"

"You can take the bed," I say, unable to believe the words coming from my mouth. "I can sleep there. I'm shorter. I'll fit better."

He pauses and then sits up, assailing me with the sight of his defined torso, bunching and contracting. His forehead furrows into a stop-fucking-with-me look.

"I can't let you do that," he says.

"Why not?"

He opens his mouth and closes it again. "I don't know. I just can't."

"Don't be silly. Just take the bed. You look ridiculous squished on that little couch. I'll check again tomorrow at the front desk. Maybe another room has finally opened up. I can handle one night."

He runs a hand along the back of his head, mussing his damp hair, conflict flitting over his face. He inhales, and his shoulders drop. "It's a huge bed," he says. "We could share it."

I lift an are-you-kidding-me eyebrow, and he raises his hands in supplication.

"Look, you slept on top of me last night, and I found it in myself to restrain any inappropriate urges."

He places a hand over his chest. His bare and extremely chiseled chest and I have to drag my attention to his face.

"I promise to be a complete gentleman. That thing is the size of a football field. You won't even know I'm there." I sincerely doubt that, but he's making sense. "Of course, if *you* don't think you can control yourself, I wouldn't blame you."

I narrow my eyes, ignoring the X-rated thoughts I'm already having.

"Of course I can. Get over yourself, Gallagher."

"Then what's the problem? We're both adults. I'm sure we can handle it. Don't be so immature, Tris."

My nose flares. He will not out-mature me. Of course I can sleep in the same bed as him and control myself. Who does he think he is? Besides, this makes us even for last night. I don't want to live in a world where I owe Rafe anything.

"Fine," I say. "But put on a shirt."

I stomp into the bedroom, his laughter following in my wake.

Things were so much easier when he was still firmly listed under the bad guy column.

The bed looks so inviting after the hard floor last night, and I pull back the fresh duvet, sliding in and reveling in the coolness of the crisp sheets against my bare skin. I wish someone could bottle this feeling.

A moment later, Rafe enters the room, tugging a white T-shirt over his head. A tiny (big) part of me is disappointed he listened. Why does he choose *now* to do as I ask? He stops with his hands on his hips, and we look at each other as the weirdness of our current predicament settles.

"No one at the office can ever know about this," I say.

He arches an eyebrow, and that *disdain* is so inexplicably delicious that I'm tempted to offer myself up for his pleasure. He could do anything he wanted to me. *Gah.*

This is stupid. He's right. We are both adults, and we can be mature about this.

"Well, stop staring and get in, honey," I say, patting the bed.

The joke breaks the tension, and I'm rewarded with a smile that only touches half of his mouth as he walks to the other side and slips under the covers.

We both lie down, staring at the ceiling.

I'm holding my breath. I think he is, too.

A moment ago, I was exhausted, but now every hair and cell and inch of my skin are wide awake. I swear I can feel his heat filtering by osmosis across the massive bed.

Maybe I wish it weren't so big. What if I slid just a tiny bit over? How bad would that be?

"Good night, Tris," he says in the semi-dark, his voice rough and low.

"It's morning." My own voice does something similar, and I swallow the bundle of nerves in my throat.

"Then good morning."

At the soft rustle of the sheets, I turn my head to find him already watching me.

"Good morning, Rafe. Sleep tight."

Chapter Fifteen

*W*hen I awake, the bed is empty. Sunlight filters around the edges of the slatted blinds, and I sit up, attempting to quell a flare of disappointment at finding myself alone. A moment later, I hear Rafe through the cracked door on the end of a phone call.

I hesitate. I should probably give him some privacy. But I also kick the blankets off and tiptoe closer on silent feet across the cool white tiles. From my narrow vantage point, I see he's pacing the living room, his phone pressed to his ear. I'm officially Rafe's creepy stalker.

There's no anger in his voice, but there's a strained set to his shoulders and a withered defeat in his tone. "Hannah, we've been over this."

I go completely still. I shouldn't be listening. This is none of my business, but a sick part of me needs to know. Maybe a small part of me understands that Rafe being free and available means I'll be forced to confront the fears I've been clinging to for years. Will I ever be ready for a relationship again? What about with someone I work with? Would he also betray me if things went wrong? I'm not sure if I can handle that again.

A wave of nausea spirals straight to my feet.

It would be safer if Rafe got back together with Hannah. For me.

And if not, I'll have no choice but to consider that *other* Rafe who could easily smash my heart into splinters. The Rafe who comforted me last night and held my hand and chose to stay with me instead of abandoning me. The Rafe I pushed away, but who always existed in my periphery like the moon circling the earth.

But maybe I have nothing to worry about. Years ago, I thought he was flirting with me, and then he started dating someone else. Until two days ago, he'd never even *smiled* at me. He can barely tolerate me.

All we've ever done is argue, and maybe I'm the only one who considers that a form of foreplay. I recall the disagreement we got into a few months ago because we couldn't decide on the calculation of a pressure vessel.

He's just trying to keep the peace, given our proximity. The blankets and the apology and defending me against Evan— it turns out Rafe is simply a better person than I ever gave him credit for.

Rafe huffs out a sound of irritation. He storms across the suite and stuffs his feet into his gym shoes lying by the door. He slams it behind him, cutting off his voice and leaving an abrupt, echoing silence.

I wait, watching the door, wondering if he's coming back. After a minute, I steal into the kitchen and notice a cloche-covered plate on the counter. The remnants of a meal sit on another plate next to it. I lift the lid to find a burger and fries with little silver cups of both ketchup and mayo nestled on the side. Something in my stomach flutters.

Standing at the counter, I scarf the entire thing down, one ear peeled for Rafe's return.

Rain has started falling again, so I decide to go for a jog on the treadmill. I change into gym clothes and tie on my shoes, which I managed to salvage from the mud pit.

When I leave the suite, the hallway is empty. I wonder where Rafe has gone.

A few minutes later, I emerge at the gym level to find it deserted. Everyone is probably resting after the storm, but I have too much pent-up energy pooling along my nerves.

I head for the bank of treadmills, stepping onto one and pressing a few buttons. It sings to life with flashing lights. A powerful blast of air-conditioning pebbles my skin as I set my water bottle in the holder and punch a few more buttons on the display. I set it for sixty minutes before the belt whirrs to life.

Putting in my earphones, I break into a slow jog as it speeds up. I crank up the volume on my "Running for Your Life" playlist, preferring it to be as loud as reasonably possible to help lose myself in the rhythm. Plus, it prevents anyone from talking to me.

I'm twenty minutes into my run, sweat breaking out on my forehead, when a presence appears next to me. I shoot a dirty look to whoever chose the machine next to mine when a dozen others sit empty.

It's Rafe.

He's changed into snug black shorts and a sleeveless top that hugs his torso in all the right ways. Valleys of shadows and light play against the dips and curves of his arms and his face.

My obsession that's not an obsession has never been more obsessive.

I tear my gaze away, focusing on the view outside.

I sense his movements. His eyes on me. He drops his water bottle in the holder and punches some buttons as his treadmill speeds up.

His pace kicks up, and I feel him peering over at my dashboard. I narrow my eyes as he smirks and very deliberately increases the pace on his machine so he's going 0.1 miles per hour faster.

I think not.

I jab the button, upping my tempo just above his. He lets me run there for a minute as I steal glances at his profile. After a moment, he pointedly increases his speed again.

Now I'm getting annoyed. I should just stop. This is so dumb. I have nothing to prove. I could run faster if I wanted to. I don't need his validation. But he is so ridiculously smug that I fantasize about a roundhouse kick to his ego.

Despite my annoyance, there's something weirdly calming about competing with him in a pointless battle of wills. It's our safe place. Our normal. It helps settle all these bizarre new feelings that surfaced last night.

So, I lean into it.

A feral noise tears from my throat, and I increase my speed again.

But this is hardly fair. Rafe descended from giants and has legs like a giraffe. Of course he's faster, but I can't let him win. Not again. Today, Daddy's connections won't help him.

He increases his speed, and I match him with a glare, daring him to do his worst.

That wins me the twist of a smile that would make the Joker look like Mary Poppins. With fifteen minutes left on my clock, sweat is pouring off me in rivulets. It slides down my face and down my back. My chest is tight, and I really want to stop. This is brutal. But I can't.

We keep running, paces matched, my breath practically fogging the air. A stitch forms in my side, stabbing me with fiery lashes. I press my hand against it, willing myself through the pain.

With a few minutes left, I up my speed one more time. Who needs lungs, anyway? This is the home stretch, and wings sprout from my ankles as I ascend to the plateau of the runner's high.

Rafe maintains his pace, watching me before he turns forward again.

My smile is smug as I keep running, my heart about to liquefy in my chest. I'm this close to collapsing when a miracle parts the heavens, and my treadmill suddenly slows, easing me into the cooldown. I want to melt into a puddle, but I take a deep breath and plant my hands on my hips for balance. A knifing ache stitches in my side, but I resist the urge to massage it as the treadmill slows to a stop.

I uncap my water and drink half the bottle as Rafe continues his pace. With an eyebrow raised, I give him my most withering smile before I hop off the machine, making my way for the changing rooms.

As soon as the door closes, I collapse against the wall, bending over as I gasp for air and clutch at my side. I drag myself to the bench, where I lie panting for several minutes.

Dammit. Why did I let myself get caught up in his stupid game? As my racing heart slows and the feeling returns in my limbs, I do allow myself an inward smile.

After chugging back another bottle of water, I'm recovered enough to make it back upstairs. My legs are shaky and rubbery as I pass through the gym, noting Rafe is no longer on the treadmill.

I head to the elevator and up to our room to take a shower.

When I emerge, Rafe has returned, also freshly showered and wearing jeans and a T-shirt. He's sitting on the balcony with a beer open on the table beside him. I lie on the other chair and fold my hands over my stomach. I refuse to let him see how much he drained me.

"I showered downstairs," he says.

I look over, searching for some sign of his earlier conversation with Hannah, finding it written in the lines of his face as he turns to study the horizon.

"You okay?" I ask.

He turns to look at me. "Yeah, why?"

I shrug. "No reason."

We sit in silence, accompanied by the crashing sounds of the sea.

He picks up his beer and points it towards me, offering me a sip. I shake my head because I've never liked the taste. He tips his head and takes a long gulp. I watch the line of his throat as he swallows, noting how his bicep swells against the sleeve of his shirt.

"How are your legs?" he asks, his gaze wandering over my lower half, spreading over me like molten sugar. I resist the urge to tuck them away.

"Fine," I lie. They feel like rubber, and my hamstrings are already tightening, an ache settling in my quads. "Yours?"

"Never better," he replies coolly, but then he winces as he shifts.

My self-satisfaction knows no bounds.

"What's that?" I ask, pointing to his lap. It looks like a sketchbook.

"Nothing." He flips it over and throws me an ominous look. "None of your business."

If he thinks I'm letting *that* go, he's never met me.

"Let me see," I say, holding out my hand and curling my fingers in a give-it-here gesture. I'm sure I caught the lines of a sketch. Rafe *draws*?

"No," he says, tilting the book away from me.

"Ra-a-fe," I say, affecting my most authoritative voice, drawing out his name.

He snorts. "You can't boss me around."

He attempts a stern look, but I catch the corner of his mouth twitching up.

"Look over there!" I shout, pointing off in the distance, and he tips his head towards me and scoffs.

"You've got to be kidding me. That was so sad."

I flatten my lips. It really was.

I begin to stand, and he stuffs the book behind him. So, I pretend that my right knee buckles, crying out as I catch myself on the edge of his lounger. It's only a partial feint because, holy shit, are my legs sore.

"Are you okay?" Rafe leans forward and grabs my wrist.

I am dirtier than a cafeteria food fight, but I wince, committing to the bit. I reach around him and snatch the sketchbook.

"Aha!" I hold it over my head and jump, grimacing because that actually hurts.

I retreat as Rafe stands and backs me against the railing.

"Don't move," I say, clutching the book against my chest and holding my hand out towards him. "Take another step, and I'll throw it over the railing."

I'm the worst right now, but curiosity is eating me alive.

He stops, balling his hands into fists.

"Tris," he says, a warning in his voice that gives me a sick little thrill. "Give me that."

"I will," I say. "I just want to have a look."

I hesitate, searching his face, trying to determine how upset he is. If he really wants me to stop, I will. But he doesn't move; he just watches me before his chin dips in the barest nod of acquiescence.

I flip open the book and inhale a surprised gasp.

It's the view from our balcony sketched out in various shades of grey, and it's absolutely breathtaking.

The light and the details are perfect—an unblemished mirror of the horizon.

I look up and sense him bracing himself for a blow, but I have no intention of hurting him. I hate that it's what he expects.

"This is incredible," I say, flipping to the next page, revealing more scenes of the beach. Stills of flowers and glasses on tables, water beading on their surfaces. There are sketches of places I recognize from back home, each more gorgeous and lifelike than the last. There are hands and eyes and pieces of people. Lips and hair and noses. There are even several pages of desserts—towering cakes and stunning constructions pieced together with macarons and whipped cream. I wonder what inspired them.

"These are amazing. You're incredibly talented."

I look up again at him, and his shoulders drop with a relieved exhale. "You think so?"

I furrow my brows. "Of course. Surely you know how good these are?"

He shrugs. "It's just a silly hobby. Something I do when I've got shit on my mind."

I stop on an image of a tree in a park, the leaves so lifelike it feels like I could pick them off from the page. "Well, if this is just a hobby, you're amazing at it."

I keep flipping, and my breath catches again as I open a portrait of Hannah. I blink.

"That's old," he says in a way that sounds like he's explaining himself. "I did that a long time ago." I shake my head. Who am I to question drawings of his ex-girlfriend?

I keep flipping and then I nearly drop the book.

My heart stops, stutters, takes a moment to catch up.

There's a sketch of me. Here. Sitting on this balcony, looking out at the water, a pensive look on my face. He's captured me so perfectly that the air in my chest twists and bends in on itself.

He takes a step closer, hovering in my space.

"I, uh," he says, rubbing the back of his neck. "I hope you don't mind." I flip the page again and find another drawing of me, but it's from back home. I'm at my desk, one shoe kicked off, a pen tucked into a makeshift bun. I recognize the dress I bought a couple of months ago.

"Why are you drawing pictures of me?" I ask, my voice hushed to a dumbfounded whisper.

Our eyes meet, and the silence between us grows thick and amorphous, ballooning into life-altering proportions.

His brown eyes glow like fall leaves drenched in sunlight, and his lips part ever so slightly. But then a curtain falls over his expression, and he snatches the book from my hands.

"No reason," he says. "I draw what's around me." He stomps into the suite, but I'm not done here. I follow him inside, close on his heels like a misbehaving puppy. "What?" he snaps. "Stop looking at me like that."

"Like what? You're the one drawing pictures of me. Can I see it again? Are there more?"

"No. I told you, it's nothing. People are hard. I was practicing. It's nothing. I draw random people all the time."

"Like who?" I cross my arms over my chest, my limbs weak and rubbery for an entirely different reason now. I can't leave this alone.

He throws up his hands. "I don't know. Margaret Thatcher."

I almost choke on my tongue. "Margaret *Thatcher*?"

He lets out a long breath, pinching the bridge of his nose. "It was the first name that came into my head."

"So you draw me, your girlfriend, and dead female politicians?"

"No, I...she's not my girlfriend." He makes a noise of frustration and begins walking away.

"How was Margaret Thatcher the first name that popped into your head? Do I remind you of an old white lady?"

I continue following him, and he whirls on me.

"No! Of course, you don't. I was just—I don't know, okay? Leave me alone."

His glower is as dark as a midnight sky, and his evil glare is charged to full capacity. He stands before me, towering like a mountain, and the bright flash in his gaze makes my heart stumble.

He takes another small step, moving so close that I'm drowning in the radiant heat of his body. My pulse races, and I go fluttery and hot. My breath saws through my chest like a nest of burrs.

The tension thickens, growing solid, wrapping itself around my hips and chest and limbs. My mouth parts in anticipation because I get the strangest sense that he's about to kiss me.

And I want it. I *want* it.

Then he blinks, and his lip curls and my heart sags against my ribs, leaking between the spaces.

"Just leave me alone," he snarls. "Don't touch my things again."

Then he wrenches open the door to the hallway and slams it behind him.

Chapter Sixteen

*R*afe doesn't return for the next few hours. I feel terrible about what I've done. I'm a complete asshole, and I owe him an apology. I shouldn't have stolen his book, and I shouldn't have threatened to throw it over the balcony. I also shouldn't have given him such a hard time about his drawings, but I sort of lost my tenuous grip on reality when I found myself in those pages.

The rain falls heavily as I lie in bed staring at the ceiling, my blanket clutched to my chest. The remnants of the storm continue, though it's not nearly as ferocious. Still, it's enough to make me anxious. Thankfully, I have a lot on my mind to keep me distracted.

Why are there drawings of me in Rafe's sketchbook? The one from Hawaii makes a modicum of sense, I suppose. We're sharing a room and can't seem to get away from each other. I'm an easily accessible subject. But the one at my desk. What is that about? Why did he draw that, and how did he get all the details so right?

What stood out the most was how beautiful I became under the strokes of his pencil. Is that how he sees me?

My breath hitches when I hear the door open and then close. I hear Rafe kicking off his shoes in the living room and entering the second bathroom.

A few minutes later, his shadowy outline fills the doorway. He proceeds across the room and slips into his side of the bed, saying nothing as he settles on the farthest edge of the mattress. Even if he's angry with me, his presence is comforting.

We lie in silence for a few moments until I whisper into the dark, "Rafe, about before. I'm sorry. I shouldn't have taken your book. That was a shitty thing for me to do."

He shifts, rolling towards me and propping a hand under his head. "It really was. You are the worst. I'm going to draw you with a tail and horns next time." He smirks at my crestfallen expression. "I'm kidding. I forgive you. I shouldn't have been drawing you without your permission."

The knot in my chest eases. "Thanks," I say. "I really am sorry. You didn't do anything wrong. If I'm honest, it's a little flattering."

That earns me a grin, and I swear it's bright enough to illuminate the entire room.

We look at each other in the dark, and I have no idea what to say. I've never been at a loss for words with Rafe.

"Are you okay?" he asks a moment later. "It's raining pretty hard."

"I'm okay," I whisper. "Just a little nervous."

I feel the mattress dip as Rafe shuffles closer.

"You can hang on to me if it helps," he says softly.

Without thinking about it, I roll towards him, and he wraps his arms around me. It's then I realize that he didn't listen to me, and he's shirtless. My nose presses into the hollow of his throat, where I inhale the clean smell of his skin.

My hands slide up his back, my fingertips exploring a velvety soft layer covering unyielding flesh. His chest heaves out a ragged sigh as his hand smooths over the curve of my hip and slides along my ribs. His thighs tangle with mine, and I (not so) briefly wonder how he'd feel on top of me.

"Better?" he asks, interrupting my wayward thoughts. I nod into his chest. This has to be wrong, but it feels so right.

All I can smell is him. All I can feel is him, and it's doing stupid, erratic things to my body. I'm sure he must notice the skip of my pulse and how I've just grown a hundred degrees warmer.

He almost kissed me earlier, but then he didn't, and bitter disappointment lingers on my tongue. There's no use pretending anymore.

"Rafe, why did you draw me?" I whisper.

The silence drags on so long that I don't think he'll answer, but then he says, "Because I draw things that are beautiful to me."

Inhaling a shaky breath, my hand slides to his chest, where I feel his heart beating in a steady, soothing rhythm.

"Thank you," I reply. For the way he's holding me. For calling me beautiful. For making me feel safe in this moment.

"Get some sleep," he whispers, tucking me closer.

And that's how I fall asleep cradled in Rafe Gallagher's arms for the second time.

The next morning, we're sitting through yet another session on leadership styles, only this time they're being very clear on how it relates specifically to WMC culture.

I shift in my hard plastic seat, crossing and then uncrossing my legs. I can't get comfortable. I'm bored and antsy, and I can't stop thinking about how Rafe held me last night. I'm a pent-up comet of kinetic energy hurtling for the earth's surface.

An older white man who heads up the HR division drones on about WMC's commitment to diversity and inclusivity, and it's all I can do to rein in a river of caustic laughter.

I recall what Rafe said about the new board chair calling for changes, but this room is so vanilla that we comprise the most boring ice cream shop in existence. Maybe those efforts are genuine, but they have a very long way to go. It's galling to listen to this ode to a company culture that has never existed before. What's even more galling is the grim understanding that this is what I've given the last five years of my life to.

The lecture moves on to strategic planning and goals for the future as my attention wanders across the room to Rafe. I'm a cat to a sunbeam. A teenager to a reckless plan.

He's wearing all black today. Dress pants and boots. A button-up shirt rolled to the elbows. He looks even more like the Rafe who might have a secret lair hidden underneath a mountain.

Finally, the lecture ends, and we move on to the next activity. They want us to get to know each other better. While our offices are scattered across the country, WMC breeds careers, not jobs. Apparently. Meaning we might work alongside one another for the next few decades.

Decades. Suddenly, I feel like an escaped prisoner surrounded by snarling police dogs.

The first exercise is to find your "match." Everyone has a square of paper attached to their backs, and we wander the room seeking our other half. One woman has the words *peanut butter* taped to her shirt, while another has *jelly* on the other side of the room. Someone else has *oil*, and then I notice *water* pass me by.

Once we find our pairs, we're supposed to converse using open-ended questions and find three nice things to say about the person.

This is absolute torture.

Three executive members, including Diane Hart and David Gallagher, sit on the edge of the room, observing us. I catch Rafe watching his father with eyes like knife points.

"Am I wet?" a voice asks.

"Excuse me?" A petite white woman with blond hair stands in front of me with an expectant gaze. I think her name is Natalie.

"Am I wet?" She twists so her back is towards me and points over her shoulder.

"Oh," I say. The piece of paper taped to her shirt says *Juliet*. "Um, that depends."

"What does that mean?"

I squeeze my lips together, caught up in my immature joke. A nearby snort alerts me to Rafe listening to our conversation.

"Just what I said." I open my hands in a helpless gesture. "When you find your other half, you probably are."

Natalie narrows her eyes and storms off without another word. I look over to where Rafe is talking to someone, and our gazes meet in mutual amusement.

I continue my way through the room.

"Am I food?" I ask. *Sort of.*

I turn to someone else. "Do I go *well* with food?" *Yes.*

"Am I spicy?" *A little.*

"Am I white?" *No.*

"Am I black?" *Yes.*

"Am I pepper?" *Yes.*

Feeling proud of myself, I begin searching for my soulmate, salt.

I pass a Homer, a Tweedledee, and a Mac. I catch sight of Rafe also searching through the crowd. He ducks around someone, and then we come face-to-face.

"Turn around," I say.

"You turn around."

I cross my arms. "Fine." I twist around and look over my shoulder, noticing that his eyes dip below the region of my back. "You're salt, aren't you?"

He bends at the waist. "At your service, my spicy companion. Though I really think I should have been pepper because I'm just so hot."

I snort. He isn't wrong. "I'm amazed your ego hasn't sunk the island of Maui into the sea."

He grins, not the least bit offended by my comment. "Okay, lay it on me, Malik. Three nice things about me." He holds up his hands. "But *try* to limit yourself to only three. I don't want anyone getting jealous when you can't stop. We already know you think I smell nice."

My nose flares at the reminder of what I mumbled in a half-coherent daze the other night. My cheeks flush, and I cross my arms, trying to ignore his smirk. "Excuse me, but you go first. Three nice things about me."

"We'll take turns," he counters. "A compliment for a compliment."

I huff out a breath. "I couldn't have just matched with some random person and faked my way through this?"

"You're stuck with me now, Trishara."

There's an implication in that statement, his words settling between us like a triangle squeezing itself into a circle.

I scan him from head to toe, searching for the most innocuous compliment I can deliver. I will not fluff up his ego any further. But wow, he looks good today. Then he runs a hand through his thick, shiny hair, and my brain turns to mush. "You have fantastic hair." The words slip from me of their own volition, hanging in front of me and slapping me in the face.

Rafe's eyes dance as he moves a little closer. The surrounding cacophony surges as everyone engages in animated conversation. But we have entered a bubble. All the noise and the distraction melt away until it feels like we are the only people left in the room.

"I think you smell good, too," Rafe says, his voice low, his mouth close to my ear. "Last night in bed, it felt like drowning in strawberries and creamy vanilla frosting."

His voice drops to a rough growl on the last three words, causing a pulse to throb low in my stomach. We both look around the room, making sure no one heard. I'm pretty sure this isn't what the HR department had in mind when they set us on this exercise.

It's my turn again, and I swallow. Hesitating. But caution is for suckers, and I take a running leap off this cliff. "I love your forearms," I say, my voice breathy as I steal a glance down. "They're beautiful."

He follows my gaze and raises that soul-destroying eyebrow. "Is that your kink, Trishara? I would never have guessed."

My throat is so tight that I have to suck air through my nose.

He makes a fist, and my breath explodes—the dusting of hair and the way his veins pop against the golden color of his skin. I *hate* how much I think about those arms.

Only a few inches separate us as we cast more guilty looks about the room. Everyone has found their pair and are chatting like long-lost friends.

But Rafe and I don't need to get to know one another. We've spent years in orbit moving like planets, parallel but never crossing. I already know what I like about Rafe. Until a few days ago, I swore it was nothing, but now I'm not so sure.

"I love the way you charge through life as though you don't give a shit what anyone thinks," Rafe says, and those words find a secret place where all my fears and insecurities fester.

Rafe moves closer, his lips so close to my ear that I can feel his heat and smell his skin. I reciprocate, standing up on my toes as I take my turn. "I think your drawings are the most beautiful things I've ever seen, and I had no idea you were capable of such...depth. You are bold and confident and have this way with people that makes them feel important, and I think someone must have told you that your art wasn't special because how could you think it was anything but extraordinary?"

My thoughts surface unbidden, but as I stand there with the recollection of those pages, I'm struck with certainty that's what I saw in his art. They were pencil sketches rendered from yearning and desire. All these years, I've been entirely misjudging some fundamental facet of Rafe. He is deeper and wider than the Grand Canyon. I might make fun of his ego, but the truth is that I'm drawn to his self-assurance. I admire the way he can charm a room.

He goes completely still, and I *feel* his breath catch.

Then his gaze finds mine, and the corner of his mouth turns up into yet another new smile I memorize for safekeeping. A smile that tells me the next words from his mouth have been carefully, painstakingly designed to destroy me.

Soft lips brush the shell of my ear. "Your ass is so fucking hot in that skirt, I want to fall to my knees and worship it."

My heart stops. Literally stops. I hold my own funeral on the floor of a hotel ballroom covered in threadbare carpet, hideously patterned to hide a decade of coffee stains.

Rafe Gallagher just told me my ass is hot. I know it is. I bought this skirt expressly for how hot it made my ass look. But he just said it out loud, and the result is an exhale on the tightly knotted bow we've been keeping on this wrapped package.

We are so far over the line of the rules I set for myself that I have to squint to see them stretching in the distance. But maybe I don't mind.

His hand lands on my hip, gentle but firm, fingers digging in with the barest pressure. He turns his head ever so slightly. His mouth brushes my cheek, and I stand perfectly still like I've been turned into marble through a spell cast by a meddling fairy godmother.

Screeeeeee!

Whistle Mouth blasts through our suspension of time, and I have never wanted to take that plastic whistle and *shove* it down her throat more. Rafe and I snap apart, turning to face the front of the room with everyone else. I feel like a lighthouse, my face so flushed and hot I could signal ships in the night.

I feel Rafe standing behind me. My elbow and shoulder brush

his chest and his stomach, and then there is the barest touch of the edge of his hand. It ghosts over the curve of my ass, and every cell in my body is dedicated to the relentless pursuit of imagining his large palm cupping and kneading and...I want it so badly that it becomes the first tier on my hierarchy of needs. If I can have this, I'll never need food or water again.

Whistle Mouth is saying something, but I can't hear anything over the roar in my ears and the pounding in my heart and the ache between my thighs. I'm going to faint here in front of everyone.

She claps her hands and blows her whistle again. "Okay, every-one move!"

The room breaks apart, and I look behind me to find Rafe looking at me with the whisper of a knowing smile.

It takes all my willpower to turn away and proceed to the next activity.

Chapter Seventeen

We don't talk about it. We let it inflate like a giant balloon sucking all the air from the room. I Google how to turn myself into a mind-reading amoeba, desperate to know what's running through Rafe's head.

What I do know is that the bed we've been sharing feels a lot smaller, and last night, there was so much energy humming through my bones that I could have powered a small city. I've accepted my fate as a wide-eyed zombie destined never to sleep again. I respect the hotel's request and resist the urge to ask if there are any more rooms, but I'm this close to snapping.

Eventually, I must succumb to a version of rest because Sunday arrives, and we have the day off from lectures.

"What are you up to today?" Rafe asks.

He's sitting at the glass table in the dining area, eating the room-service eggs and bacon we ordered. I pick up my book, which I haven't touched since the plane ride, and stuff it into a large tote along with sunscreen, flip-flops, headphones, and a sarong.

I've already changed into a teal high-waisted bikini patterned with large white lilies. He's watching me intently as I move about the room. If I drop my book and am forced to bend over to retrieve it with my back to him, that is purely coincidental.

"Spending the day poolside with Lan and Gabrielle, consuming numerous cocktails, and working on my tan. You?"

He shrugs and takes a bite of eggs. "I'll probably go to the gym, and I'm supposed to have lunch with my dad later." He says the last part like he's bitten into the skin of a grapefruit. I want to offer comfort but resist my desire to touch him. This primal need has become a constant tug of war, and I'm afraid of what it will set off. I feel like dynamite on the verge of detonation.

"Okay, well, have fun?" I say instead, and he makes a derisive sound as he attacks his food. I hesitate, wondering if I should stay.

This is clearly a sore spot, but I've been waiting all week to sit poolside with my friends, and I must keep Rafe at a distance. A few kind gestures and one panty-melting comment don't change anything.

I tell myself that Rafe's unhappiness is not my responsibility, though something about that sits like a lead brick in my stomach. Nevertheless, I pick up my bag and sling it over my shoulder. "See you later."

"Yeah," he replies as I turn and leave the room.

"Let's take a selfie," Lan says, holding up her phone. "Crowd in." Gabrielle and I sit on either side, our cheeks pressed together as she snaps a pic. Gabrielle sneaks a sloppy, wet kiss onto Lan's cheek and laughs as they collapse into a hug.

"Ugh, you two are so cute," I scoff. "You're making me sick."

"You're at a conference with like a hundred straight dudes,"

Lan says. "Surely you can find someone to turn that frown upside down."

She places her fingers in the corners of my lips and stretches them up until I bat them away, laughing.

"I refuse to date anyone at WMC," I say with a scoff.

"You don't have to date them, *dah-ling*," Gabrielle intones, lowering her sunglasses and peering over at me. "Just *do* them."

I sip my rosé and point my glass in her direction. "That either."

"C'mon, what about Andy?" Lan asks as we all turn to eye the man in question. He's just arrived with some friends, who are all gathered at the bar on the opposite side of the pool. As if sensing our attention, he looks over, raising a hand towards us.

"I don't know," I say. "He's cute, but eh..."

Honestly, I'd actually kind of forgotten about him. Between the storm, Rafe's sketchbook, and the incident with my ass, I've let a string of texts from Andy go unanswered. Whatever attraction I first felt has become a wavering penlight compared to the million-watt spotlight of Rafe's confusing attention.

"What about the guy with the muscles and the sexy eyes? Your sworn enemy?" Gabrielle asks, sipping on her drink.

"Gabrielle!" Lan says, affronted.

"What? I'm not blind. That guy is *hot*, and he has sexy eyes. Relax. I think your eyes are sexy, too."

Lan rolls said eyes and sits back in her chair. "Gabrielle has a point," she says. "You looked kind of intense during that whole 'say three nice things' game the other day. What was happening there?" She waves a hand in my direction.

I peer into my glass, avoiding her gaze. "Nothing. We were just talking."

"Looked like more than just talking," Lan says in a singsong voice.

My thighs press together as I remember not just the words Rafe said but how he said them. Like the hero in a romance novel about to sweep me into his arms, carry me up to his tower, and make love to me until I can't breathe.

No, he is still the villain. The bad guy. He would take me to his underground lair, not a fairytale castle. Fuck, why is that prospect even hotter?

"Hi there." I am pulled from my thoughts by Andy's voice. He's smiling at the three of us as he settles on the end of my lounger. "How's everyone doing? I've sent you a few texts, Tris. Everything okay?"

"Sorry about that." I search for a plausible excuse. "My phone has been acting up." He nods as if that seems reasonable and then looks around the pool area. "Your attack dog not here today?"

"My attack dog?"

"Tall guy with the angry face?"

I snort. "No. I don't know where he is."

Andy shifts, moving a little closer, his hip brushing over my toes. "If you don't have plans tonight, there's a trivia contest at the Sand Dune Bar."

Andy lays a hand over the top of my foot and squeezes. I don't think I like the assumption in that touch, but I let it rest there, not wanting to cause a scene.

"I'm amazing at trivia," Gabrielle says, and Lan nods. "I've heard they give out huge prizes."

"How about you?" Andy asks as his hand slides to my ankle, circling it with his fingers.

"I'll see," I say. "I'm kind of tired. I might just call it an early night." I shift my legs, hoping he'll take the hint. He doesn't.

A moment later, a Rafe-shaped shadow falls over us, and we both look up to find his laser-eyed focus on Andy's hand, still gripping my leg.

This is all very annoying, but I'm also grateful Rafe's alpha stupidity causes Andy to back away. I should be furious at Rafe and his caveman antics, but my inner feminist is taking a nap. She understands that sometimes you need to counter one point of male nonsense with another.

"I should have known the mutt wouldn't be far," Andy drawls as he stands.

Unfortunately for him, Rafe is taller and wider and definitely angrier. While I don't understand what Rafe is doing, I don't interfere because I didn't want Andy touching me, anyway.

Rafe's jaw hardens into iron as he locks stares with Andy.

Gabrielle clasps her hands as though this is an afternoon soap opera and not my actual life. Lan braces a protective arm in front of her, clearly worried that Rafe and Andy are about to start throwing punches.

Thankfully, Andy takes a step back before anything drastic happens, and he looks down at me. "Come to the bar later. I'd love to hang out some more." Then he tosses a dirty look at Rafe and walks away.

Then Rafe looks at me, and his expression combines all the sides of Rafe. It's not the pure evil glare, but his dark lord mixed with a hint of protective bear and a smidge of sultry wolf. It's there for a heartbeat, and then before he says anything else, he too turns and walks away.

The three of us sit in stunned silence when Gabrielle blows a low whistle. "I mean, if you're looking to get laid, I don't think you'll have any trouble, my friend. Those two might even agree to do it at the same time just for the chance to have you."

She takes a sip of her water and bats her eyes innocently.

"Shut up," I say before Lan and Gabrielle burst out laughing as I drop my face into my hands.

Chapter Eighteen

I agree to attend trivia night after Lan and Gabrielle promise to play offense against Andy. I haven't quite settled on my feelings about him, but we've chosen a code word in case I need someone to step in. *Coconut* shouldn't be too hard to work into a tropical setting.

I'm dressed in a two-piece outfit made of flowing pink silk dotted with tiny white flowers. It's a crop top with short puffed sleeves and a sweetheart neckline paired with a high-waisted skirt that is a little on the short side of professional. It's a lot of skin, but I've spent the day at the pool, and I'm glowing. I strap on a pair of wedge sandals and head to the lobby to meet Lan and Gabrielle.

As I approach, Lan whistles and waves her hand like she's just touched a hot stove.

"Are you trying to cause a riot?" she asks. "'Cause those boys are going to tear each other to pieces with their teeth when they get a load of you in that."

I look down at myself. "Should I change?"

"No way," Gabrielle says, linking her arm with mine. "You look amazing."

"Rafe probably isn't coming," I add as we start walking.

"Did he tell you that?"

"No, but I haven't seen him all afternoon. He must be off brooding somewhere."

"Hmm," Lan says with a knowing air. "He's got that brooding thing down to an art form."

I roll my eyes. "C'mon. My buzz is in danger of wearing off."

We make our way through the hotel's wide marble hallways and exit through the rear entrance to arrive at the Sand Dune.

It sits directly on the beach, where a dozen flickering torches backdrop a long bar. Sleek white couches surround low wicker tables, all connected by wooden boardwalks interspersed with small pools floating with tiny flickering candles.

As we enter, Andy waves us over to a U-shaped seating area. He's sitting with some guys from the conference, along with some women I don't recognize.

Thanks to WMC's unbalanced gender ratio, they've clearly had to go hunting for reinforcements. Thankfully for them, at least a dozen wedding parties are also staying at the resort, so there are plenty of bridesmaids ripe for the wooing.

Andy pats the seat next to him, and there is no mistaking his assessing look as his gaze rakes me from head to toe. I resist the urge to tug down the hem of my skirt. Maybe I should have worn something less revealing.

He shouts down the line to make room for me and my friends. As I sit, I'm immediately squished against him as Gabrielle and Lan squeeze their way onto the sofa. Is it too soon to call *coconut*? I talk myself down from overreacting.

"When does trivia start?" I ask, tugging back a piece of hair that blows across my face.

"Soon," Andy replies with a smirk, leaning closer. "You look great."

"Oh, this old thing?" I joke and then immediately look away, uncomfortable and wondering why I agreed to this. I'd honestly rather be in my room watching the water and reading my book or having a quiet dinner with my friends.

As we all make conversation, the noise swells, and the energy picks up, and it's obvious everyone started partying a while ago. While more and more people find their way to the bar, I'm jostled from every side, and my skin itches with the uncomfortable sensation of being hemmed in. I consider a plan to politely extricate myself.

Then Rafe walks into the Sand Dune. My attention zeroes in on his presence instantly.

His dark hair tosses in the breeze, and he wears navy shorts, a blue fitted T-shirt, and a large silver watch that *does* things to me. Did he wear that because of what I said about his arms?

A surge of bodies nearly squeezes me off the couch, so I take the opportunity to escape.

Stumbling a few steps through the sand, I right myself.

Rafe also finds me immediately.

It's then I understand who I wore this outfit for. His gaze meanders slowly from my face down the length of my body, traveling past my mouth and over my breasts, sliding to the hem of my skirt and my barely covered thighs, and this . . . I don't mind.

Lan catches my eye, and I nod to assure her I'm okay.

"Excuse me," I say to Andy, though I'm not sure if he can hear me, and then walk away.

I stride in the opposite direction of Rafe. I don't know why, but I'm struck with a premonition: If I approach him, I'll fall into a black hole from which I can never return.

Or maybe I just want to see if he'll follow.

I wind through the sand, passing laughing crowds and flickering torches, heading towards a bar to order a drink.

A booming voice erupts over the sound system, signaling the start of trivia night. A wave of bodies coalesces towards a stage set up just beyond the bar's perimeter. Apparently, the prizes range in significance from free trips to impressive sums of cash, and the competition is fierce.

I ask for a glass of wine, and while the bartender fills my request, I sense a warm presence behind me. The bartender deposits my drink on the bar and looks up.

"I'll have a Big Swell IPA," Rafe says over my head. The bartender nods and plucks a glass bottle from a basin of ice, cracking the top and handing it over. I pick up my glass and take a sip, willing myself not to look at Rafe.

There's a lot that needs to be said but is probably better left alone. And I don't think I'm ready for any of it.

We both turn around as the announcer explains the rules of the game to dozens of eager onlookers.

"You playing?" Rafe asks, tipping the neck of his bottle. Finally, I turn to look at him and shake my head.

"No, I think I'll sit this one out."

Through some form of silent agreement, we drift away from the bar, ending up on the edge of the crowd. Lan and Gabrielle have muscled their way to the front, both grinning with excitement.

I notice Andy poke his head up like a gopher, scanning the area.

Worried that he's looking for me, I shuffle behind Rafe, using him as a shield. He looks over at Andy and then down at me, his mouth stretching into a satisfied smile.

I return it with a scowl and focus on Lan and Gabrielle instead. The announcer fires off questions to each participating pair with a velocity that has my head spinning. Rafe and I stand together, watching as Lan and Gabrielle maintain a one hundred percent response rate. I clap furiously and cheer for each right answer.

"This is kind of intense," Rafe finally comments before looking at the empty glass in my hand. "Another one?"

"Sure." He takes it from me and turns to walk away.

Again, I notice Andy searching the crowd, and I catch the back of Rafe's shirt, my fingers brushing a solid wall of muscle.

"Wait for me," I say. He stops and gestures for me to walk ahead.

We order our drinks and look at each other like we're not sure what to do next.

"Do you want to sit?" I point to several empty couches in the far corner of the bar.

He nods, and we make our way over, sinking down side by side to watch the trivia from afar. For a few minutes, Lan and Gabrielle nail every question as I sneak glances at Rafe's profile. He's sporting a layer of stubble, and wow, it's sexy. My legs slide together as I think about how that would feel against my skin.

Stop. It.

But I'm not the only one staring.

His gaze is drifting down my thighs, lingering for a beat before meeting my eyes.

By the light of the torches, I make out flecks of gold and orange in his irises. They're the color of cinnamon and nutmeg. Leather club chairs and log cabins and acorns scattered across the forest floor.

The barest smile teases his mouth, and I imagine sinking my teeth into his bottom lip. A sheen of sweat breaks out on my forehead due to a heady combination of tropical humidity, several glasses of wine, and just a hint—okay, more than a hint—of raging hormonal lust.

"Nice dress," he says, his eyes glittering as he lowers his head to whisper into my ear. "You look good enough to eat."

My response is a sharp inhale that straddles a wobbly line between a gasp and a moan. I'm acutely aware of his arm and leg touching mine. I can't take my eyes off him and the snug shirt that molds to the lines of his chest and his abs. The tilt of his hips as he leans back with his legs spread just the right amount.

If a fairy godmother arrived to grant me three wishes right now, one would be x-ray vision. How? *How* did I go from hating Rafe Gallagher with every drop of my soul to desperately wishing we were both naked?

And then he twists the knife deeper.

His hand hovers over my knee, and every one of my senses homes into his almost touch like the neon red dot of a sniper. His gaze flicks to mine, seeking permission, and I nod.

His touch is light and gentle, yet it feels like an explosion. We both focus on his fingers as he traces circles on my skin. They drag higher, just an inch, and I feel it absolutely *everywhere*. It's slow. It's torturous. I grip the leather sofa with my hands to keep myself from falling.

Electricity sparks through my veins as my chin tips up and my knees inch apart. His pupils spread, and his eyes turn black as the bottom of my stomach drops from beneath me.

"Rafe," I say because I'm so agonizingly turned on that I need to feel some part of him on my tongue.

"I'm sorry about this afternoon," he replies. "Lunch with my father was a disaster, and I was in a mood."

Right. I completely forgot that I'm supposed to be annoyed about something. I was much too relieved to see him, not only to shield me from Andy but because I wanted him here. I try not to examine the root of that thought too closely. But now, I can't think with him touching me. I remove his hand from my leg and try to focus on what he's saying.

Finally gathering my wits, I ask, "What *was* that about?"

"I shouldn't have done that, but that guy is such a tool, Tris."

My momentary arousal morphs and sharpens, and now I'm angry. "It's none of your business who I talk to, Rafe. There is no plane of existence where you have any say over me."

He runs a hand through his hair in a clear sign of distress. "I know that. My father was pressuring me about the training program and—" He stops and looks at me. "It just made me a little crazy seeing that fuckwit touching you."

My heart does a little flip at his words. "It's also none of your damn business who touches me."

"Tris, that guy is a dick. He's only after one thing. To score with one of the few women attending this thing so he can say he did it."

My reaction is the epitome of disbelief. Did he just imply that Andy was only interested in me for bragging rights? And why does that hurt so much?

"Fuck you, Rafe. Just because I don't look like your supermodel ex-girlfriend doesn't mean someone else can't find me attractive." I leap from my seat before he can say anything else.

Tears build behind my eyes. *That asshole.* I can't believe I was starting to trust him. I storm through the bar and towards the hotel, marching underneath a stone awning lined with thick marble pillars.

"Tris," Rafe shouts after me, and I pick up my pace. I will not let him see me cry. I will not let him hurt me anymore. "Please." He runs up and catches my wrist. "I'm sorry. I didn't mean it like that."

"Then what did you mean, Rafe?" I whirl on him. "You thought you'd first go all possessive asshole, decide who can and can't touch me, and then insult me to my face?"

He says nothing, just looks uncertain for a moment, so I turn and storm off again. Then he finds his voice.

"Wait," he says, and I whirl on him one more time.

"What kills me is you came to me apologizing but then blamed it all on your father instead of taking accountability for your behavior. Just leave me alone."

"Please," he says, and it's fused with so much emotion that it actually makes me stop. "I'm sorry. I keep saying everything wrong around you. What I said there, I didn't mean it like that. I just meant a guy like that will never appreciate how amazing you are. How smart and funny and bright. A guy like that only wants a notch on his bedpost. He'll never understand you."

The ground tilts. I sway and nearly lose my footing. Then I scoff because that's a much better reaction.

"And *you* will appreciate those things?"

"Yes," he says.

It's only one syllable, but it's stuffed full of so many things yet to be said.

He's staring at me like he's tumbling through freefall.

Every pithy response I wish I could come up with shrivels in my throat.

I'm not sure who moves first. A beat of silence drops before Rafe's mouth crashes into mine. We kiss. We kiss like it's our last moment on earth. Like at any second, this will be taken away.

I panic, then do the complete opposite of what I want and shove him, hands pressed flat against his chest. We tear apart and just *stare* at each other.

Rafe's eyes have gone so dark, they're deep black pits of glittering stars. That was a terrible idea. But I don't care. He is beautiful and warm, his lips swollen, his hair mussed.

"Tris, I'm sor—" I don't give him a chance to finish yet another apology because I am tired of *sorry*s, and right now, I regret nothing. I grab the fabric of his shirt and yank him down as our lips meet.

He grunts as his hands circle my waist, my back hitting cool marble. Ferocious palms and long fingers grip the backs of my thighs, and I'm lifted up, my legs trapping his waist. Our mouths part, hovering an inch away, eyes open wide as I plummet down the rabbit hole. One hand braces the side of my neck, his thumb running down the center of my throat as we sip on the forced exhales rushing in and out from our lungs.

Rafe's hand slides down my rib cage and smooths against the curve of my ass. He squeezes as he again captures my mouth with his. A slick slide of tongues and teeth and lips is punctuated with a tilt of his hips and the arch of my back.

He's hard enough to knock down buildings. I feel it infinitely in the soft, wet ache between my thighs. He moves, thrusting and grinding, followed by an agonized moan. My hands find his shoulders and his chest and his stomach, finally discovering their happy place in the nest of his thick hair. I grip it, tug it, pulling him to me harder. This isn't enough.

Somehow, he understands because his tongue dives deeper until we drown. We are the burn of heat and fire and every conflicting emotion I've ever felt for this infuriating man.

A break on the rocks.

A star dropped from the sky.

This. Is. A. Reckoning.

Ships sink. Tornadoes spin. Volcanoes erupt.

No one has ever kissed me like this.

He breathes my name, and I say it back because this is all I am right now. He tastes like sunshine and longing, and I lap up every drop. His hands wander to the underside of my skirt, fingertips skating the dangerous edge of my underwear.

His mouth moves down my throat, burying in the curve of my neck as he nips and bites at my skin, mapping a voyage across the range of my collarbone and over the valley of my breasts. I want this to last forever. Our pulses clash, our mouths tangle, our hands are greedy.

But then Rafe swerves from my lane, pulling back and lowering me to the ground.

I feel his absence burying into my chest like a wreath of thorns.

"Fuck," he says. "Fuck. I'm sorry. I shouldn't have done that. Tris, I'm sorry."

It's another *sorry*. We're sorry again, but he's right. This was a terrible idea.

I begin, quietly and appropriately freaking out.

"You kissed me," I say, not sure if it's an observation or an accusation.

Rafe's nostrils flare, taking the latter bend in the road. "You kissed *me*!"

"You started it!" Though I'm not really sure if that's true.

"You continued it," he counters, and *shit*, that is totally true. "I shouldn't have done that."

I know why *I* shouldn't have done that, but why shouldn't *he* have done it? My stomach twists as bile creeps up the back of my throat.

He laces his hands at the back of his head and paces. The hem of his shirt lifts, and I catch a sliver of his Midas-touched stomach. My fingers twitch with the desire for more.

The feel of his hands and his mouth have now been tattooed onto me with ink and blood.

"Fine. That's just fine," I snap.

Nothing has ever been less fine.

I am such a fucking liar.

So, I'm left with no choice but to glare at him and then run away.

Chapter Nineteen

I stand in line at the check-in desk with my arms crossed and my toe tapping the marble while a family of nine hundred and forty-three people, all draped in floral-patterned shirts, crowd the reception area. It's been fifteen minutes already, and I'm this close to hauling someone back by the collar and bulldozing my way through.

After storming away from Rafe last night, I didn't see him again until this morning when I found him asleep on the couch. I guess our days of sharing the bed are over. Belinda finally responded to one of my many emails, claiming the room mix-up was an accident. She added that she called the hotel, and they had no other rooms to offer before assuring me we'd be just fine staying together. Thanks. So helpful.

But it's no matter—today, I'm finding a new room for Rafe if I have to build it myself with some rusty nails and planks of desperation. I know they didn't want me to ask again, but I'm losing my mind.

This morning, I dressed in my grey pencil skirt and a black T-shirt dotted with crystals. When I left the room, Rafe didn't stir, and I harbor suspicions that he was pretending to be asleep. It seems like something he'd do.

Now, I'm waiting in the lobby, praying another room has opened up, but the human glacier wall in front of me isn't moving. Nine hundred people need one million rooms, and I'm going to die waiting here.

I check my phone. This morning's sessions are starting soon, and I'll be late if I don't get going, but I can't spend another minute in that room with Rafe. It took me forever to fall asleep last night, even after I made use of my Sona 2 cranked up to level 12. But that totally backfired because it only made me think about Rafe and that kiss even more.

My thighs squeeze together with the intense recollection of Rafe's iron-hard erection nestled between them. My hand flutters to my throat as I feel the burn of his mouth on my skin. I wonder if my Sona 2 has a power booster I can attach or something. This isn't good. I have to think of something else.

"You coming?" I jump nearly a foot, entirely absorbed in my horny daydreams. It's Andy, and he's giving me an expectant look. "Class is starting soon."

I look back towards the desk where the crowd is still six rows deep. These people probably took up every available room, anyway. I sigh. I'll come back later and try again.

"Sure," I say. "Do you know where we're going?"

"Yeah. Allow me to escort you." He gestures with a flourish, and I give him a tight smile because he's trying to be cute. And he is cute. Maybe I need to give him a chance. It's not his fault that Rafe appears to make him look bad every time he comes near me.

I stretch my smile wider, ignoring how forced it feels. If I'm considering breaking my personal stalemate and giving my attention to a man at WMC, then it should be this one. Or some other one. Or literally anyone who isn't Rafe.

"I lost you last night," he says as we walk towards the conference rooms. "You missed some good trivia."

"I wasn't feeling well." I touch my forehead with the back of my hand as if to convince him of my lie.

"Are you still sick?" He frowns at my hand, and I snatch it away. I'm being ridiculous.

"No." I shake my head. "Nothing a good night's sleep couldn't cure."

"Oh, I'm glad to hear that." He rubs his chin, looking a little unsure of himself. "I was wondering if you wanted to get some dinner tonight? I hear there is a mean seafood spread at the Coconut Lounge."

I don't really want to. What I want is to survive this day, get Rafe out of my room, and spend the night with my smutty romance novel. But I already know that even if he's physically removed from my presence, my imagination is vivid, and my obsession with Rafe is as familiar and inevitable as the sun rising over the horizon.

So, I look Andy in the eye and put on a smile that I hope is convincing.

"Sure, I'd like that."

"Awesome," he says, releasing a relieved puff of air.

We've just arrived at the conference room, where lines of tables are set up in rows. A whiteboard announces the day's activities with bold black lettering that spells out *Aptitude Test*. I sigh. Another test.

"Should we say seven?" Andy asks, and I nod before he smiles and finds his seat. Lan and Gabrielle wave me over, and I slide in next to them, pulling my bag over my head and setting it on the ground.

"You missed our victory last night!" Gabrielle exclaims. "We won!"

"Amazing! What did you win?"

They exchange a pleased look. "A private yacht tour for four, including all the food and drinks you can consume," Lan says.

"Congrats. That sounds incredible."

"You'll come along, right?" Lan asks. "It's going to be so fun."

"Sure. Of course. I'd love to. What about the fourth?"

Gabrielle's expression turns sly. "We thought you might want to invite someone?"

Their gazes slide to Rafe, who's settling himself across the room. His eyes find mine, and my cheeks warm as I turn back to my friends.

"Um, I'll think about it."

"Okay," Lan says. "We'll go sometime next week. We're think-ing the night before the training program announcements."

I nod, fiddling with the pen in my hands. "Sure. Thank you." They both look so hopeful that I don't have the heart to tell them I won't be inviting Rafe, but we'll cross that bridge later. There's still time. Maybe I'll find someone else to fill this inconvenient ache in my . . . chest.

Several pieces of stapled paper are dropped in front of me, and I pick them up, trying to focus on the task at hand. Whistle Mouth stands at the front of the room, eyeing us with her unearned supe-riority. "Today, you will undergo a series of tests to determine your aptitude in specific areas such as verbal, numerical, or log-ical reasoning, as well as how you think, learn, communicate, and remember. There is no grade, and you cannot give a wrong answer. These tests are simply designed to determine your capacity to function in various contexts."

I'm sure I'm not the only one thinking about how scary that sounds, as evidenced by the low murmur cycling through the room. We are *definitely* being graded on our answers.

Whistle Mouth calls for silence, and the room descends into the drone of concentration, the scratch of pencils, and the soft sounds of shuffling paper.

The first question is simple, and I nearly laugh at how obvious it is.

Which word describes you best? I'd rather be:

Thinking

Listening

Leading

Doing

Communicating

My pencil hovers over the empty circle next to *leading*, because I'm sure this is the correct answer. For a moment, I'm torn between responding the way they expect and how I really feel. I do want to lead, but maybe I'd actually rather be listening, and maybe *that* would make me a better leader.

Because I can't seem to help myself, I look over at Rafe to find his head down and his dark hair falling into his eyes. I've done a lot of things in the past few weeks that some might call career-limiting moves. I blackmailed my boss and then made out with his son. And I can't stop thinking about doing it again. The making out. Not the blackmail. Though I'm not ruling it out for future consideration.

Rafe said his father was pressuring him about the training program, and it occurs to me that it's probably already been decided. I never stood a chance, and my answers don't matter.

So, I look back at my paper and mount my own quiet rebellion by choosing to answer honestly. Maybe it really is time to give up on this and accept that while WMC was the only option I had five years ago, that isn't true anymore. Despite everything, I've had the opportunity to cultivate many skills that would make me a valuable asset somewhere else.

Plus, I'm so tired of trying to win over a corporation that refuses to be won.

I darken the circle next to *listening* as pressure releases me from the box in which I've been contained. Maybe I'll learn something important about myself instead of just being the person I think they all want me to be. I run through the rest of the questions on this test and every other one, being as honest and true to myself as I can.

Several hours later, we're all tested out and finally allowed to go free. A low hum drones through the room as everyone discusses their answers and the questions. Rafe is watching me in a guarded way, but I turn away. I don't know what I want to say to him, and I feel a headache coming on as pain forms behind my eyes.

My phone rings as I'm walking back to the suite. It's Molly. I've been remiss in providing her with updates, so I dig out my earphones before answering and am greeted with a petulant lower lip thrust that would put most toddlers to shame.

"Hi," I say. "I know. I know."

"Where. Have. You. Been?"

"Busy?" My gaze darts away, knowing she's about to call me on my bullshit.

"Trishara. Tell me what's going on this instant. Why do you look so guilty?"

I look around. I'm alone, but I lower my voice anyway.

"We kissed."

She leans in closer to the screen, scrunching her nose. "Who kissed?"

"Rafe. Me and Rafe—"

Molly lets out a screech so loud I almost drop the phone as she finishes off the final shreds of my eardrums that Whistle Mouth hasn't already claimed.

"You kissed!"

"Yes. Stop freaking out!"

"Just a kiss?"

"Yes! Why?"

Her eyes grow so wide they fill the screen. "Why?! You kissed. I am so excited!" She screams again, and I flinch. "I can't believe you stopped at a kiss and didn't fuck each other senseless with all that pent-up *angst*."

"What are you talking about? There is no angst!"

She rolls her eyes. "Tris, you can't possibly expect me or anyone to believe that you haven't been into Rafe for years."

I open my mouth and close it. "What do you mean, anyone? Who else knows this?"

She laughs, covering her mouth, the screen blurring as she folds at the waist. "Him?"

"You know my rule on dating at WMC."

"I do, and I understand why you think you need to cling to it. But what happened was years ago, and rules are made to be broken. Rafe isn't Leo. If you'd pull your head out of your ass, you would have realized that a long time ago."

I press my lips together. "I don't know if I can break this rule."

"Yes, you can. Especially when the reason is six-plus feet of gorgeous."

"Shut up," I say. "He's not that good-looking. He's a seven at best."

Molly snorts so hard I worry she's blown a nostril. "Yeah, sure. You basically melt every time he walks into the room."

I sag against the wall. "Molly. It was the most amazing kiss I've ever had. I can't stop thinking about it." Her smile stretches so wide I can see every one of her teeth.

"And now?" she asks.

"Now, we yelled at each other and are pretending like it never happened."

She blows out a breath, fluffing the bangs that have fallen over her eyes. "Typical."

"I'm going on a date with Andy tonight," I add.

"Excuse me? Why?"

"'Cause I can't stop thinking about Rafe."

"I'm sure that must make sense in your mind."

I rub my temple as my head starts to pound. "Molly. I gotta go lie down."

"Okay. Tris—I want details *immediately* when you both finally cave."

"We're not having sex," I declare just as an elderly couple shuffles by where I'm standing in front of the elevator. They regard me with judgment, and I hunt for a rock to climb under.

"You are definitely having sex," Molly says. "You've finally cracked the pull tab, and it's only a matter of time before the pressure blows off the lid."

"Well, that's very poetic," I say, and she snickers.

Is she right? Do I want her to be?

Just then, Rafe appears around the corner and stops to wait for the elevator beside me. Molly screams again, shouting Rafe's name so loud my ears nearly bleed.

"Rafe! Hi, Rafe!"

I pull out my earbud, but that's a rookie mistake, because the tinny sound of her voice fills the air. I make out the words *kissed*, *fuck*, and *Trishara* before I slam the disconnect button in mortification. When I get home, I'm going to tie her up, throw her in the back of my trunk, and dump her in the Chicago River.

The elevator chimes, and Rafe and I step inside. I refuse to look at him, but I can see his reflection in the shiny metal door as he watches me from the corner of his eye. Did he hear that? If I pretend it never happened, then it didn't. Sure, that works.

When we arrive on our floor, I practice my hundred-meter dash and bolt for our room.

Slamming the bedroom door behind me, I pop some painkillers and fire off a text to my parents to let them know I'm alive.

Then I decide to take a nap. I set an alarm for my date with

Andy and flop on the bed, thinking of bottomless brown eyes and messy dark hair as I drift off to sleep.

The alarm goes off sooner than I'd like. I jolt awake, blinking through the fogginess of sleeping in the afternoon. I flop onto my back and stare at the ceiling for several minutes before I will myself up. Still dressed in my skirt from earlier, I pull down the zip, let it drop to the floor, and step out before heading for the closet.

I pick a halter sundress that falls past my knees. Something very different from the outfit I wore last night, lest I give Andy any unintentional ideas.

I put on some light makeup and brush my hair, deciding not to fuss with it too much. While my headache has somewhat subsided, a throb persists behind my left eye. I consider texting Andy and canceling about a thousand times, but then I think about Rafe and our kiss and the montage of filthy dreams I just had.

I need to try *something* to get him out of my head.

Eventually, I convince myself to leave. When I enter the living room, I spy Rafe on the balcony talking on his phone. The door is slightly cracked open, and I can just make out the sound of his voice. I turn away to leave, hoping he won't notice me, when I hear him say Hannah's name.

I shouldn't have done that.

That sick feeling and Rafe's words come back from last night. I can't help but think of Leo in that moment. He was always taking private phone calls, too. Checking in on his other girlfriend while

I sat in the dark like a fool. I know it's not the same situation, but it still feels a bit too close to home.

Rafe kissed me last night, and now he's talking to Hannah again.

Resolving to move past Rafe, I head for the Coconut Lounge, where I agreed to meet Andy. Is there an irony that *coconut* was my safe word last night?

He's already waiting for me in shorts and a T-shirt at the entrance. Rafe wore something similar last night, but the effect is completely different, and I scold myself for comparing them. The point of this date is to stop thinking about him.

Andy. I am focused on Andy. Or anyone besides Rafe. I'd have dinner with a cactus right now.

I flash the brightest smile I can summon before we're led to a table on a balcony overlooking the water.

The waiter runs over the menu options, and we place our orders. I'm quiet because I'm not feeling well and don't really want to be here. Thankfully, Andy doesn't seem to notice as he keeps up a stream of chatter. At least he's got that going for him.

We're interrupted by other WMCers passing by and saying hello a few times.

The date is fine. There's nothing specifically wrong with Andy. He's attractive and clearly smart, but I can't keep pretending I'm ever going to be into this. I already promised myself that he would have to be worth it if I took the chance and broke my rule about dating someone at the office. And I know Andy isn't.

Once dinner is over, he suggests a walk. I'm about to say no when I think of that suite with its closed walls and Rafe filling every corner. I'm torn between wanting to run back to him and staying as far away as possible.

I agree to the walk and immediately regret it because what could be more romantic than walking on a beach in Hawaii with the wind tossing our hair backdropped by the soft, harmonious sounds of the hotel bars and restaurants? Eventually, we stop and admire the clear star-strewn sky.

"You've been quiet tonight," he says.

"It was just a long day," I reply, giving him a small smile. "Sorry."

"No worries." He falls quiet for a moment, and the tension creeps between us. This would be the perfect moment to kiss if we were in a movie. It's a romance setting come to vivid life.

"You look beautiful tonight," he ventures, and I consider making a joke about how I know that, but I've done that before, and it always seems to catch men off guard. What I'm supposed to do is pretend I don't think I'm beautiful and act like he's the one handing this knowledge to me.

"Thanks," I say instead, and he steps closer. I don't move back because if he wants to kiss me, I'll let him. I haven't stopped thinking about Rafe at all tonight, and maybe a kiss from someone else will force him out.

Andy's head lowers, and he brushes his lips against mine, and...it's nice. He presses a little more firmly, and...it's fine. This is all fine.

Wow, this is nothing like Rafe. *This* is a kiss I'm used to. This is a kiss I've experienced plenty of times.

But I've looked into the sun and cant ever go back. Rafe has ruined me forever.

I break away and step back. This isn't working. The only thing I'm thinking about is Rafe. This was a dumb idea.

"Thanks for dinner," I say. "It was nice."

"You're going?" Andy asks with a question in his eyes.

"Yeah," I say again, putting my hand to my forehead. "Sorry, I guess I still haven't recovered from last night. Thanks again. Dinner was great. I'll see you later?"

"I'll walk you back to your room," he says, his tone taking on a shred of aggression that I don't care for.

"That's okay," I reply, yanking my arm from his grip. "Stay here and enjoy the beach. It's a gorgeous night. I heard the others are meeting at the Rainbow Bar. You should join them."

I keep my tone light.

Andy clenches his jaw.

"Sure," he replies after a moment.

Maybe a former Trishara would feel bad about how I've acted tonight. I should never have agreed to this. I used him to get someone else out of my system, which was a dick move, but it turns out he's also kind of a dick himself, and I'm already moving away.

"Good night," I say, trying to sound brighter than I feel, relieved when he doesn't try to follow.

Before I go upstairs, I detour to the front desk, intending to ask about another room. Thankfully, the reception area is now blessedly free of Hawaiian-shirt-clad families.

However, my old friend Kalena is there, and her smile falters as I approach.

"Hi, me again." I give her a little wave. "Just wondering if any rooms have opened up yet?"

"I'm sorry, but the room we had is gone now."

"What room?"

A furrow creases her brow. "I called up and spoke with Mr. Gallagher earlier. He said you'd no longer be needing a second room, so I gave it away. I apologize if I misunderstood. I can certainly let you know if anything else comes free, but we've just filled right back up again."

My mouth opens as I freeze.

"We're hosting a lot of conferences and weddings," she adds, clearly prepared for me to make another scene.

"He did what?" I ask.

Kalena blinks. "He said you were fine and wouldn't need a second room. Again, I'm sorry."

I shake my head. "No...that's okay..." Now I'm completely puzzled. "This afternoon? Today?"

"Yes," she says, looking around as if she thinks she's about to get in trouble. "He seemed quite certain."

This afternoon. After he told me that we shouldn't have kissed. After we'd just spent the day avoiding each other. After he moved back to the cramped couch. After he was on the phone with Hannah.

"Thanks," I say quietly.

I turn away and head for the elevators, more confused than ever.

Chapter Twenty

I spend the entirety of the next two days scrutinizing Rafe from across the room, wondering what's going on in his head. I wish I could crack it open and read what's written inside.

Why did he refuse the second room? What's his game? I try not to think about it while simultaneously thinking of nothing else.

After we're done with our classes on Thursday, I head to the gym for a workout, setting myself up in the weight area. Nothing gets out my stress and anxiety like lifting a lot of heavy things. I haven't been as dedicated as I am at home, but in my defense, there has been a lot going on.

Of course, I'm a few minutes in, my earphones blasting, when Rafe shows up and sets up next to me. I pull out an earbud, the metallic sounds of music audible above the hotel's choice of generic motivational music. He looks at it and then at me, and I think we're both remembering Molly shouting at him through the phone.

"You'll damage your eardrums playing your music that loud," Rafe says as he lies down on the bench and begins pressing an enormous set of dumbbells. I choke out a laugh.

"Oh, thanks for the tip, Dr. Gallagher."

He gives me a sort of half grin–half grimace as he works. I

become momentarily rooted to the spot as his triceps bunch and his chest heaves as he completes each rep. When he's done his set, he drops the weights and sits up, peering at me.

"Tris." I jump and meet his gaze as he drags a finger down the corner of his mouth. "You've got drool there."

My nostrils flare, and I resist the urge to check because, honestly, it might be true.

"Shut up," I say and wince. I hear him chuckle as I turn away and replace my earbud. We spend the next hour dancing in each other's spaces.

I came here to release the tension in my shoulders, but I'm only growing increasingly aware of Rafe and the sheen of sweat glistening over his muscles. After a while, he pulls off his shirt and wipes his forehead, and if I wasn't drooling before, then I definitely am now. I pull out my earbuds again.

"Excuse me," I say, pointing to a large white sign on the wall. "Rule number nine says shirts must remain on in the workout room."

He pretends to scrutinize the sign, squinting and rubbing his jaw. Then he winks. "So go report me."

I almost laugh, but I hold it in. Our push and pull has always relied on maintaining the façade that I'm not enjoying this. And I wonder if it's the same for him.

He returns to what he was doing, and I stare at his back, not at all distracted by the shadows and hollows of his muscle, and why is the light so good in here? He looks over his shoulder and grins, and my chest twists with a lurch.

I think about my night with Andy and how much I wanted to escape, but with Rafe, I want to remain suspended here forever.

We're not even doing anything—we're barely speaking—but over the past two weeks, his presence has become a constant that makes me feel just a little more...whole. We went from two people standing on opposite sides of the room to whatever *this* is.

His gaze catches mine, a small smile playing on his lips, and I wonder if he feels this, too. He said we shouldn't have kissed, so maybe not. But that kiss was too hot not to have meant anything to him. So maybe something is also holding him back.

After finishing my weights, I head to the stretching area. When Rafe is done, I get up, dust my butt off, and grab two bottles of water from the fridge, handing one over.

"Thanks." He uses his still doffed shirt to twist off the cap and takes a long drink. If that fairy godmother returned, I'd use my second wish and ask to be turned into that water bottle.

Fuck, I need to get out of here.

I make my way for the elevator with Rafe on my heels. We stand at opposite ends of the tiny box as it fills with his scent and his entire presence. The light bounces off his abs and his chest, and I will myself to stare at a spot just above his shoulder so he doesn't catch me gawking again.

"You're strong," he finally says, and I arch an eyebrow.

"For a girl, you mean."

"That's not what I said."

"No, but it's what you meant," I challenge because I can't help *pushing* him.

"Don't put words in my mouth. It's not what I meant. It was a compliment, freely and unsarcastically given."

I bite my lip. "Fine. Thank you."

"Your form is very nice," I say, immediately blushing at my unintended double entendre.

Rafe gives me a wicked smile that might be my new favorite.

I think he likes this, too.

The bell dings and we arrive at our floor and enter the suite. The one we're still sharing because Rafe turned down the second room. I'm dying to ask why, but something makes me hesitate, perhaps worried the answer isn't the one I'm hoping for.

"You can take the first shower," he says.

"I thought you were back to using the other bathroom?"

He lifts his brows and tilts his head. "Is it okay if I keep using the shower?"

"Yeah, of course. I'd never force someone to take a bath against their will."

He smirks. "Not a bath person?"

"The only thing they're good for is handwashing delicates and the occasional two-person, post-sex cleanup."

We both freeze, tiny fractures forming in the space between us.

I meant that to be funny, except we kissed, and it was so hot, and I've just uttered the word *sex* in front of Rafe, and now that's the only thing I'll ever be able to think about again.

He hesitates, his fist tightening around his water bottle as it crackles.

"Right," Rafe says, rolling his shoulders.

"Help yourself," I say, gesturing towards the room.

"You sure?"

"Yeah, I need to cool off a little."

I'm still burning up, partly from the exercise but more because

I've worked myself into a tizzy. Rafe is standing inches away, still not wearing his shirt, and I need him to get dressed immediately.

"Please, go put something on." I make a face of disgust no one would ever buy.

That earns me another wicked grin before he disappears into the bathroom. And yep, that's definitely my favorite smile.

A short while later, I emerge from the bathroom clad in sweats and a tank top, my wet hair loose around my shoulders.

Rafe sits on the balcony, looking at his phone.

"I was going to order dinner—you want something?" he asks, looking up.

"Of course I want something," I say, picking up the menu card from the table. "Scallops Alfredo." I flip the card over. "And the chocolate lava cake." Rafe nods and calls down to room service with our orders.

"Can I get you something to drink?" I point towards the kitchen.

He arches a skeptical eyebrow. "You're going to serve me?"

I'm about to smother him with a pillow, but he's laughing, and I plant my hands on my hips. "Don't get used to it."

"I would never." He raises his hands in mock surrender. "I'd love some sparkling water. Thanks."

I nod and disappear inside. Our food arrives shortly after, and we settle on the balcony in our designated lounge chairs, with the small metal table between us. There are a dozen other places we could dine in the suite. Somewhere we could eat without our knees brushing together, but I think that maybe we both know that.

I'm so weirdly grateful we've moved past the kiss and are speaking normally again. Maybe we'll pretend it never even happened. But despite all my reservations about getting closer to anyone, I already know that isn't what I want. No one has ever kissed me like that. How can I let that go?

I can't.

When his knee touches mine, there is more electricity in that tiny brush of nothing than a whole entire kiss with Andy. I can't ignore it. I can't pretend. And I need to reconcile that with myself. I also need to know what's going on in his head.

Apparently, I'm not the only one having *thoughts*, because as soon as I open my mouth to say something, Rafe beats me to it.

"I want to apologize again for the other day," he says. "I shouldn't have behaved like that at the pool with Andy. Of course, it's entirely up to you who you talk to, and it's none of my business. I'm sorry I went all caveman on you. He's just such a dick."

He picks up a napkin and wipes his mouth. "I was in Cleveland for a meeting where I first met him a few months ago. A group of us went for drinks, and the things he was saying about the women in his office . . . Well, he's just not a good guy." He raises a hand. "But that's all to say I had no right to do any of that."

I sigh because none of that really surprises me. "Do I want to know what he said?"

Rafe presses his mouth into a straight line. "There was a ranking system."

"Ew," I reply, mentally banishing Andy to the graveyard where potential hookups go to die. Then, I shovel an extra thick layer of dirt over his plot. "That's why you had that weird tension between you on our first night."

"I might have told him that he was a shithead, and he didn't take too kindly to that."

I huff out an incredulous laugh. "No, I don't imagine he did." I study his face briefly and then ask, "You said your dad was giving you a hard time that day?"

He nods with a grim press of his mouth as he runs a hand through his hair and looks out towards the water. "The training program. He thinks it's imperative for my future and is convinced it'll *motivate* me."

"Motivate you into what?"

He clasps his hands and looks down at them before he meets my gaze. "Wanting *his* life. As his only kid, he wants me to follow in his footsteps. WMC has been his entire identity for his adult life, and he can't see any other future for me."

"But you don't want that?"

"I don't. Not at all."

I study him as he watches me, perhaps waiting for my reaction.

"You don't want any of this, and they gave you the team lead promotion."

He shakes his head before he gives me a strange look.

"What? Why are you looking at me like that?"

He exhales a long breath. "You already know you should have gotten it. You always meet your KPIs. Your team was the fastest. You're brilliant and a great leader. Everyone can see that, and it should have been a no-brainer."

My gaze narrows, wondering where he's going with this. "And?"

"And I debated ever telling you this, but I went to my uncle and told him I didn't deserve the position and that he should give it to you."

"Because you didn't want it," I accuse.

"No. Because you're the one who deserved it. Tris, you're so damn capable and brilliant, and the truth is, you're the reason I'm even half-competent at my job."

I shake my head, "What does that mean?"

"Working with you made me want to be better. Even if it isn't really what I want, I've tried to make the best of it, and I don't really know why we became so competitive with one another, but you'd get that determined look in your eyes, and I . . . wanted to impress you. But there's no doubt that you are so much better at this."

His words sink between us like a lead balloon.

"So, what happened when you went to Charles?"

Rafe inhales a long breath. "He told me the decision had been made, and if I didn't want it, they'd give it to Rory. I didn't want to tell you because I thought knowing that idiot was their next choice would hurt even more."

I say nothing for a moment, blood thundering in my ears. It's then that I understand I never stood a chance. I'd convinced myself I was second best, but I wasn't even a consideration. It's a cold slap in the face. A dose of reality. A hearty shove reminding me that the only person who can break me out of this rut is me.

I leap up from my seat and brace my hands against the balcony railing. Immediately, he follows.

"Talk to me," he pleads.

"Rory?" I ask. "They were going to give it to *Rory*."

I want to puke.

He nods. "It felt like I had no choice but to accept it. Rory would have been so much worse for everyone. For *you*. Fuck, I've been trying to get him fired for years, but this company can't seem to pull its head from its ass even when someone is that toxic."

"I thought he was your friend?" I ask, scrutinizing his face.

"He's not my *friend*." He looks so mortally offended by my question that I blink. "He just won't leave me alone. He thinks that because we're related, I owe him something. I tell him to stay away from me, but the asshole does what he wants. I can't stand him."

I huff out a breath that is part disbelief and part defeat.

My hands squeeze the railing as I will my tears not to fall. Rafe stands silently next to me, tension radiating between us. I grip the railing as I bend forward and belt out a scream of frustration.

"Tris, what can I do?"

"I don't know!" I yell, throwing up my hands.

"You have every right to be angry. I'm going to fix this. When we get home, I'll try again. I will try harder." He looks so agonized that I almost feel sorry for him.

I shake my head, my eyes drifting shut. "No. I don't want you to do that."

"Tris—"

"No, please. I know you mean well, but I don't know what I want anymore."

"I let you down. I'll never forgive myself for that."

I look at him and am surprised by the open, raw expression on his face.

"You mean that?"

"I do. I really do. I am truly sorry. Tris, this place doesn't deserve you."

My answer is a rueful smile. "Maybe I'm finally starting to get that."

Once again, I face the water, and he leans next to me, our elbows propped on the railing. I feel the brush of his arm, and I steal a glance over. We've spent years as drifting tectonic plates working our way against each other's edges. If we keep shifting, could we fit together?

I breathe out a long sigh, realizing that I've made Rafe the poster child for my personal stagnation when he was never truly the villain. I can't change the world on my own, and I can't change WMC, nor is that my job. I've been so scared to move on, but it's time to face the reality I keep refusing to see.

I'm reeling from the fact that he asked his uncle to give me the promotion. But maybe a part of me isn't surprised anymore that he'd do that for me.

Part of me is angry that he thought he could be my white knight, but maybe it was the right thing for him to do. And they would have given it to Rory instead. I should have known that all along. Maybe in his own way, Rafe did what he could. He can't change the world overnight, either.

But there's something else I have to know.

"Why did you have me moved from your team?"

He bites the inside of his lip, wariness flickering across his expression.

"I thought that's what you would've wanted."

A tightness grips my chest. This he did for me, too?

I squeeze my eyes and run my hands over my face. "I thought it was because you couldn't stand the idea of working that close to me."

The admission exposes a raw nerve, but maybe we're revealing all of our scars tonight.

"No, that wasn't it at *all*," he says softly, and I sense he wants to say something else, but then he looks away.

"I keep a file on Rory," I say a moment later.

His eyes widen. "You do? Of what?"

"All the crap he says. Screenshots of the shit he posts on social media. I'm sure it won't ever matter, but it's there just in case."

"Good. Hang on to it," Rafe says, a note of admiration in his voice.

"So, then, what do you want for your life?" I ask.

He hesitates, uncertainty etched into his features. He's holding something back.

"Tell me. I want to know."

I see it then. Something boiling just at the surface that craves the release of freedom. He studies me as if he's weighing his next move. We are full of truths right now, and I sense he's about to assign me as the catcher in his trust fall.

A moment later, he lets out a loud sigh and picks up his phone from the lounger.

He unlocks it and then looks at me before opening an app and handing me the phone. I furrow my brow, taking it from him. I'm looking at someone's Instagram account. It's full of food. Desserts, to be specific. Stunning, beautifully crafted, colorful desserts.

Towering perfectly iced cakes. Plates of smooth rainbow-hued macarons. Chocolate and lemon tarts decorated with perfect swirls of cream and jewel-hued berries. I give him a quizzical look, and he worries his lip, watching the phone in my hand.

I tap on a video that shows someone decorating a cake with perfectly precise lines of icing. Familiar hands. Hands attached to the most perfect forearms I've ever seen. Ones I've fantasized about an embarrassing number of times. A moment later, a face fills the screen. A face I've studied with such dedication that I could tell you the exact latitudinal and longitudinal coordinates of that soul-shattering dimple.

I look up, finding a wariness in his expression that twists my heart.

"You're a...baker?"

He grabs the phone. "Never mind. It's stupid, I know." I yank the phone from his grasp and hold it against me. I am *not* failing this trust fall.

"*Excuse me.* But this is *not* stupid."

I scroll through the photos. There are thousands and thousands of likes and comments on every single one. People gushing over him. People fawning over his talent. People asking for his hand in marriage. I keep scrolling, tapping on his live video feed, and there he is, smiling and talking to the camera as he walks through a cute Hawaiian bakery full of colorful macarons. I turn up the volume, and there he is. Charming Rafe. Charismatic Rafe. The Rafe he's always been for everyone but me.

He's talking to the camera, explaining to his followers why he's in Maui as he describes the setting in loving detail. Comments pop up on the screen.

Swooning, declarative, and totally in love with Rafe the Baker.

I remember the drawings in his sketchbook of those elaborate desserts. His disdain for the dry lemon tarts in the airport. Now it all makes sense.

"The Dessert Wolf?" I ask, reading out the name of his account.

He shrugs. "Rafe sort of means wolf in Old English."

Of course it does.

"This is incredible. And amazing. I literally couldn't be more surprised or pleased if you'd told me you were my fairy godmother here to send me to the ball."

His shoulders drop, and he lets out a slow breath. I can practically feel his tension melt away, but I'm also confused by his reaction.

"You really think so?"

I nod and then shake my head. I have never, ever seen Rafe Gallagher anything but fully and totally confident in himself, but he looks like a lost little boy seeking approval.

"I really think so. What the hell, Rafe? How did I not know about this? I definitely would have liked you better if I'd known you could make me cake."

His eyes darken a little. "Hardly anyone knows about this. My family, Hannah. That's it. I keep it quiet."

"But why? You're incredible." I scroll through a few more images, marveling at these actual works of art. He shrugs, but there is nothing casual about the gesture.

"My father disapproves. He thinks it's a waste of time and I'm an embarrassment to him. This is also why I need *motivating*." He doesn't say what else his father believes, but I can guess what David Gallagher thinks of his son's desire to be a pastry chef.

"I went to Vegas for a two-week course with Victoria Avery last year. She was amazing. Her chocolate sculptures are masterpieces."

I've just scrolled to a string of photos from those same two weeks. Poetry. True honest-to-goodness poetry rendered in chocolate. Flowers and clocks and even a rocking horse so lifelike, I can easily imagine a child riding it. "Hannah was so pissed I used two weeks of my vacation time for it. She wanted to go to Italy. So, as a compromise, we stayed at the Venetian. She sat by the pool the entire time, angry, while pointing out all the reasons this wasn't as good as the real Venice. But it was one of the most formative experiences of my life."

The ache in his voice surprises me. I've spent the last two weeks delving into the layers of Rafe, but he keeps revealing new ones I would never have guessed existed at all.

"This is what you want to do?"

He shrugs again. "I don't know. Maybe I want to work in a restaurant or open my own shop? I've never really let myself think about it too much. Remember when I said I caused my mom a lot of stress? This is mostly why. I swear that almost every time I see my parents, my dad and I fight about it, and it kills her. I hate doing that to her."

"Oh," I reply because this is truly one of the saddest things I've ever heard. I've returned to the video of him in the macaron shop as he talks to his adoring fans and shows off his purchase.

"Wait," I say, looking up at him. "The macarons. You knew they would go stale and wouldn't survive the trip back home. You didn't buy those for Hannah."

Rafe's eyes spark, and he rubs the back of his neck. "I've always loved how you eat even the cheapest piece of sugary birthday cake as though it's the most decadent thing ever to cross your lips."

I frown. *"What?"*

"In the office, when it's someone's birthday and they buy some shitty cake, I love how much you enjoy it."

He laughs at the look on my face because I'm not sure if I should be flattered or horrified. Cheap grocery store cakes are my guilty pleasure, and what the hell? He was noticing how I *ate* them?

"Hannah hates it too. She politely requested I never breathe a word of my 'hobby' to any of her friends." He shakes his head. "It's another reason we broke up. She thinks it's too risky to bank on this as a career, and…it hurt that she wouldn't even try to believe in me. I actually make a pretty decent amount from my social media accounts, but no one believes this is a real job."

I blink, trying to arrange all of these pieces into some kind of order.

"So, you bought the macarons for *me*?" I blurt out.

Good job, Tris. That's the important part here.

His smile turns sheepish. "Sorry, it was stupid. I walked past the shop and had to look inside, and I thought you'd love them. I don't know what I was thinking. I'd changed my mind about giving them to you by the time I'd made it back here."

"It's not stupid," I say quietly, my heart tying into weird twisty knots. "That's really sweet."

He bought them for me. Not Hannah. Why does that mean something?

We watch each other for a moment, silence blooming between us. It's not uncomfortable or tense—it's an endless runway stretching into possibility.

The chocolate lava cake I ordered is sitting on the table. I pick up the fork and take a bite, closing my eyes in ecstasy because it's really, really good. Rafe watches me intently, and I spear another forkful and hold it out for him.

"You're a fan of dessert, then?"

"Yeah." He wraps his hand around mine and the fork perched in the air. "I am."

I wave my other hand in a sweeping motion. "And yet, you look...like that."

He snorts. "Why do you think I work out so much?"

I huff out a laugh and cover my mouth as a spray of chocolatey crumbs dusts the air. "That's why I exercise too."

He grins and then pulls my hand towards his mouth as he wraps his lips around the end of the fork. Good grief, I could watch him do that every day for the rest of my life.

I gesture to him again. "You do a much better job at that whole chiseled abs thing," I joke, taking another bite. Rafe's expression turns serious as he takes the fork from me and spears another bite.

"You're perfect, Tris." His voice is so intense that my breath catches, and my heart trips over itself. "Absolutely perfect. Don't ever let anyone tell you otherwise." He holds the fork to my mouth, and I take the bite, chewing slowly, unsure of how to respond.

I swallow the cake and tip my head. "Why did we never talk about any of this before?"

He chews and swallows before giving me a penetrating look. "We didn't get off on the best foot for some reason."

"Right," I say, thinking of all the reasons I pushed him away when we first met. Five years ago, those reasons defined my entire existence. They became the hard-and-fast rules I lived by, making me so fucking afraid of allowing anyone in.

I convinced myself that this was how I wanted to live.

And now I'm realizing just how much that might have been to my detriment.

Then he adds, "Maybe the universe wasn't ready yet. Maybe we needed this place and this moment first."

I smile. I like the sound of that.

"I feel like after all this sharing, I should invite you back to the bed," I say. "That couch looks miserable."

The corner of his mouth crooks up. "It's not so bad."

I scoff. "Fine, then stay there."

Then, I open my mouth like a baby bird, and Rafe smirks, taking another piece of cake and feeding it to me.

Chapter Twenty-One

*O*nce we've polished off every last crumb of cake, we lie on our respective lounge chairs, enjoying a comfortable silence. Something irrevocable has changed between us over the span of a single conversation that feels like it's been building to this moment for years.

As the sun sets, squeals from below draw me up from my seat. I hang over the railing to see a wedding party making all the noise. A bride in a fluffy white dress hangs off the back of her groom, surrounded by bridesmaids in diaphanous mint-green dresses and groomsmen in dark suits with satiny green ties.

Rafe stands next to me, leaning his elbows on the railing. He's close enough that our arms press together, and I notice every inch of him. Every breath and every slight shift. We watch as the wedding party poses for photos, shrieking and laughing.

My phone buzzes, and I pull it out of my pocket, noticing it's a text from Andy. I look up, and Rafe quickly averts his gaze. He was totally looking at my screen.

"I forgot there's an event tonight," I say. "Some kind of mingling thing."

Rafe glances at my phone and then at me. "If you want to go with him, you should."

I snort and shake my head. "He was already a two at best, but after what you just told me, he's a minus ten."

Rafe laughs. "He's a what?"

I snicker and tell him about Brian and the question he asked me on the day of the retreat announcement.

"He called himself a seven?" Rafe asks with a laugh. "Nah, he's a good guy."

"He is," I agree.

Rafe grins, his eyes sparkling. "What did you rate me?"

My cheeks heat. "No way, we're not doing this."

He laughs and nods at my phone. "Do you want to go to the thing?"

"Not really." I slide my phone back into my pocket. "You?"

Rafe shakes his head. "Nah, I don't think so."

Our gazes meet and then pull away. Maybe neither one of us wants to admit we want to hang out here alone.

We return our attention to the wedding party, still taking pictures on the sand.

"We should crash the reception," Rafe says casually, his eyes bright with mischief.

My mouth falls open. "Could we do that?"

He lifts a shoulder. "Couldn't we?"

"That would be very devious."

He smiles. "But also really fun."

"Have you ever crashed a wedding before?"

"No. Have you?" he says in an accusing way that's half teasing and half serious.

"This was *your* idea! I've never crashed a wedding."

The bride and groom move towards the shoreline, where the

bridesmaids gather their dresses around their knees and run into the surf, kicking up water. The harried photographer follows behind, snapping pics with one of the two giant cameras strapped to her body.

"It does sound much better than another boring WMC event. How would we do it?" I ask.

He tips his head in consideration. "We'd need to dress up a little. Do you have something fancy to wear?"

I roll my eyes. "Of course. Do you have something fancy?"

He looks at me from the corner of his eye. "Fancy enough."

"What would we do?"

"Eat some food, mingle, and pretend we know the happy couple. Get some free drinks."

"All the drinks are free here," I point out.

"Let's not get bogged down in details, Trishara."

I let out a laugh. "What if we get caught?"

Rafe turns to face me, one arm on the railing as he leans a little closer. "I had no idea you were such a rule follower, Malik."

My breath catches. He smells so good. Like the shower he just took, and the chocolate cake, and I marvel at the column of his throat as he swallows, wondering what it might be like to lick it. "If we get caught, we'll run. Maybe we'll have to leave the country and live in exile on a deserted island forever. I hope you like pineapples."

"Well, now, you're just mocking me."

He grins, and his eyes sparkle. He's smiling at me again, and I can't help but feel like this is an extra special one, just for me. My heart stutters in my chest.

I look at the wedding party again. Their guests mill about,

elegant in their suits and dresses with glasses of champagne perched in their hands.

"Okay, let's do it."

"Yeah?"

"Yeah. I'll go get changed." Rafe's smile grows even bigger. "I had no idea you were such a rule *breaker*, Gallagher."

He smirks and runs a hand through his hair. There's no way he doesn't understand what that does to me. "You're learning a lot about me tonight."

I pause and scan him from head to toe, enjoying the view and taking my time before I meet his eyes. "Yeah. I guess I am."

"Maybe I'll learn something about you."

He's blushing, and it's adorable.

"You can certainly try."

I wink and head to the bedroom to change.

About thirty minutes later, Rafe knocks on my door.

"Are you ready yet?"

"I'm coming," I shout. I'm wearing the killer red dress I bought in Chicago. It's just as perfect as I remember. It's sexy and hot, and I feel amazing in it.

The long skirt sweeps to the floor with two high splits on each side, reaching my hips. The low neckline reveals the swell of my breasts, and I've curled and scooped my hair into a high ponytail to show off the open back.

I complete the look with a pair of delicate gold earrings, long enough to brush the curve of my neck. I've put on plenty of dark eye makeup and opt for a nude lipstick, coated with shiny gloss.

After another knock, I stuff my phone and other essentials into my handbag. "Coming!"

Finally, I open the door to find Rafe pacing back and forth.

He's gorgeous in a pair of dark dress pants, shiny black shoes, and a fitted white button-up layered with a dark grey vest. I am practically swooning at the sight of his sleeves rolled up to his elbows. He's combed his hair back, but that errant piece that always comes loose is already attempting an escape.

He turns at the sound of the door and then stops dead, his hand running over his mouth and then his chin.

"Fuck," he breathes as he drinks in every inch of me. "You look incredible." His voice is rough, and he clears his throat.

I put a hand on my hip. I passed his trust fall, and it's time for him to return the favor.

"I know I do," I reply, and a beat passes before his smile stretches wider. He strides over and takes my hand, pressing it to his chest.

"You're not just beautiful. You're so fearless and confident." He leans closer as his mouth brushes the shell of my ear. "It's sexy as hell."

I'm flying. He didn't get weirded out by my comment.

"You clean up pretty nicely, too, Gallagher." He stares at me for a few more heartbeats, then holds out his elbow.

"Shall we?"

"Let's go crash a wedding."

I giggle because there's something euphoric about this. About this thing the two of us are doing together. Just us on the same side. Our secret. Something that exists between only me and Rafe Gallagher.

The man who, two weeks ago, was someone else entirely.

The elevator dings, and the doors slide open at the ballroom level. With more than one wedding happening tonight, we survey each set of wide double doors, leading to three different celebrations.

"Which one should we go to?" he asks.

"I think we can both agree that we *must* celebrate Kevin and Stacy," I say.

"Who?"

"Our couple from the beach. Those are the names I gave them."

He snorts. "I think we can agree on that."

We approach the largest room, where I recognize the mint-green dresses and our bride and groom.

"Perfect, this seems to be the biggest wedding," I whisper. "Maybe no one will notice we don't belong."

Rafe stands straighter and takes my hand, threading his fingers through mine. He's holding my hand again. What is the appropriate reaction? I lack the very specific life experience needed to navigate this small but definitely significant act of affection.

He tugs me against him. "Just look like you belong, and no one will question it. Not in that dress."

His gaze turns heated as he scans me again, and my stomach dips. This overpriced garment has already more than paid for itself. I'll have to send flowers to the woman in the boutique who suggested it. Or maybe I'll throw her a parade.

We stride to the door and nod at the two women sitting at the table.

"Hi!" one of them chirps. "Friends of Melissa or Derek?"

Darn. I really liked Stacy and Kevin. "Both," Rafe says smoothly. "Old friends from college." He says it with such confidence that even I find myself believing it. The woman nods eagerly.

"Enjoy. Bars are in each corner. I highly recommend the

signature cocktail." She bats her eyelashes at Rafe, and who can blame her?

He's still holding my hand as we enter the ballroom. It's decked out in more mint green and hues of peach. We head to one of the bars and order the recommended signature cocktail.

"Orgasm on the beach." I read the sign on the bar top, feeling my cheeks heat. Well, that's subtle. Usually, that would be funny, but I'm thinking about that kiss again. The way Rafe's mouth and hands scorched my skin. The way it seemed like he wanted to consume me.

"Tris?" Rafe is asking, and I've gone off into daydream land again. He's holding two short glasses with pinkish-orange liquid and passes one to me. I sip at the drink, and we drift to the edge of the dance floor.

"Mmm, this isn't bad," he says as I scan the room, wondering if anyone is questioning who we are, but no one is paying any attention; they're too busy enjoying themselves.

"We probably should stay out of sight of Stacy and Kevin," Rafe says.

"Good plan."

After a few minutes, Rafe takes my glass and places it on a table.

"Wanna dance?" Rafe holds out his hand, and I study him.

"What?" I ask.

We've gone from hand-holding to dancing, and not one part of me isn't wondering what could come next if I'm brave enough to let him in. Can I trust Rafe?

The strange thing is that I feel like I can. We spent so many years butting heads, but maybe that was also a form of trust I placed in him. Nothing we ever did crossed a line, and I wonder if some part of me always recognized that I could push him because he would never have gone too far. Maybe I was testing to see if he'd always come back.

"We're going to dance," he answers. "That's what you do when you crash a wedding."

It's not a question. Just a statement that underscores the enormity of how far we've come in such a short time. We still haven't talked about the kiss. We're still pretending it never happened, but it's the only thing I can think about. I'm somewhere between a blissful release of endorphins and impending doom as I wonder if it was all just a fluke, never to be repeated.

But I'm almost positive he's thinking about it, too. His eyes dip to my mouth and then lower to the not entirely accidental siren call of my exposed skin before quickly looking up. Every inch of me tightens.

"Is that okay?" he asks.

"Yeah." I smile and slip my hand into his, a shiver rushing to my toes.

Maybe we can finally become something else. Maybe it's time to file away my sharp edges. Maybe I needed to hold him at a distance until I was ready to risk my heart again.

He leads me into the center and wraps an arm around my waist, pressing his body to mine. Over the next few hours, we dance and mingle. I've never smiled so much or laughed so hard. We cheer when the couple cuts the cake (camouflaging ourselves behind their guests) and discuss its merits as we devour an enormous slice.

"Moist and has a good crumb," Rafe says, chewing thoughtfully. "Icing is a little sweet."

"I think it's perfect," I say, licking a dollop off my finger. Rafe's eyes follow my tongue with a sort of hunger that makes me weak in the knees.

"You and your fondness for sugary icing. You wound my baker's heart."

"You said it was cute," I counter, taking another large bite and chewing with vigor, making ostentatiously appreciative noises.

"I don't think that's what I said," he replies drily, his mouth crooking into a smile as I offer him a half-hearted glare.

We polish off our cake just before a slow song comes on the loudspeakers. Rafe takes my hand and pulls me into the middle of the dance floor, placing his warm hands on my waist.

"Now we're slow dancing?" I loop my arms around his neck.

"It's just a night of endless firsts," he answers, pulling me in closer, his hands sweeping up my back, along my exposed skin. *Fire.* It sounds so clichéd and ridiculous, but actual fire runs through my veins as I suck in a breath.

He pulls back and reaches up to tuck a strand of hair behind my ear. "You aren't cute, Tris, you're utterly fucking beautiful."

His low voice sends me into freefall.

"Are we going to talk about it?"

We both know I mean the kiss.

His head tips, and his hand slides to my shoulder and then down my arm, pulling up a shiver.

"We could talk about it, but honestly, I'd rather just do it again."

My eyebrow arches. "I thought you said you shouldn't have done it?"

That earns me a rueful smile. "It just threw me off. Don't listen to me. I'm a complete fool."

I snort. "Well, that is true."

His expression turns serious a moment later. "Tris. Do you think we could move past this thing between us? We've been sharing a room for two weeks and somehow made it work."

That reminds me of something I've still been wondering. "Wait . . . why did you refuse the extra room they offered?"

Guilt passes over his expression. "Maybe I was starting to like sharing." His gaze meets mine with an unflinching look. "I thought maybe we were becoming friends?"

Friends.

I stop, looking away for a moment, overcome with a complicated avalanche of emotion I'm not quite sure what to do with. I've been handed the hot potato and have nowhere to send it.

"Yeah. I think we are."

He tightens his grip on me, pulling me closer in a way that doesn't feel exactly *friendly*, but I'm not complaining as all my thoughts and feelings collide in a tangle. His hand slides down my hip, and I brush the collar of his vest.

"Why don't you ever dress like this at the office?" I ask, adjusting the knot on his tie.

He quirks his mouth. "Do you like it?"

"I do," I say, a bit more breathlessly than I intend. He looks amazing. I want to devour him. I want to dip him in sugar and suck on him like a lollipop. "I said you were an eleven out of ten. Maybe even a twelve."

He blinks before his face stretches into a grin. "I think you're a thousand out of ten."

"Always trying to one-up me, aren't you, Gallagher?" I joke, and he chuckles.

"In this case, I'm absolutely right." His hand slides up my arm, and then his finger runs under the strap of my dress. "You never dress like *this* at the office." His hands continue moving, smoothing down the bared swath of my back.

I laugh. "This is hardly office appropriate."

I mean, that was the entire point of this dress. I just never imagined I'd be wearing it with Rafe.

His eyes darken. "You're right." He leans down, speaking directly into my ear. "I'd rather it was balled up on the floor with my face between your thighs."

My breath turns to mud, and my pulse thunders in my ears.

We've stopped dancing. We're standing in the middle of the room, surrounded by strangers. The lights have dimmed, forming a private circle no one can enter. His hand slips to my lower back as Rafe pins my hips against his, where I feel the rock-hard evidence of his arousal.

"This is what you do to me," he says softly. "Ever since we got to Maui, I've been barely able to concentrate. All I can think about is how much I want to kiss you, taste you, fuck you. I've jerked off in the shower so many times, my palms are raw."

Heat floods between my thighs. This is so hot. Rafe is a dirty talker, and if that fairy godmother arrived to grant my third wish, this is exactly what I would have asked for.

I let out a sound of mock indignation. "That is *my* shower."

His laugh is low as he presses me closer. His hand drifts lower, sliding through the opening in my skirt, coming to rest in the crease of the back of my thigh. "If I slid my hand into your panties, would you be wet for me, Trishara?"

"Yes," I whisper as I cling to the collar of his vest.

There's no use denying it. After everything he's just said, no part of me wants to.

"I want you. I want you so much," he says.

His breath is ragged, his cheeks flushed. I look into his face. His perfect, beautiful face.

I pause for a moment, suspended in this space, ready to plunge headfirst into this thing that's been forming since that day I crashed into him five years ago.

"I want you too," I finally answer.

His exhale feels like a sigh of relief, spilling out everything we've kept held so tightly to our chests.

His hand wraps around the back of my neck, and he lowers his face. My lips part in anticipation of another earth-shattering kiss.

"Who are you?" A voice jolts us both. A woman in a wedding dress stands with her fists on her hips, her shoulders curved with aggression. "I don't know either of you. What are you doing here?"

Shit. We're busted. Rafe is now holding my hand, and he squeezes it. We're in this together.

"Stacy!" I say. "Don't you recognize me?"

"My *name* is Melissa." Um. Oops.

"Melissa. Right. I guess we're at the wrong wedding?" I look at Rafe, adopting a confused expression. His lips press together as he tries to hold in a laugh.

"Security!" Melissa yells at the top of her lungs. The band stops playing, and every eye is turning our way. "Security!"

"We should probably run," Rafe says. "Our island of pineapples awaits."

He tugs my hand, and I grab my skirt as we spring out of the ballroom. Melissa chases after us, screeching at the top of her lungs.

"She's going to kill us," I say.

"We had a good life," Rafe replies as he jabs the elevator button. We watch the numbers for a few seconds, but they don't move.

"Come back here!" Melissa shouts, shaking a fist. "What are your names?"

"This way," Rafe says, pulling on my hand, and we launch into the stairwell. I'm laughing so hard I can barely stand.

"My shoes," I cry. "I can't run in these shoes."

Rafe picks me up and hauls me over his shoulder as he pounds up several flights. When it's clear that arresting wedding crashers isn't on the priority list for hotel security, he stops and puts me down. My sides ache from laughing, and I lean against the wall, gasping for breath.

"That was amazing," I say, wiping the tears from my eyes.

"You called her Stacy," Rafe says, howling.

It lights up his face, and he's truly never been more beautiful. I can't stop staring. I can't believe he kept this from me for so long.

He stops when he notices, and our gazes lock.

There's a pause, and the entire world comes to a screeching halt. The wind and the stars and the ocean and our breath and our hearts all cease and just...stop.

Rafe is on top of me in an instant. His hands cup my face, and his mouth presses to mine, and this feels like magic. With my back pressed to the wall, his tongue licks the seam of my mouth. I open for him as we meet in a slick slide of needy, hungry kisses.

His hands roam down my arms and my sides and my hips, where he grips them with a fierce kind of possession. We kiss and we kiss while our panting breaths fill the quiet stairwell.

A door slams below, pulling us apart. We probably should find somewhere better to do this. Because sentences have become too hard, I loop my arms around Rafe's neck and say, "Upstairs. Now."

Chapter Twenty-Two

Rafe scoops me into his arms and wrenches open the door. We find ourselves on a quiet level. He strides to the elevator and pushes the button, all without dropping me.

"I can probably walk now," I say.

His arms tighten around me. "Nope. You're mine tonight, Malik."

This feels a bit like my fantasy of Rafe the Villain carrying me to his underground lair.

When the door to the elevator slides open, he rests my butt on the handrail, punches the number to our floor, and is kissing me before the doors have time to slide closed. My legs wrap around his waist, and we kiss until we have no choice but to come up for air.

When we reach our suite, he kicks the door closed and carries me to the bedroom before standing me against the wall.

"Arms over your head," he demands. He crowds against me, one hand pinning my wrists, his mouth dragging down the skin of my throat as his other hand covers my stomach. "Spread your legs."

I consider protesting simply out of habit but decide I like this side of Rafe. I do as he asks, but for good measure, I add, "You're so bossy."

His low rumble shudders through me as his eyes meet mine. "You're loving it. Admit it."

Why is he right? If this were regular life or the office, I'd never let him order me around, but like this, with that fire in his gaze, it's making my stomach flutter. His mouth captures mine as his hand slides into the folds of my skirt, his fingertips brushing the crease of my thigh.

"Rafe," I say as he nips the skin on my shoulder. "Can you promise this stays between us? We're just dealing with this weird tension. We're *friends*." I emphasize the last word like an exclamation point. I need this to be meaningless. I can't let myself feel something real, only to be betrayed again.

He pulls up to look at me, amusement dancing in his gaze. "Sure, Tris. If that's what you want."

Something in his expression and his tone makes it sound like he's humoring me, but I let it go for the moment because he's doing things that make me forget the answer to two plus two.

With agonizing slowness, he runs a finger along the edge of my underwear and between my legs. I gasp, my back arching against him. He pushes aside the fabric, fingers sliding along my wetness as he makes a low sound of approval. He circles my clit with his finger, applying an exquisite amount of pressure.

I moan, and he releases my wrists before wrapping his hand around the side of my neck, his thumb tracing up the curve of my throat.

"I want to hear those noises you promised," he whispers against my mouth, recalling my pithy comment during the storm. He kisses me as his fingers slip between my legs and along my seam again before one slides inside me. I gasp, my hips tilting as he slowly pumps out and then in.

"Yes, just like that. How loud can I make you scream, Tris?"

He thrusts into me, adding a second finger as he fills the needy, wet ache swelling in my core. His thumb circles my clit as he pumps a few more times. I can already feel myself spiraling, my thighs clenching, and my stomach fluttering.

He removes his hand and slowly drops to a knee, planting kisses down the center of my chest and my stomach and then against the fabric just below my navel. He looks up with that signature predatory Rafe gleam as his big, warm hands slide up my bare thighs.

He's the villain about to ravish the princess, and I am here for all the ravishing. Reaching down, he circles my ankle and lifts my foot, placing it on his knee. Then he drags a finger down the inside of my leg until he reaches my shoe. I shiver at his touch, my hands clutching the wall for balance. Carefully, he undoes the strap, removes my shoe, guides my foot back to the floor, and then repeats the process with the other side.

Rafe is on his knee, taking off my shoes. I'm having trouble processing this. I ignore the voice reminding me to be careful. That I have rules about getting involved with anyone at the office. But I push it down and shove it away because I want this. I don't want to be scared anymore.

He places my shoes next to him, and then his hands are on me again. Slowly, with his eyes pinned to mine, his palms graze over my hips before his fingers hook into the waistband of my thong. He pauses, tipping his head in question. I nod because I don't think I can speak. My heart is wedged firmly in my throat.

He slides the fabric down, his fingertips dragging along my skin and his thumbs lightly brushing between my thighs. I tremble like the string of a plucked guitar as he lifts one foot and then the other before tossing my thong away.

When he hooks my knee over his shoulder, I bury one hand in the thick waves of his hair, the other flattening to the wall at my back. It feels like I'm falling and floating all at the same time. My hips tilt in supplication as his tongue makes its way to my center. I moan and gasp. He tastes and nips and sucks, and it's been so long, and *holy shit* Rafe is fantastic at this.

"Fuck," he murmurs into my skin. "You taste as good as I imagined."

He returns his two fingers, slipping inside me as his tongue works in rough circles. He takes his time, teasing apart the shreds of my composure.

He groans in appreciation, feasting and savoring in a way no man has ever done before. His enthusiasm borders on feral, and this is more decadent than a seven-tiered cake layered with French buttercream.

His fingers curl, finding the spot where tension spirals into ever-tightening ripples. I can't last much longer. His mouth closes over my clit, and he *sucks*. I twist up and up and up, and then I explode, granting him his wish when I scream. He finishes his exploration with his tongue as if he can't get enough. Eventually, he pulls away, placing soft kisses on the inside of my thigh. Then he stands, crawling up my body like a panther before he presses his mouth to mine.

"How did that compare to your little toy?" he asks with a sly smile, and I bark out a laugh.

"You're obsessed with that thing."

He props an elbow on the wall and gently runs a finger along the ridge of my collarbone. "When you all but confessed that morning, I almost came right there," he says. "I wanted it to be me."

I wanted it to be him, too.

"You win," I answer. "An eleven out of ten."

He grins before kissing me again, and I start pawing at his clothes.

Buttons. Why are there so many buttons? His vest and his tie and his shirt fall to the ground, and I run my hands down his chest and his abs. He holds still as he allows me to explore his body, savoring the dips and edges and planes. The caps of his shoulders, the swell of his biceps, and the solid muscle of those perfect forearms.

This is my holy grail. My summit to Everest. As I run my hands along them, he lets out a breathless laugh at my obvious reverence.

"What's with you and my arms?" he asks. I grin up at him.

"I've got a thing for them."

He flexes, and the stretch in his tendons has me swooning. I could get used to this.

He leans down to kiss me while I undo his belt and then his pants. My nails scrape along the plane of his stomach, tracing the ridges along his hips. He moans into my mouth as I delve past the waist of his boxer briefs to find his cock. His hips jerk as I stroke him with a firm grip. He's warm and hard and impressively *solid*.

His fingers slide under the straps of my dress. "I need you out of this immediately."

He wastes no time, peeling the fabric off and pushing the red silk over my hips. I watch it flutter to the floor like a pile of rose petals.

His arms form a cage on either side of my head, and he drags his gaze over every inch of me, his eyes pooling into dusk. "You are so beautiful," he says, his voice thick and low. "You have no idea how much I've wanted this."

His hips press into mine, his erection grinding into my stomach. I shove his pants over his hips, dragging down his boxer briefs. When he's naked, he presses up against me, and the lush heat of skin on skin tears away every last fragment of my feeble defenses.

His large hands cup my ass before he lifts me up, my legs circling his waist. All those hours at the gym find their use as he effortlessly carries me to the bed, where he lays me down and stretches out over me. It feels like the world is moving in slow motion but also rushing past me at the speed of light.

"Rafe, we're naked," I say because I need to call attention to it. Because when I opened the door to discover we were sharing the Orchid Honeymoon Suite, I never imagined this was where I'd find myself.

He laughs, and I'm not sure I've ever appreciated just how great his laugh is. It lacks any thread of self-consciousness, loudly proclaiming for the world that he's here and he's amused. I want to hear it again. Suddenly, I lament all the years I wasted not hearing that laugh.

"We are. Is that a problem?" I get a new smile. One that's hazy and a little drunk. I love this one.

"No, but what will Belinda write in the company newsletter?"

I'm rewarded with another unabashed laugh, and then he's kissing me. His body crushes mine, hot and heavy, and for tonight, it's *mine*.

I ignore the voice in my head, reminding me to be on my guard.

My hands tangle in his hair as I pull him closer. Our tongues slide, and his cock thrusts against the needy ache begging to be filled.

"Do you have a condom?" I ask.

His expression falls, and he makes a sound of frustration. "Fuck. No, I don't."

I arch an eyebrow. "You came to a Hawaiian resort for three weeks without supplies?"

His response is a rueful smile. "I have no idea what I was thinking."

"Well, it's a good thing someone is prepared." I wriggle out from under him and run to the bathroom, digging through my toiletries bag. When I return, Rafe is perched on the bed on his knees, looking like an erotic Disney prince awaiting his queen. This I could get used to, too.

As I reach the bed, he snags my wrist and spins me around so I land under him again.

"Who were you planning to have sex with?" he asks, ripping open the box.

"I don't know, but it sure as hell wasn't you," I deadpan.

"Then, call me the luckiest bastard in the universe."

His words are possibly meant in jest, but I sense something significant buried within them.

He tears open the package, and I watch as he rolls the condom over his erection.

Then Rafe collapses on top of me, his mouth capturing mine in a soul-stirring kiss I feel straight to my marrow. His skin is velvet as I run my hands over his back and his shoulders and down his chest. He whispers in my ear, telling me I'm beautiful, and I am so *lost* in this.

Finally, I feel his hard cock sliding between my legs and slowly easing into me. Bit by bit, he inches in with small pumps, stretching me, filling me. When I'm not sure I can take it a moment longer, he thrusts to the hilt. Our breath shatters into jagged pieces as he waits for me to adjust, studying me with a gaze that feels like the bottomless depths of a midnight canyon.

"Tris," he says softly as he pulls out and thrusts into me slowly, over and over, my fingers gripping his shoulders, digging into muscle and skin. His hand slides under my back, tilting my hips as he drives into me faster. I watch the tendons in his neck, the flush on his face, the wild light in his eyes. I pull his mouth to mine as we move together in waves of skin and heat, and no one, *no one*, has ever made me feel quite like this.

His hand hooks behind my knee, lifting it as he gently sinks his teeth into my calf. My back arches off the bed as he angles into me, driving deeper and harder and faster.

"Rafe," I gasp.

"Look at me," he rasps. "I want you to look at me."

I meet his gaze, and something crucial traverses our once-uncrossable divide.

We dissolve in a fog of lust and desire, underlined by the barbs and cuts we've delivered over the years. Verbal punches and kicks and jabs that were about something entirely different from what either of us understood. They've smoothed away, leaving softer curves and edges.

I feel like I'm frothing over rapids as I paddle madly to shore, trying to find my breath, trying to find solid ground that isn't there.

I crash, my body bowing up to meet his, my cries filling the air. Rafe loses control, his movements stilted and frantic as he thrusts again and again and then shudders out an exultant moan as his orgasm rocks over every inch of skin.

We stare at each other, our lungs expelled of breath. Both entangled in an emotion I'm not sure either of us knows how to name.

"Wow," I finally say because it's the only way to adequately encompass all the layers I need to dig through.

"That was incredible," Rafe says, his voice deep and rough like bricks dragged over concrete. He clears his throat, but there's no clearing the hunger in his eyes. They're a night sky glittering with a million points of light.

We both smile, and I'm struck with the sense that, again, this smile is only for me. The thought is both thrilling and terrifying.

"I want to do that again," Rafe says. "All of it. I want to taste your mouth and eat you out and fuck you until the sun comes up, Tris."

I slide my hands into his hair and pull his face to mine.

"I think that can be arranged."

Chapter Twenty-Three

"Morning," Rafe murmurs into the curve of my throat. He's wrapped around me like a blanket, and I snuggle into him, refusing to think about how good this feels. I'm tumbling through a black hole that's sucking me into a void of nothing, but I close my eyes and cannonball straight into its heart. I'll deal with the fallout later.

"Morning." I twist to face him, the band of his arm tightening. Before I can say anything else, he's kissing me. Last night was full of firsts and seconds and, let's be honest, thirds and fourths, and as Rafe rolls on top of me, it's clear we're going for fifths, and I am one hundred percent here for this.

After we're done, I groan into my pillow, "I don't want to leave this room."

It's Friday morning, and it's almost the weekend. Rafe slides from the bed and begins gathering up his discarded clothing.

"Let's call in sick." I roll over and bare myself, tearing the blanket away. "I'll let you do whatever you want to me."

He's tugging on his pants, and I lick my lips and aim my pointed gaze below his waist. His eyes turn black as coal as a low growl rumbles in his chest. "Don't tempt me."

I rise to my knees, piling my hair on top of my head with a

seductive smile. I can see him weighing his options as he steps closer, his hand sliding into the hair at my nape.

"Later," he says with obvious effort. "As soon as we're done today, we are meeting back here, and we aren't leaving this room for the entire weekend. I haven't even scratched the surface of all the filthy things I want to do to you."

He kisses me quickly and then turns to leave the bedroom.

"Did you *really* just say that to me and walk away?"

He tosses a wicked grin over his shoulder as he disappears into the second bathroom.

"Fine," I call, collapsing in a heap on the bed. "Don't be surprised if you find yourself here alone."

I hear his cackle from the other room as if he knows there isn't any universe in which I'd make good on that threat, and I hate that he's absolutely right. Wild unicorns won't keep me from this bed.

I blow out a sigh because I can feel the stirrings of a headache. Forcing myself up from the bed, I hunt down my painkillers, hoping to chase it away.

"Why do you have so many pills?" Rafe appears in the doorway and gestures to the counter. He's buttoning up his shirt, and I mourn the loss of the view.

"These are for daily prevention, and the rest are for dealing with the pain when they don't work." I wave out a hand, showing off my collection.

Rafe narrows his eyes. "What causes them?"

I shrug and squeeze toothpaste onto my toothbrush. "I don't know."

"You've been to a doctor?"

I toss him an exasperated look. "Yes, Rafe. I've been to a doctor. Many of them. Over and over."

"You've had an MRI? Seen a neurologist? Is it a tumor?"

I pinch the bridge of my nose. "Of course I have, and it's not a tumor. I promise. It's just something I have to live with."

He tucks his shirt into his waistband and buttons his cuffs, much to my disappointment.

"Taking all that medication can't be healthy."

"It's this, or spend half my life in bed writhing in agony."

"I don't like it," he says, his brows drawing together.

"That makes two of us. Now get out so I can take a shower."

"I've seen you naked, Tris," he says, eyebrow arched.

"Yes, but you're annoying me now."

His face cracks into a smile, and he laughs to himself as he leaves, but not before tossing another wicked look over his shoulder.

Once he's gone, I can't help but smile, too.

An hour later, we find ourselves suffering through today's lecture. We agreed to sit on opposite sides of the room in some wayward attempt to remain focused. But to no one's surprise, it's not working at all. I find myself stealing glances at Rafe every 0.02 seconds, only to find him doing the same. I couldn't explain today's topic if my life depended on it.

As the facilitator drones on, I feel his eyes traveling up my legs. I purposely wore a short, swingy skirt, entirely intent on being distracting because I'm annoyed that he refused my request to stay in bed. After another glance, I attempt to focus on the facilitator, but my thoughts are a million miles away.

A moment later, my phone buzzes from where it sits on the table.

Rafe: I can't stop staring at your legs.

I smile at the screen before I swipe it open and type back.

Me: Who is this?

I return my attention to the front of the room, knowing my reply has probably earned me that villainous glare.

Rafe: 😳

Rafe: I can still taste you. It's making me insane.

My pulse skips. Rafe is also a dirty texter. That fairy godmother does good work.

Rafe: Uncross and then cross your legs the other way.

I don't look at him as I reply.

Me: Seriously?

Rafe: Yes

Finally, I allow my gaze to slide to him. His hands sit balled on the table, one clutching a pen in his hand while his intense stare practically peels back the layers of my clothing.

Me: First, roll up your sleeves.

His smile morphs into deep satisfaction as he reads my text. Our gazes meet, and he doesn't waver as he slowly unbuttons his cuffs and rolls them up as if this is exactly what he intended all along.

When he's done, he rests his arms on the table, and I bite my lip because even after having his mouth on every inch of my skin and spending the night without a stitch between us, I still can't get enough of him like this.

He tips his head, his expression reading *okay, your turn*.

I sneak a self-conscious glance around the room, but no one is watching.

Some people are pretending to listen to the facilitator. Most are looking at their own phones, and a few are nodding off after returning late from last night's event. I can't imagine we got more than an hour of sleep either, but I have never been more awake as I turn back to Rafe, watching me like a hawk perched in a tree.

With our gazes locked, I slide one leg off the other and slowly cross them the other way. His smile tips up, zeroing in on me like an eagle spotting a mouse scurrying along the forest floor.

Rafe: That was so fucking hot

My stomach detaches from my body and plummets to the ground. No one has ever made me feel this needy.

Rafe: This is agonizing

Me: You're the one who made us come here. We could be back in our room right now doing...other things.

Rafe: I think those break-out rooms are empty.

Me: ??????

I pretend not to know what he's suggesting because the thought is both mortifying and completely electrifying. Who is this man I was so sure I knew?

I'd formed him in concrete and clung to it with obstinacy. From that very first day when he'd stolen the air from my lungs, I'd convinced myself that everything about him was wrong for me. I'd lumped him with the rest of the men who couldn't be trusted with my heart. But this Rafe isn't the Rafe I cobbled together with scraps of a humiliated heart and a bruised ego.

This Rafe is passionate and edgy. He sends filthy texts, and he's looking at me with a sparkle like compressed rock in his eyes. But maybe I also missed it because he's been hiding who he is, too. He's also had to fit a mold that's choking off his air because his family won't support his dreams.

As my thoughts tumble like dice on a gameboard, Rafe stands, gives me a wink, and then disappears through a door at the back of the room. No one is paying any attention, and I go equally unnoticed as I slide out of my seat to follow a minute later.

I enter a narrow, carpeted hallway with doors leading to

smaller breakout rooms furnished with tables and chairs. The heavy door closes behind me, muffling the facilitator's drone. There's no sign of Rafe, so I proceed slowly down the hall, peering into each room.

When I reach the end, Rafe's hand appears out of nowhere and grabs me, pulling me inside and pushing me up against the door as he locks it. He wastes no time trailing kisses down my throat and along my collarbone.

I arch into it, grabbing his hips. "If you'd just taken me up on my offer this morning, then we wouldn't be in this situation now."

He lets out a maniacal laugh. "Maybe. Or maybe this was my plan all along. Isn't it kind of hot knowing we might get caught?"

I choke on a giggle as Rafe backs up until he hits the table.

I stand nestled in the *V* of his legs while his hands grip my ass, pulling me against his swelling erection. They slide under my skirt as he bites my nipple through the thin material of my top. This is so wildly inappropriate that it makes every line of my body tighten in anticipation.

It goes against every notion of office decorum I've imposed on myself, but after Rafe's confession about the team lead promotion last night, I think I'm over caring what anyone at WMC thinks. Besides, Rafe has a way of making this feel both exciting and safe.

He spins us so I'm now against the table. "Turn around," he whispers in my ear, and I do so immediately.

He grabs a fistful of my hair, tipping my head up. As he sucks on the curve of my neck, he grinds his cock into my butt. His other hand slides up my leg, tugging up my skirt so it's gathered at my hips. His fingers slide between my thighs as he rubs against the thin silk.

"Fuck, I can't get enough of this mouth," he says as he kisses me deeply, and heat grows roots through all of my limbs.

He bends me against the table and pulls down the back of my underwear, dropping to his knees. I feel him spread me apart as his tongue strokes me from front to back. "I missed that," he says, letting out a low groan of satisfaction.

"It's been like three hours," I say.

"You're my addiction now, sweetheart. Get used to it."

Next, I hear the sound of his zipper, and I clench my thighs in anticipation. Last night, we agreed we were okay without condoms since I'm on the pill and we've both been tested. He grips my hips in his strong hands and slides into me with a moan.

"Yes," I cry as he strokes in and out. With my palms pressed flat against the table, I shove my hips back, craving more. I breathe out a moan as Rafe presses his chest to my back and covers my mouth with his large hand.

"Shhh," he says, but I can tell he's laughing.

"You wanted to get caught," I mumble against his fingers.

"No, I just wanted the thrill of maybe getting caught," he says, voice rough as he grips my hip harder.

"You like it when I'm loud," I argue.

"Tris, stop talking. I'm trying to get you off."

Whatever I was about to respond with dissipates as he slides a hand between my legs and continues driving into me. I muffle my cry in the crook of my elbow as I break apart on the crest of an insane vision-blurring orgasm. Rafe bands an arm around my waist, continuing his frantic pace until he groans into the back of my neck and follows me over the edge.

We remain locked together as we catch our breath. I look over my shoulder, and Rafe covers my mouth with his with a kiss so deep that my knees buckle.

A whistle shrieks through the walls, immediately followed by the sound of moving chairs and a hundred voices.

"I think they're taking a break," I whisper.

"Shit, they're really loud. How thin do you think these walls are?"

I burst out laughing and cover my mouth with both hands. Rafe is tugging up my underwear and smoothing my skirt over my hips before he tucks himself into his pants and zips up. I spin around, wrapping my arms around his neck, kissing him as his hands slide down my backside.

"That was insane," he says, dropping his forehead to mine.

I nod and he gives me a crooked grin, brightness reflecting in his eyes.

The muffled thunder of chatter signals that this morning's session has ended. We open the door to find a stream of people heading for the bathrooms at the end of the hall. I step out and come face-to-face with Andy.

"Hi!" he says brightly. "I texted you…"

His voice drops off as Rafe appears behind me. I watch him catalog our current state. Hair mussed. Faces flushed. Clothing askew. Only a fool couldn't put two and two together.

"Hey," I say, matching his cheeriness with an inward cringe, hoping to deflect his thoughts to anywhere but what Rafe and I were just doing. "Sorry about that! I went to bed early last night. Lunchtime?"

He narrows his eyes, and it takes all my willpower not to roll mine. Does he really think I owe him a damn thing?

"Yeah, lunchtime," he says after a moment.

Rafe wraps his arm around my waist in an entirely unnecessary show of possessiveness. I hate that I kind of like it. But instead of leaning into it, I lightly elbow him in the stomach and then roll my eyes at him instead. I duck past Andy, adjusting my skirt as my cheeks flame.

"Gotta go to the bathroom," I say with a wave and, like the adult I am, run away.

A few minutes later, I'm standing at the mirror attempting to smooth out my hair and splashing a bit of cold water on my cheeks. It's then I notice a poster taped to the wall advertising a massive dessert buffet in one of the hotel's restaurants happening tomorrow.

While snapping a photo, I see Lan emerge from a stall. She passes behind me and starts washing her hands, giving me a sly smile in the mirror.

"Hi," I say.

"How'd you enjoy the session?" she asks, tucking a black strand of hair behind her ear.

"It was...fine?"

She bursts out laughing.

"I *saw* you leaving right after a certain tall, dark, and handsome someone else left."

She blinks, her lips pressed together like she's trying to contain a smile.

"Did you hear us?" I ask, my cheeks turning red again.

She snorts. "Was there something to *hear*? I was learning all about WMC Purcell company culture. That's *all* I heard."

I study her for a moment and then decide it's better not to know.

"Come on," Lan says, linking her arm through mine, still laughing to herself.

We find Rafe waiting near the door with his back to the wall and his arms crossed over his chest. Our gazes meet, and his soft smile makes my stomach do this weird little flip.

I hold up my phone and point to the screen and the photo of the dessert buffet poster.

"Look at this." His eyes light up as he reads it, and that also does another weird thing to my heart. "I know we had other plans this weekend, but maybe we should take a break for some sustenance?"

He assesses me from head to toe with a heated look and cocks his head. Lan pats me on the shoulder and speaks into my ear. "If you're going, count me and Gabrielle in. If not, you might want to at least wait to get to your room next time."

She winks and then saunters off with a snicker. Is she serious or just giving us a hard time?

"You don't mind?" Rafe asks when she's gone, reading the details on my phone.

"Mind? This sounds like my actual idea of heaven. Throw in a halo and some cherubs lounging on white fluffy clouds, and it'll be perfect."

He wraps an arm around my waist and pulls me in close. "Okay, but after that we're meeting back in our bed."

My heart squeezes again at the way he growls *our bed*. If this keeps up, I'm going to have a heart attack.

A chime dings from Rafe's phone, and he pulls it out of his pocket. I glimpse the name "Hannah" on the screen, and that squeeze morphs into a wave of nausea.

Rafe blows out a long, weary sigh. "Sorry. I better get this," he says before pressing his lips to my temple. I stiffen. He's answering Hannah's call. "I'll be out there in a minute."

It's a reminder that I need to put the brake on my feelings. I need to stop before I fall too far into this. I have rules for a reason. I've already broken my WMC embargo, but I can't let myself feel anything real. This is just a fling. A casual hook-up. That's all I'm comfortable with.

He returns to the breakout room. The same room where he just bent me over the table and made me see stars. The door closes with a click that feels like a slap to the face. A moment later, I hear the muffled sound of his voice. I briefly consider eavesdropping but then decide that way only lies madness. He said they're broken up, and it doesn't matter anyway. I need to remember this is only physical, and he hasn't promised me anything.

My legs are hollow as I head to the room where lunch is being served. I gather some food and sit down with Lan and Gabrielle. But I can't taste anything, and I quickly give up.

The hot, itchy feeling creeping down my spine amplifies when Rafe doesn't return for the entire break. He slips into his seat on the other side of the room just as the session is resuming.

I don't want to look at him. I'm terrified of what I might see.

My phone buzzes.

Rafe: I can't wait for dessert later.

Rafe: And I don't mean the buffet.

Rafe: 👅 🍑 🐱

I snort and cover my mouth because he's a horny fourteen-year-old. But it's also weirdly adorable. I look up at him, and he winks. The tension loosens in my chest.

He's giving me another new smile.

It's so genuine and warm and sparkly that I start to feel bad for doubting him.

Still, part of me can't let this go.

Can I trust that smile? They're all new to me—maybe I'm only seeing what I want. I trusted Leo, too, and look where that got me.

I look at Rafe's phone clutched in his hand like a ticking time bomb. Maybe I'm making too much out of this. He told me it's over between them.

But then why does she keep calling?

And why does he keep answering?

Chapter Twenty-Four

Me: Hi.

Molly: OMG YOU DID IT.

Me: What? How could you know that?

Molly: I could just feel it in that "hi."

Me: No, that isn't a thing. You're a thousand miles away.

Molly: Am I right?

Me: ...Yes

Molly: YESSSS. You owe me $50.

Me: I—what?

Molly: We bet $50 you'd have sex.

Me: No, we did not.

Molly: Well, I bet someone.

Me: Geez. DO NOT tell anyone. This is just a while we're in Hawaii thing.

Molly: Ooh. I don't care for that.

Molly: How was it??

Me: The best I've ever had.

Molly: ☺☺☺☺☺

Me: I think I'm screwed.

Molly: At least you got screwed first.

"You ready?" Rafe asks, pulling my attention from Molly. I'm on the balcony, and he stands in the doorway casual in a black T-shirt and jeans, but he makes it look effortless and dreamy. I tuck my phone into the back pocket of my white denim shorts and nod. We head downstairs to the Rosewood Dining Room to meet Lan and Gabrielle for the dessert buffet.

The hostess seats us at a spacious booth facing a huge circular table in the center of the room, laden with colorful, towering stacks of sugary treats.

"Are you planning to film this?" I ask. "Your followers will love it."

Rafe tosses me an uncertain look before he glances at Lan and Gabrielle. I wish he didn't feel the need to hide or be ashamed of this.

"Followers?" Gabrielle asks, leaning forward and waggling her eyebrows. "What followers?"

I nudge Rafe with my shoulder. "Show them."

His brow scrunches. "It's nothing."

"It's not nothing. Let me show them? Please? I promise they'll love it."

He offers me a tiny nod. I pick up my phone, open my Instagram app, and find his account. I followed him the first chance I got. Lan and Gabrielle lean forward as I point the screen in their direction.

"Wow," Gabrielle says, taking the phone and scrolling through his feed while Lan looks over her shoulder. "What's going on here? This is you?"

She taps on a video, and Rafe pops up, waxing about the characteristics of an ideal shortbread crust. While they watch in rapt attention, I watch Rafe, gauging his reaction. It's heartbreaking to watch the way he shrinks into himself, but I reach out to grab his hand and give him a confident smile. He *needs* to understand how amazing this is and that everyone who's made him feel bad about it is wrong. Their judgment says way more about them than it does about him.

Gabrielle and Lan are still clicking through photos and videos as they *ooh* and *ahh*. With every exclamation of delight, I notice Rafe's tight shoulders drop from his ears.

"By the way, you haven't followed me back yet," I say in mock offense.

He pulls out his phone, taps at the screen, and finds my profile. His expression is thoughtful as he scrolls through the sporadic selfies, random food shots, and occasional vacation pics I share with all six of my rabid fans.

He looks up at me.

"Sorry, I get a lot of follows. I don't even notice anymore," he says sheepishly.

"Oh, look at you. One minute, you're embarrassed, and the next, you're giving me starlet attitude," I tease.

He clicks the follow button and then leans over, stretching his arm across the back of the booth, and says softly, "I'll follow you anywhere, Tris."

I frown. What is *that* supposed to mean? He's watching me with a reverent look, and it's slowly dissolving the shell of the meager armor I've cloaked myself in. Something in my chest cracks, does a 180, and then slides back into place. I swallow because, suddenly, I can't breathe.

I notice Lan and Gabrielle are watching us, their heads tilted with wistful expressions.

"Aw," Lan says, pretending to wipe a tear from the corner of her eye.

"Stop it," I say, snatching my phone from Gabrielle and then pointing to Rafe. "Let's go. It's time for dessert."

It comes out harsher than I intend. Why did his comment rattle me so much?

He follows me to the buffet, and I watch as he circles it like Michelangelo assessing a raw hunk of marble. Rows of jewel-toned macarons sit nestled between glistening berries and slices of mango, peaches, and watermelon. Delicate stacks of mille-feuille are arranged alongside petit fours coated in pale pink, lilac, and mint-green icing. Crystal goblets are layered with cream and chocolate and fruit in mini parfaits. Cakes, so many cakes, are decorated with fine sugar cages and fondant orchids so lifelike they seem plucked straight from a garden.

Rafe pulls out his phone and turns on his livestream as he begins filming, describing everything in loving detail. His passion and his adoration for this are so obvious.

"Lime madeleines with grapefruit icing. Raspberry and rose eclairs. Brown sugar meringues with white chocolate mousse and lavender syrup," he recites, rattling off the names from printed tent cards.

He's mesmerizing to watch, his smile brighter than the sun. I'm sure every one of his followers must be head over heels in love with him. He looks away from the phone and over to me with a smile and something achingly tender in his expression.

I'll follow you anywhere, Tris.

I descend into an abyss as I understand why those words affected me so much. They dig in, talons out, and scrape away the lie I've been telling myself for five years.

I have feelings for Rafe.

I'm not delusional. Of course, I always *felt* something, but it was something I manipulated into carefully skirting the edge of real emotion. It was overwrought and unrealistic, like a story you tell yourself to get through the day.

It was infatuation. It was obsession. It was fascination. It wasn't real.

I refused to let it be anything else.

He's returned to his work, snapping photos, angling his phone this way and that.

This wasn't supposed to happen. Rafe is my rival. *Was.* And now, he isn't. Not even a little bit. Was he ever? No. I did this to myself by pushing him away the very first time we met. And despite all of that, he never actually left. He existed in my sphere, challenging me and giving me what I needed until I was ready to break down the walls I erected around myself.

"Will you take this for me?" he holds out a small white ramekin filled with a pink mini soufflé. I blink up at him, trying to pick up and arrange my thoughts.

"You okay?" he asks, his brown eyes brimming with concern.

I love those eyes. They're rocky trails winding through forests. They're warm spice cakes and mugs of tea sipped at sunrise. They're autumn landscapes rendered in vivid technicolor. How could I ever think they were evil?

"Yeah, I'm fine." I reach for the plate. "You're not going to put me in the photo?"

"Not if you don't want." He cocks his head. "Though you'd be the most beautiful thing on my feed."

The way he looks at me makes me wonder if he's in the murky backwoods of something real, too.

I'll follow you anywhere, Tris.

"Maybe we'll work up to that. I'm not quite ready for fame."

He grins and brings his phone closer, snapping a few pictures at different angles. He shows me the result. Only my hands are visible, backdropped by the splash of my pink polka-dot shirt blurred in the background. I'm no expert, but even I can see the light, the color, and the composition look like that of a professional.

"You're really, really good at this."

"Thanks," he says with a smile that somehow manages to be both vulnerable and proud.

"Rafe," comes a voice, and we both look over to find David Gallagher holding a plate topped with a slice of pineapple cake.

He eyes his son before his gaze falls to the photo still visible on Rafe's screen.

"Dad," he responds, his pride from a moment ago shriveling into decay.

Diane Hart also stands at the dessert table, looking us over as she selects items from the buffet.

"You skipped breakfast with me and Bruce this morning to do this? Take pictures of cake?" David asks as his lip curls in distaste.

I've never wanted to punch his smug face more.

Rafe missed a meeting with his father and the CEO?

I blush when I think about what we were actually doing around breakfast time.

"You promised you'd take this retreat seriously," David continues.

"I promised I'd come," Rafe says quietly, his voice strained. "That's all."

David's nostrils flare ever so slightly, and I see red.

I snatch the phone from Rafe's hand and hold it out to David.

"Do you see how good he is? Can't you see how much he loves it?"

David Gallagher and I already have a complicated history, so what's one more transgression?

"Tris," Rafe says, laying a hand on my shoulder. "You don't have to do this."

"I'm sorry, but your dad should recognize your talent even if he refuses to respect it." I shake the screen at David again. "Look at all these likes and how many followers he has and the comments he gets. They *love* him."

David stares at the screen for several long moments while I notice Diane watching all of this go down. Great, I'm making a fool of myself in front of her again.

But I'm angry for Rafe, and I don't care right now.

Then our gazes meet as the barest hint of a smile hugs her bright pink lips before she resumes her dessert selection.

David's gaze has moved past the phone and is now focused on Rafe as father and son engage in a silent standoff.

"Don't bother," Rafe says, addressing me while he keeps his eyes on his dad. "I've heard it all before."

Rafe grabs my hand. "C'mon." He tugs me away, refusing to look back. I cast a glance over my shoulder to see David watching us as we return to our table.

"Are you okay?" I ask as he collapses into the booth, his head dropping in his hands. Lan and Gabrielle are still getting treats from the buffet, and I give him a moment to collect himself.

He looks up at me, his expression vulnerable. "I'm fine. Thank you for trying."

I shrug and rub his back. "I was about as successful as when you tried to stick up for me," I joke, and he looks at me and smiles. "Do you want to leave?"

He shakes his head as he glances across the restaurant. David has returned to his seat on the far side of the room.

"No." He slaps his hands on the table. "Absolutely not. He's not ruining our day. Let's go eat."

Two hours later, Rafe and I ascend on the elevator to our suite, sugar running through our veins. Thankfully, David and Diane left shortly after our confrontation, so we didn't have to speak with either of them again.

"That was all so good," I say, licking the corner of my lip, where I can still taste the chocolate sauce from my last profiterole.

"Stop," Rafe says, pushing me against the wall and caging me in his arms. He bends down and licks the chocolate away.

"Hey, that was mine," I protest.

He chuckles and then we come together in a crushing kiss of berries and honey and a flavor that is distinctly Rafe. It's intoxicating and heady, and I'm falling so hard that it feels like I've just plunged headfirst off a waterfall.

This is bad. This will probably destroy me. I remember the moment when I knew Leo would be bad for me, but I went for it anyway, ignoring my cautious inner voice. But this feels totally different. Rafe might ruin me, but not in the same way. What if this could be okay? What if I could let go and allow myself to slide into this?

If I ever want to be in a relationship again, then I have to find a way to trust someone.

Rafe's hand slides under the hem of my shorts, fingers skating the edge of my underwear, and it feels like the only thing that could stop me is if the cable snapped and this elevator plummeted twenty stories to the ground.

Even then, with all of my bones shattered, I'd want to keep kissing him.

We arrive on our floor intact, and the elevator doors slide open with a ding. Rafe hooks his hands under my thighs, my legs trapping his waist as he carries me to our door. After some fancy maneuvering, we get it unlocked and tumble inside.

My feet slide to the ground, and I press my hands to his chest, pushing his back against the door. My palms splayed flat, my fingers quest over the toned, hard muscles welded together to create the perfect armature of this man. Slowly, I memorize every line and angle before falling to my knees.

"Tris," he hisses as I lower his zipper one torturous inch at a time, looking up at him with an innocent doe-eyed smile that I hope ruins him, too. His erection tents his boxer briefs as I yank down on the waistband.

I wrap my hand around his thick cock, licking the tip and swirling my tongue around the head before drawing him into my mouth. With an agonized moan, his head thunks against the door.

"Oh fuck. Tris," he groans as his fingers thread through my hair. With my hand and my mouth, I lick and suck and pump, feeling him grow bigger and harder as his hips tilt with rhythmic thrusts. I slowly peel him apart, making him come undone as I revel in this power and the sounds he's making as he melts under my touch.

After a minute, he pulls me up and flips me around, so now I'm the one against the door. He sucks on the curve of my throat as he unbuttons my shirt.

"I have to confess that I've fantasized about you on your knees," he says as he cups my breast.

"You have?"

He pulls away to look in my eyes with a mischievous glint. "Yeah, but it wasn't quite like that."

"How?"

He tugs down the zipper of my shorts and eases them over my hips. "First, I'd call you into my office and tell you to close the door." My shorts drop to the floor as my chest flutters with tight breaths. "Then I'd tell you to close the blinds."

My breath turns sharp, scraping the back of my throat. "Okay. I close the blinds. Then what?"

I work on his T-shirt, lifting the hem and pulling it over his head. My nails drag down the planes of his chest and his stomach and the *V* of his hip creases as he leans down and brings his mouth to my ear.

"I tell you to remove all your clothes except your high heels. You're in those man-eating black ones with the red soles. I fucking love those shoes."

An involuntary whimper seeps from my mouth as he strips off my shirt and yanks down my bra cup before he leans down and sucks on my nipple. My back arches against the door as he grinds his hips into mine.

"Then you get on your knees and crawl to me." My thighs clench because that sounds super hot. "Then you stop at my feet and slide your hands up my legs." His thigh finds its way between my knees as he presses his leg to my pulsing center. "Then you undo my pants and suck on my cock."

I'm squirming against his leg, trying to find the relief of friction.

"The HR department is going to lose its mind," I gasp.

He lets out a low, dark chuckle as he unhooks my bra, still grinding his knee between my legs.

"When you're done, I lay you on my desk, where you spread your legs, and I feast on your pussy until you're a quivering, boneless mess."

I wonder if you can orgasm just from the sound of a man's voice?

"You really thought about that?"

"Intensely," he replies with a smile. "Do you have a fantasy, Tris?"

I look away, suddenly self-conscious, but he catches my chin and directs my gaze back to him, his lush brown eyes full of determination. "Tell me."

I bite my lip and give him a shy smile. "I pictured you as an evil villain dressed in black," I say, and I can tell he's already enjoying this. "You'd sling me over your shoulder and steal me away to your stone tower or your high-tech lair, where you'd have your way with me."

He's grinning now. "Oh, we are definitely making that happen. Airbnb must include *villainous lair* as a search option." I sputter out a laugh that comes up short because that's a future plan, which means he's thinking about us beyond this room and this resort, and I can pretend all I want, but I kind of like the sound of that.

I want to let go. I *want* to let him in. Maybe I'm ready for that.

But then we're interrupted by the buzzing of his phone. He digs into the jeans hanging off his hips and pulls it out. I catch the flash of Hannah's name on the screen, and he silences it and tosses it on the nearby counter.

"Sorry about that." He leans in again, but I place a hand against his chest, holding him back.

"She calls you a lot."

"I'm sorry. There's nothing going on with her, I promise."

I stand up straighter, pressing my palms to the door at my back.

"Clearly something is going on, Rafe."

He's about to respond, but I don't give him the chance, not sure I want to hear what comes out of his mouth. I was wrong about giving this a chance. It's safer if I just keep my feelings out of this and let this be casual and temporary.

"Never mind. It's fine. We're just having fun, right? We agreed. This is a Hawaii thing only. It's none of my business."

There. I wipe away everything *real*, like the lines on a chalkboard.

He tilts his head, searching my face. "Is that really what you want?"

"Yes. I'm already breaking my rule about getting involved with anyone at work."

His brows furrow at that. "Why won't you date someone at work?"

"Because it's . . . a bad idea."

His expression of confusion deepens. "I don't understand. We wouldn't be breaking any rules. There are tons of couples who met at the office."

I pin him with as stern a look as I can, considering I'm mostly naked. "It's not that."

"Then what is it?" He cups the side of my face, his eyes brimming with concern. "What happened?"

My mouth opens and then closes. I've kept this story so close to my chest, but maybe it's time to come clean. I've lived in fear of everyone's judgment, but if I tell Rafe, his horrified reaction might be what I need to break away from this infatuation.

So, I tell him about Leo. All of it. How we dated and he lied to me. And about how he betrayed me and violated my privacy, leaving me to the wolves.

"They called me a ladder-climbing slut and...so many other vile things I can't even repeat," I say, trying to steady my voice.

Rafe clenches his jaw, his eyes flashing. He places his palms on either side of my head and leans in. "He broke the law, Tris. None of that was your fault. Please tell me you went to the police."

I scoff. "And what would they have done? I gave him permission to take that photo. They would have said what everyone else did—that I was asking for it."

His shoulders drop, and he exhales a sharp breath.

He's angry, but it seems like it's on my behalf.

"No one would hire me. That's why I took the job at WMC. It was two years before I stopped receiving anonymous dick pics. I had to change my number and email three times before they stopped."

His expression brims with fury. The vengeance of a James Bond villain about to enact his plan to fry the earth with his giant laser. He rubs a hand down his face.

"Fuck Tris, I'm so sorry that happened. That's despicable. Where is he now?"

I shake my head. "He's still running his company, probably screwing over a stable of other young women."

He wraps me in his arms, dropping his chin to the top of my head.

"What's his last name?" he asks.

"Why?" I look up at him.

He shrugs. "I'd kind of like to find him and rip out his spine."

That dispels the tightness in my chest, and I choke out a laugh. He isn't judging me for my mistakes.

He cups my face in his hands and gives me a penetrating look.

"Tris, I want you to know that I'd never do anything like that to you or to anyone, if that's what you're afraid of."

The earnest look he's giving me surfaces so many emotions I'm trying to tease my way through. I *do* know he wouldn't have shared a photo like that. I've always understood he's not that sort of man. I want to trust him, but I can't let my heart slide any further until I'm sure. I'm enjoying my time with Rafe, but I don't know if we can ever be more.

So, I might as well enjoy it while I have it.

"Rafe," I say, looking up at him. "Get some clothes on. Dress pants and shirt."

"Why? Where are we going?"

I point to the far corner of the room. "Nowhere, but we have a fantasy to play out, and that desk should do the trick."

His eyebrow arches as he realizes what I'm suggesting.

"You sure?" he asks. "Are you okay?"

"I'm fine. I promise."

He hesitates, studying me. "We'll talk about this again."

I shake my head. "No, there's no need. Now, are we doing this or not?"

I plant my hand on my hip and raise my eyebrow. He leans in and kisses me so deeply that I can barely catch my breath. Then he pulls away and practically flies to his bathroom to change. I head to the bedroom to find the heels he mentioned.

"Miss Malik, I need to see you in my office immediately," he says sternly as he approaches, still buttoning his shirt.

"Coming, Mr. Gallagher," I say in a high, breathy voice, and we pick up where we left off.

Chapter Twenty-Five

A few days later, I'm sitting in a golf cart coasting down the paths of the Naupaka Golf Course. It comes to a grinding halt at hole 11, skidding on the gravel. Diane Hart slides out from the seat, elegant in crisp white shorts and sleeveless polo. Her blond hair is tied into a low ponytail, held back with a white visor.

She marches up to the tee box, where the grass is so vibrant and green it looks like it's been spray painted. I hate golfing, but professional necessity has forced me to become at least somewhat competent.

We're in the middle of a tournament and I ended up on a team with Diane and two other white men whose names I've already forgotten. Ted? Chris?

Lan and Gabrielle are both on other teams, and Rafe was grouped with his father; Paul Stuart, another VP; and Bruce, WMC's CEO.

When Rafe found out, he swore under his breath, and the cold look in David Gallagher's eyes suggested he heard his son's protest. I'm not sure if they've spoken since the incident in the restaurant.

To make up for it, Rafe has been sending me a stream of texts all day that alternate between complaining about the tedious conversation and ogling me. His team is playing behind ours, so at least we can share the occasional glance when there's a backup.

Diane wiggles her butt, adjusting her stance as she peers into the distance, preparing for her shot.

> **Rafe:** Your legs look sexy in that skirt. I can't wait until they're wrapped around my head later.

> **Rafe:** Oh FFS... they want my "thoughts" on the merger between WMC and SynEng. KILL. ME.

I search through the trees, but Rafe is still on the tee box of hole 10.

Diane swings and hits her ball with a thwack, sending it straight down the middle of the fairway, where it lands just a few feet from the hole. Of course, she's an amazing golfer. Is there anything this woman can't do?

Ted and Chris (or whatever their names are) blow out appreciative twin whistles as Ted (or maybe it's Chris) steps up to the green. Diane returns to where I wait with my driver gripped in a hand. I stuff my phone back into the pocket of my bright yellow golf skirt.

"Wow, you're really good," I comment.

Diane picks up her water bottle and takes a long sip. It's sweltering under the peak of the midday sun. When I discovered I was grouped with her, it took me about six holes to stop panicking. I've finally managed to dial down my nervousness from a stroke-inducing one hundred to a manageable palm-sweating ten.

"I had to get good," she says. "More deals are done out here than inside the walls of any boardroom."

I know it's true, but I hate hearing it. It's just another barrier standing in my way.

"You're taking lessons, right?" she asks, assessing me with a critical eye.

"I have in the past," I venture. "But I'm not really sure golf is my thing."

"You're up!" Chris/Ted (Chred?) calls from the tee box. I nod at Diane and make my way up the gentle slope. With my driver angled in front of me, I stretch my arms and drag up the tips from said lessons over the years. It's been a while since I've been out on the links, and I'm definitely rusty.

I pull back and swing, connecting to the ball with a satisfying crack. It goes flying down the middle, veering slightly and landing about ten feet short of the green. It's not a terrible shot. I'm a little bit impressed with myself.

When I turn around, Rafe and his team are just pulling up. He's gorgeous in pale grey shorts and a fitted teal polo. The shade is glorious against his tanned skin and dark hair.

After giving him a quick wave, I hop back into the cart with Diane.

A few seconds later, I feel my phone buzz in my pocket.

"You know, I asked to be paired with you today," Diane says as I'm about to reach for it.

"You did?"

She steps on the gas, and the cart lurches down the path.

"I noticed you on the first day, and the way you stood your ground against David's boy was inspired. It's obvious you know how to handle yourself in this world." I try to hide my shock. That stupid Ferris wheel argument with Rafe impressed her?

"And the way you took on David himself in the restaurant? I doubt anyone's put him in his place like that in years." She barks out a gleeful laugh, and I sense that Diane Hart and I are kindred spirits in more ways than one. "You need that kind of fearlessness to succeed." Again, I try to control my reaction. I was convinced she must've thought I was a monster, talking to him like that.

She guns the cart as we bump over the fairway. "I was also very interested in your test scores. Did you know that in a room of a hundred respondents, you are the only one who scored 'listener' as a leadership style?"

My heart lurches, wondering if she means this as a good thing or a bad thing. What did my tiny act of rebellion garner when I'd chosen the answers I wanted rather than what I thought they wanted to see?

"I was?"

She nods as we pull up to the green. One-half of Chred has just knocked his ball near the hole, and I'm up next. I choose an iron and give my ball a light tap. It lands on the green with a plonk and rolls about three feet from the hole. While I wait for Diane and the rest of Chred to putt, I check my phone.

> **Rafe:** You're seriously killing me with that skirt. Do you have any idea how good you look hitting the ball? Promise me you'll leave it on later when I fuck you on the dining table.

My thighs flex. Rafe and I have had sex on literally every surface of the suite. On the kitchen counters, the sofas, every chair, the floor, and the balcony in every position we could conceive. Physically, I am the happiest girl in the world. (Emotionally, I'm a kindergartner finger painting.)

Diane makes short work of her ball, sinking it in with a light tap, followed by me and then Chred again. We slide back into our carts and rumble to the next hole.

"Anyway," Diane says, picking up our conversation. "I was very impressed. It's rare to have someone stand out in a sea of like-minded employees. Everyone thinks the same, or pretends to, and it's damaging to a company's culture. We can't be our best without different points of view. Have you given thought to where you'd like your career to go at WMC?"

I try to contain my excitement at her question. "Absolutely," I say. "I want to follow in your footsteps. You've inspired me so much."

Though her façade remains cool, I can tell she's at least a little pleased by my fawning.

"I'm happy to hear that. I've nominated you for one of the training program spots." My stomach leaps. "There's one more person whose vote you need, but I'm confident he can be swayed." She offers me a wink.

"Thank you," I stammer out. "That means so much to me." I can't believe this. Do I actually have a chance? I'd all but abandoned WMC in my thoughts, but learning I could win a spot starts to reel me back.

"It's not an easy road," she says. "As a woman, you'll have to put up with a lot of bullshit." I huff out a breath and sink back into my seat.

"Yeah, I've noticed."

Her smile is tight as we come to a stop behind Chred's cart. The team before us is still on the tee box, so we sit back and wait.

"As a woman of color, you'll face even more scrutiny." I draw my eyebrows together, surprised at her bluntness. "I know people who look like me prefer not to say these things out loud, but it's true. And I realize that's unfair, but you can't overcome obstacles if you don't acknowledge the doors standing in your way."

"How do you deal with it?" I ask. "When you're judged for things they'd never judge a man for?"

Diane sweeps her pale blue eyes over me. "This is the way the world is, Trishara. You have to learn to pick your battles. Be a lion when it comes to business as you did with David and his son, but if you want to get where I am, you learn to smile, bear it, and look the other way when it comes to the other stuff. They'll never respect you for that."

Her words thud to the bottom of my heart with an echo.

"But don't you want to make it better for the next generation? Don't you want to change things so the women who come after you don't have to put up with this?"

She sighs as if I'm a child who doesn't understand. And maybe I am.

"That sounds nice in theory, but things don't change, Trishara. You need to grow the thickest skin of all to succeed in this business."

I hate her words and these sentiments. None of this feels right. Is she truly just resigned to all of it? I shouldn't judge her until I've been in her shoes. Still, she's recommending me for the training program, and maybe she's wrong. Maybe I can follow in her footsteps and try to change *something* for the better.

Lost in my thoughts, I don't say much else. As we near the end of the round, my phone buzzes and I assume it's Rafe sending me another text. Instead, it's an email from EnviroTech, the environmental start-up I applied to before I left Chicago. They want me to come in for an interview.

I read the email a few times, numb and conflicted about my next move, and then put my phone away, deciding to respond later.

When we've finished the round, Diane, Chred, and I shake hands and thank one another for the game before everyone heads to the clubhouse for a round of drinks. I've just ordered a giant glass of lemonade when I feel a hand on the small of my back.

"That was agonizing," Rafe says before asking for a beer. "Longest day of my life. How about you?"

"It was fine," I say, but the uncertainty in my voice is obvious.

"You okay?" he asks, and I nod.

"Just tired and hot and sweaty." I hold the front of my white sleeveless shirt away from my body and flap the fabric, trying to stir up a little air movement. I don't want to talk about what Diane said right now. "And some guy kept distracting me all day with his texts."

Rafe's grin is unapologetic as he accepts his beer, and we find a shady table on the balcony to sit.

"I could use a shower," I say, running a finger up his forearm with an innocent look.

"Not before I have my way with you in that skirt," he says, his voice low so no one can hear. "You promised."

"I did no such thing," I say as his hand finds my knee.

His phone buzzes on the table, and I already know who it is. Mostly, Rafe doesn't answer anymore, or so I think. If she's calling when I'm around, she must also be calling when I'm not. Is he talking to her then? What is he saying? This uncertainty is eating me alive.

He flips the phone over, frowns at the screen, and dismisses the call.

"Hannah again?" I ask, trying to keep my tone casual.

As far as I'm aware, he never calls her, and I guess that's something, but I'm grasping at a house made of paper straws.

"Doesn't matter," he says, shoving the phone in his pocket and leaning towards me. His leg presses against mine, his hand still on my knee. I'm not sure what *doesn't matter* means, but I formulate a thousand possible variations, and I hate them all. "Where were we?" He drags his hand a bit higher, my skin tingling as his fingertips tease the edge of my skirt.

It also doesn't matter what he is or isn't saying to Hannah. I refuse to let it mean something. We're having a physical relationship in a tropical paradise, and soon this will be over.

I ignore the painful twist in my stomach at that thought.

Rafe's cheeks are flushed from the heat, and a trickle of sweat runs down the side of his neck. I track it with my eyes, wanting to lick it off his skin as it disappears under his collar. I should stop this right now, but I'm not ready to let go just yet.

"Are you done with that?" I ask, turning a pointed look at his beer, of which he's drunk less than half. "We should probably get ourselves ready for the reception later."

"It's still hours away," he replies with feigned innocence, but two can play this game.

"Okay, well, I'm going to go get started. If I'm finished before you return to the room, I guess that will be a shame for you." I down the rest of my lemonade and stand up, heading for the path leading back to the hotel. It's bordered by tall shrubs and trees forming a shaded canopy overhead.

A moment later, the thud of footsteps sounds behind me. A hand snakes up the back of my skirt and squeezes my ass while an arm snakes around my waist, tugging me against a big, warm body. A mouth presses to the curve of my throat with a growl.

"That better be you, Rafe," I say.

He snorts as we check behind us to ensure no one else is following before we clasp hands and run for the coolness of the air-conditioned hotel.

A few minutes later, we burst into our room. Rafe slams the door and cups my face in my hands, kissing me deeply.

We back up one step at a time until I feel the cold edge of the dining table hit my thighs. Rafe lifts me up and sets me on the surface.

"We could do this in the shower," I say as he sucks on the curve of my neck, his hand sliding under my shirt.

"After this," he says as he leans me back, lying me flat. "This little yellow skirt has been teasing me all day."

He tugs on my panties, sliding them down my legs and tossing them away. Then he leans over me, flattening his body to mine, his hips grinding between my thighs. I feel him maneuvering his zipper, and then a moment later, the press of his wide cock at my entrance.

He wraps his hands around my wrists and pins them over my head, staring me in the eyes.

"You're amazing, Tris," he says hoarsely as he slides into me slowly. "I've always known it, but these past few weeks have shown me just how amazing you are."

I can barely speak over the knot in my throat and the intense look in his eyes. "You really thought that?" I ask.

"Absolutely."

"You're pretty amazing, too," I breathe as he thrusts into me, and my back arches off the table. Maybe a part of me always knew it as well. His gaze meets mine, and it's the first time I feel a discernible change in myself. A slow shedding of the past, revealing another version of the person I've been wanting to be for five years.

We're still moving together, heat swirling in my stomach. He leans down to kiss me, his tongue driving into my mouth as his hips pump and he keeps my hands pinned in place. Our breaths tangle and my core clenches around him as he drives into me.

This is pure, raw heat, and when I look into his eyes, I feel… safe.

I'm not sure if I'm there yet. If I'm completely ready to let go, but Rafe is the first person who makes me feel like it's possible.

Chapter Twenty-Six

The final days of the retreat pass in a blur of conference rooms, droning talks, and the occasional group activity. It's clear after three weeks of late nights, too much partying, and many hours spent sitting in hard plastic chairs that everyone is feeling the effects, leaving us all with the deflated vitality of worn-out pillows.

It's the day before they announce the training program recipients and the exec team has retreated to their whisky-soaked corner to make their decision while Lan, Gabrielle, Rafe, and I toast on the deck of a small luxury yacht as it bobs through the waves. Lan and Gabrielle still needed to collect on the prize they won on trivia night, and if you'd told me then that Rafe would be my plus-one for this excursion, I would never have believed it.

I decided to bow out of the interview with EnviroTech, tentatively hopeful after my golf game with Diane. I've given five years of my life to this place, and if I'm chosen, then I think I owe it to myself to see this through. Maybe it's a signal that things could change for me at WMC.

"Thanks for inviting me," Rafe says after we've finished our scrumptious dinner. We've spent the day on the water, cruising past islands, swimming in lagoons, and eating to our hearts' content.

"Well, we really like Tris, and you two appear to be attached at the hip these days. It wouldn't have been right to leave you behind," Gabrielle says, and everyone laughs.

"I really like her too," Rafe says, and my entire body goes warm at the inflection in his voice. Lan and Gabrielle do that thing where they tilt their heads and make swoony eyes. I scoop out an ice cube from my glass of water and toss it at Gabrielle. She screeches when it lands on her lap.

"Stop that," I say, trying to redirect the conversation. "What about you? You seem to have formed a happy little club of two."

Lan and Gabrielle exchange a shy glance that brings a smile to my face.

"We're planning to try it long distance and see how things go," Lan says as they fold their hands together, fingers entwined on the table. "We'll do weekends in either New York, depending on the training program, Seattle, or Florida and maybe meet somewhere in the middle sometimes."

"Ooh, how about Chicago?" I suggest, and they both beam at me.

"We were hoping you'd say that," Gabrielle says. I let out a squeal of delight and clap my hands. "Assuming you're there of course."

"It would be amazing if we were all in New York, too. We can go on double dates!" Lan exclaims. "But you still have to tell us, where does one go for dessert in Chicago?"

Rafe rattles off some of his favorite restaurants, insisting they must try Chicago's most famous strawberry cheesecake. As they quiz him about the best places for cupcakes and pastries and milk-shakes, I begin spiraling. We have one day left. After that, we'll get on a plane and return home.

Until this moment, I hadn't really considered what would happen if I ended up in New York for a year. Before my conversation with Diane, it had never seemed like a possibility. Rafe doesn't want to work for WMC, so would he even take the spot if he gets it like I suspect?

I hadn't given much thought to what happened after this, because I'd convinced myself this would be over once we left this place. But now, I can't help but weigh the possibilities. We could end up in different cities, and I couldn't ever have another relationship where I wouldn't see him half the time, but we could also end up in New York together, and that could mean I'd be forced to finally reconcile with my fears.

Panic swells in my gut as I consider every side.

"Wanna go for a swim?" Lan asks. "The captain said this is a nice calm spot."

Everyone is looking at me. I've gone off into my head again. I give it a shake.

"I'm good, thanks."

I need some space. I'm going to throw up. I shove my chair back and head for the front of the boat, where I climb onto the bow's sun pad, tilting my face to the warm sunlight filtering from the sky.

I'm there for a few minutes when I feel someone behind me.

"Mind if I join you?" Rafe asks, holding two small plates topped with coconut tarts. I peer over at him. His feet are bare, and the cuffs of his navy pants are rolled up. His thin white shirt is buttoned only partway, and the wind buffets against it, exposing the taut planes of his bronzed stomach and chest. He's so beautiful it makes my throat hurt.

"Since you brought dessert, sure," I say, trying to fluff up my tone, but it comes out wrong. He sits cross-legged with his knee pressed against my thigh and sets the plates down.

"You okay?" he asks. "You got up very suddenly back there."

I'm not sure I can tell him the entire truth, so I settle for a partial one. "I'm a little brokenhearted about having to leave all this and go back home. It's so lovely here." I sweep out a hand to encompass the pristine blue water and the emerald-green mountains casting afternoon shadows over the boat.

"It's been pretty spectacular," Rafe agrees, but he's not looking at the scenery. He's studying me so intensely that I swallow a thick knot in my throat.

He presses a kiss to my shoulder. "I meant what I said back there, Tris. I really like you."

Dark brown eyes reflect in a golden ray of sunlight as Rafe watches me, expectant and...hopeful? I'm not sure what to do with the tight ball of emotion expanding in my chest.

"I really like you too," I say, and the words feel like a confession and a vow.

A smile crosses Rafe's face. This is a brand-new one. This one is brighter and more beautiful than all the rest combined. I study that smile, committing it to my growing library, worried this will be the one and only time I see it.

"Why are you looking at me like that?"

"Do you know that until last week, you'd never smiled at me before?"

Rafe blinks. "What? That's not true. I smiled at you all the time."

I shake my head. "No. You smirked. You gave me a smug or sarcastic twist of your lips, but it was never a true smile. You smiled at everyone else, so I knew it was possible, but I thought it was because you hated me. It wasn't until that night on the balcony when you gave me the macarons that you smiled at me for real, and now you do it all the time, and it's...hard to get used to." His brow furrows and I quickly add, "I mean that in a good way. Your smile is the best, Rafe."

He lets out a soft chuckle as he drops his head forward.

"What's so funny?"

He takes my hand, pressing it to his chest as he tucks a strand of hair behind my ear. "Tris. That wasn't because I hated you but because I thought you hated me. That first day we met, we got off on such a wrong foot, and I guess I just got used to that being how it was between us."

"I'm sorry. It wasn't your fault." I let that hang between us. "When I bumped into you that day, I got scared. I was still broken after what happened with Leo, and you were so pretty, and I was drawn to you immediately, and...I felt this spark, so I pushed you away. I couldn't fathom the idea of losing myself to anyone ever again."

He studies me as the breeze tosses his hair and his expression becomes unreadable. Does he hate me *now*?

"I felt it, too," he says softly as the band around my heart releases. "It was like time stopped for a moment, but then you looked at me like I'd just kicked your puppy, and I didn't know what to do. You were the first person I'd ever met who I couldn't seem to win over."

I huff out a rueful laugh. "All of this was my fault."

He shakes his head. "I pushed back, Tris. It's my fault, too. I wanted so badly to get any kind of reaction from you, but I meant what I said that you made me better, and maybe this was just the path we had to take." His smile turns sly. "And do you have any idea how beautiful you are when you're angry? Fuck, it turns me on."

"Rafe!" I say, giving him a good-natured shove. "Stop it."

He's laughing, and again, I'm struck by how much I love it. "What can I say? It's true."

I sigh. "I convinced myself you were so wrong for me because that felt safer. I realize how unfair I was being now. I'd put you in a box with the rest of the Khakis."

"Khakis?"

"You know, the bland, mediocre white dudes who make up the majority of WMC. They wear pleated khakis and couldn't find their way to a clitoris if their life depended on it."

He looks so deeply affronted by my statement that I feel the twitch of a smile.

"First off, I have heard no complaints in the department of finding your clitoris, and I have *never* worn pleated khakis in my life," he says with so much passion I burst out laughing. "Whose term is this?"

I'm laughing so hard that tears are leaking from my eyes. "Me and Molly. It's our inside joke. I'm sorry. I see now that's not who you are."

I stop laughing at the expression on his face. He's looking at me like he wants to peel me open and examine every thought in my head.

"I want to keep seeing you when we get home," Rafe says with so much sincerity that his voice cracks. "I don't want this to be over."

"What about the training program?"

"I'm not accepting it no matter what happens," he says. "If my father maneuvered a spot for me, I'm not taking it. I need to break away from WMC—I just have to figure out how without causing a world war with my parents." He kisses my fingers. "And if you move to New York, then we'd figure it out. If Lan and Gabrielle can make it work, we can too."

I let out a deep breath. "Rafe…"

"Don't answer me yet. Just think about it, okay? You're the most incredible woman I've ever known. Promise me it won't be goodbye when we get home on Sunday. That it'll be 'let's wait and see.' Please give me a chance to prove I'm worth it."

"Rafe," I whisper.

Of course he's worth it. I don't have to think about it to know he's worth all of it.

I think about everything we've been through the past three weeks. Of all the things I never knew about Rafe. He's been there for me in ways I never realized, supporting me and standing in my corner. He makes me feel beautiful and alive and like I can conquer the world.

Despite how much I put him through, he wants to be with me.

And…I want to be with him, too.

Something inside of me breaks. A hard shell I've been wearing for the past five years begins to crack. Striations run along my skin, exposing bits of raw flesh.

And it's at that moment I realize I'm in love with Rafe Gallagher. Maybe a part of me was from the very start.

He's watching me so carefully that I see the flecks of yellow and orange in his eyes. I study the tiny scar on his chin and the curl that rests on his forehead. All those pieces of him I've fallen in love with, too.

He touches my cheek, fingers caressing my skin, and I fall even more.

"Say something, Tris." His voice is soft and deep. It reaches straight through to my toes, and I fall again. I kept trying so hard to protect my heart, but Rafe gathered it up, piece by piece, holding them safely in his hands.

Finally, I think I'm ready to let go.

"Rafe, I—"

BZZBZZZZBZZZ.

That *sound*. That stupid fucking sound. It rips a gaping hole through my chest, reminding me why I was keeping my heart locked safely in a jar.

"Fuck," Rafe breathes, pulling his phone from his pocket.

My laugh is part disbelief, part hysteria. "Is there even service out here? How does she keep doing that?"

He tosses me an apologetic look as the boat hits a wave, and we're rocked to the side. The phone slips from his hand and he accidentally answers it.

"Rafe?" Hannah's voice comes out tinny and hollow. "Rafe? Where are you? All I hear is white noise. Rafe? What's going on?"

We both stare at the phone lying on the deck in horrified silence until, finally, he lifts his gaze to mine. I can't tell what I see there. Regret? Remorse? Guilt? Whatever he just said, his (ex?) girlfriend is still calling him multiple times a day, and I deserve better than the third wheel. I can't do that to myself again.

I gather up the skirt of my dress around my legs and stand. "I'll let you get that," I say over the sound of Hannah calling for Rafe in the background.

Rafe reaches for my wrist, wrapping his fingers around it. "No, Tris. Don't go. I'll tell her I can't talk."

"No, you should talk to her," I say, fusing a chill into my voice. I yank my hand from his grip and shake my head, turning away so he can't see my tears as they fall while I slide back into my armor.

Chapter Twenty-Seven

The buzz of Rafe's phone haunts my dreams. Incessant, like the drone of killer bees sent to annihilate me from this plane. No...wait. That's my phone vibrating on my nightstand. Blinking sleep from my eyes, I lean over to see a number I don't recognize.

"Hello," I mumble.

"Is this Trishara Malik?" a crisp voice asks.

"Yes, who is this?" I sit up, pushing my hair out of my face with my blanket tucked under my armpits. Rafe stirs next to me, his eyes peeling open slowly.

"This is Diane Hart's assistant. She's reserved a table at the Diamond Lounge for lunch at 12:30 p.m. Dress is business casual. Don't be late."

The phone disconnects abruptly, and I'm left staring at the darkened screen.

"Who was that?" Rafe asks.

"Diane's assistant. She wants to have lunch."

Rafe sits up. "Why?"

I shake my head. "I'm not sure. During our golf game, she mentioned that she was impressed with my scores on some of the testing. She hinted at putting in a good word for me about the training program."

Rafe's smile is tentative. He reaches a hand out but pulls it back. "That's fantastic. You didn't say anything."

"I wasn't sure if she really meant it, I guess."

After walking away from Rafe on the boat last night, I kept my distance, and he gave me space. I didn't want to talk about it, and I still don't. Lan and Gabrielle could tell something was up, but they didn't say anything either, and we finished the night in awkward silence.

I fell in love with Rafe, but there are too many strings here. It hurts too much to look this in the eye, so I'm practicing avoidance as I rebuild my shield and work on falling back out. When we returned to the suite, we said very little, lying next to each other until we drifted into sleep.

It's only 9 a.m. Tonight, the ceremony to announce the winners of the training program will take place. Five lives will change—at least five—because I already know I'll never be the same again.

"I'm going to go for a workout before lunch," I say. "Do you want to come?" I want him to say no. It'll be easier to start snipping the threads if he isn't around.

Maybe he senses it too, because he replies, "I'd love to, but I should catch up on some email this morning."

"Okay." I slip out of bed and head for the bathroom.

When I return from the gym, Rafe isn't in the suite. He texted to say he was meeting up with his dad. Knowing how much stress David causes him worries me, but I put it out of my mind as I prepare for my meeting with Diane.

Rafe isn't my responsibility. Rafe isn't mine.

Diane's assistant said business casual, so I opt for a black pencil skirt and an emerald-green sleeveless blouse with a bunny bow at the neck. I slip on my black heels and use my flatiron to straighten my hair into a smooth sheen.

A short while later, my shoes click along the marble floor as I approach the Diamond Lounge. Located just off the lobby, it's a swanky space filled with plush club chairs that serves small plates and locally made spirits.

When I arrive, I give the hostess my name.

"You're the first," she says, grabbing three menus and leading me through the restaurant. As I take my seat, she sets one menu in front of me and the other two on top of the plates on either side.

"Can I get you a drink?"

"Water is fine," I say before she nods and walks away.

I texted Molly earlier about my lunch and the disaster with Rafe last night. I haven't heard back yet. It's Saturday, so she's probably out for the day, heading to yoga and the farmers' market. I can't wait to get home to dissect every moment of the past three weeks with her and then sob until I wring all these emotions out and bury them away.

A few minutes later, the hostess leads Paul Stuart, VP of southeastern operations, through the restaurant. I stand as Paul arrives and holds out a hand.

He's in his late fifties with greying brown hair and pale grey-blue eyes.

"Miss Malik," he says. "Paul Stuart. Diane asked me to join you today."

"It's nice to meet you," I say, returning to my seat as Paul sits in the chair on my left. He's fairly trim and clearly an athlete. As he sits, his eyes dip to my chest, pause at my mouth, and then lift to my eyes. He gives me an oily smile, the corners of his eyes crinkling, and my fingers itch for a panic button.

"Diane has told me you've impressed her," he says, getting straight to the point. "She wanted me to meet you, as she's secured the other votes needed to award you a spot in the training program, but I wasn't convinced yet." His tone indicates how beneath him he feels this is. How much of a favor he thinks he's doing me. I bite my tongue to prevent a career-limiting retort from flying from my mouth. I hate this guy already.

I swallow, apprehension building in my stomach. Five of six of them chose me? And now I have to jump over fences like a pony to impress this asshole?

"I see," I say, trying to keep my voice even. "And what would convince you?"

His mouth stretches into a smile that shows off a set of straight white teeth. He's spent a lot of time outside, and his skin is stamped with the sun worshipper's leathery glow. I imagine he must own a sailboat he pays more attention to than his wife. His eyes dip again, and my skin crawls off my bones.

"Where's Diane?" I ask, checking my phone, hoping her assistant has sent me a message.

"She said she'd be a few minutes late," he says. "Don't worry."

He plants his elbows on the table.

"Tell me, Miss Malik, why should I put in my vote for you?"

I press my mouth together. I hate that I have to do this. I hate that he's making me perform. Maybe it was foolish to hope this place could ever be different.

"Well, I graduated from college at the top of my class, and I've been with WMC for almost five years. Through that time, I've excelled in every project I've been tasked with. I meet and exceed my KPIs and have developed and implemented several new processes to improve efficiency...."

As I talk, I can tell he's not even listening. He sits back in his chair, pose casual, hands wrapped around the armrests. I finish my groveling through gritted teeth, checking the entrance, and hoping Diane appears.

When I've gone silent, he sits up and leans forward again.

"That's very nice, Miss Malik, but I did have something else in mind."

This time, his perusal is slow and deliberate. His eyes linger on my mouth, then my breasts, before he looks up again, and the sick realization of what he's suggesting dawns. This fucking pervert.

"I beg your pardon?" I ask, hoping I've misread this.

"Come now, Miss Malik," he says, tutting. "You've just finished telling me what a bright young woman you are."

And that's when his hand lands on my knee under the table. I freeze, my entire body seizing as it inches higher.

"I've seen you spending time with Gallagher's boy," he says. "I know you're not shy."

He winks, and my blood rushes so loud that white noise howls in my ears. My neck grows hot, and my stomach cramps as Paul gives me a coy smile. I think of Leo sharing that image of me and the endless parade of disgusting photos and texts that followed. Those men all thought I owed them something too.

Paul's hand moves higher, sliding up my thigh, and that's when I return to my body.

"Get your hands off me," I yell because what do I have left to lose? I stand up, the chair skidding away with a screech. "You vile, despicable pig. You want me to sleep with you for the sake of the training program?"

His slimy smile oozes into raw fury. Everyone heard me, their heads spinning all the way around like funhouse clowns.

"Keep your voice down," he hisses.

"I will not keep my voice down, you prick." With a thwap, I toss my napkin on the table and look up to see Diane watching us with her bright red lips parted to form a circle.

"This asshole just propositioned me," I say, pointing to him. "Is that why you invited him here?"

Her mouth opens wider and then closes. I think about what she told me in the golf cart, and I want to believe in her so badly right now. I need her to prove she didn't mean what she said and that she won't stand by and allow this to go unchallenged.

I need to see the woman I *thought* I was idolizing all these years.

Diane and Paul exchange a loaded glance.

For a moment, I witness the barest prick of worry in Paul's expression. A slight furrow of the brows, as if he's afraid someone will finally call him on his bullshit after a lifetime of getting away with everything.

But this is the lesson I learn right then: For some people, the status quo will always be their way.

Diane straightens, tugging on the hem of her jacket as she arranges her face into an ice sculpture. And then she, too, reaches into my chest, rips out my heart, and punts it across the room.

"Don't overreact, Trishara. I'm sure you're misunderstanding what Paul said." She fixes her gaze on the slimeball cowering in his chair. "Right, Paul?"

And just like that, Paul recovers. He sits up and squares his shoulders.

No one is challenging his rightful place at the top of the food chain today, and things will be as they've always been. He nods as they seal their pact in blood.

Though her expression remains stoic, I'm sure I watch a tiny piece of Diane Hart float away.

"I still would very much like to nominate you for the training program, Trishara," she adds. "Please have a seat so we can discuss it over lunch as planned."

Our gazes meet. This is a standoff. We are the bull and his red cloth waving in the wind. We are cowboys dueling at dawn, fingers twitching on our triggers.

As she watches me, I understand this is my moment to decide. Who will I be? What will my future look like? Do I do as I'm told, shut up, sit down, pretend like nothing happened? Do I secure a spot in the training program and try to salvage this career? Or is it truly a lost cause?

No. I can't do this. I can't pretend I'm okay with any of this. Diane isn't the woman I thought, and I can't have my soul whittled away any further.

"I don't think so," I say. "You can take the training program and fuck off. Both of you."

I grab my purse and stomp out of the restaurant with the weight of an entire roomful of eyes on me. As soon as I reach the door, I turn the corner and burst into tears. I sag against a wall as my heart races and my limbs shake.

I sniffle and dig into my purse for a tissue but come up empty-handed. I spot a bathroom on the far side of the lobby and scurry over, grabbing a paper towel from the dispenser. I study my tear-streaked face in the mirror. My eyes are bloodshot, and my mascara is smudged.

I can't believe that just happened. I've just lost everything for good.

I've had some pretty bad days, but this is one of the worst of my life.

A toilet flushes and a woman steps out of the stall, pulling a large suitcase behind her. She's tall and blond and gorgeous and *worst* is relative, I suppose, because the woman is Hannah.

I can't tear my eyes away as she turns on the faucet to wash her hands. After a few seconds, she notices me.

"Can I help you?" she asks.

Of course she doesn't recognize me. I've always assumed I was beneath her notice.

"Sorry. I'm Trishara. I work with your…my…I work with Rafe."

She frowns as she shakes off her hands and studies me. "Oh, right. You're the one he had to share a room with."

I'm not sure why, but I'm surprised she knows this. Something about that feels okay. He told her he was staying with me. He's a single man. There was no reason for him to hide it.

But what's going on?

"What are you doing here?" I ask.

Hannah grins and faces the mirror before digging out a tube of lip gloss from her purse. "I'm surprising Rafe."

"But you broke up." It comes out harsher than I intend.

She offers me a sharp look, annoyance flashing over her expression. "He's just behaving like a typical man. Get too close, and you know how they get scared. They're like kittens." She spreads gloss on her lips and then screws on the cap. "He just needed some time, but things will be fine with us. I got David's assistant to change his plane ticket and booked a room for us for a few nights. It'll be like a makeup honeymoon."

My stomach heaves, climbing up my throat.

I'm going to *kill* Belinda. Slowly. Excruciatingly.

Hannah hops on her toes and beams as my heart falls through my feet.

Things will be fine with them? What happened when she called last night? Did they reconcile?

No wonder Rafe pulled away this morning.

"Have you been crying?" she asks, squinting.

Hannah's presence sucked up all of my tears, but my face is still flushed, and my makeup is still a mess.

I turn to the mirror and try to clean up. "Yeah, some asshole made a pass at me."

Hannah tuts and places a hand on a slender hip. "Hmm. I guess you're pretty for an Indian girl."

I go entirely still. I'm so stunned by the awful infinite layers of that comment that I can't even speak as she checks her hair in the mirror.

"So, can you take me to him?"

I blink. Is she talking to me? "Excuse me?"

"You're sharing a room, right? They wouldn't tell me the number at the front desk, and he's not answering his phone, so I was deciding what to do when, luckily, you walked in here."

I stare at her. I'm numb. Broken from the inside and out.

"Hello?" she asks when I don't reply.

I nod. I have no fight in me left.

"Follow me," I say, my voice wooden and foreign to my own ears.

I wonder if he's returned to the suite. I check my texts, but there's nothing from him. Of course there isn't. He's getting back together with his girlfriend. The ball of anxiety in my stomach swells, making it hard to breathe.

Hannah trots behind me as we approach the elevator.

Tears build behind my eyes again, and I suck in deep breaths, trying to calm my racing pulse. I'm this close to fainting. My knees are liquid, and my limbs have turned to lead. I'm moving in slow motion like I'm drowning in Jell-O.

As we ascend the hotel in awkward silence, I can't feel my hands or feet.

Hannah looks over at me with a small, uncertain smile because I'm being weird. She has no idea what happened with Rafe, but I knew all along that this was a possibility.

Finally, we arrive at the suite. I swipe my key card and swing open the door.

Hannah pushes past me, dragging her suitcase into the room. "Rafe!" she screams as he stands up from the couch. Slowly. So slowly, like he's also sinking through the same bowl of Jell-O.

"Hannah," he says as she runs towards him and throws her arms around his neck.

I watch him. He's stiff and wide-eyed. What's going through his head?

"Surprise!" Hannah yells. "I caught the first flight out of Chicago this morning! I booked us a room so we can spend a few extra days together. I already cleared it with your dad."

Rafe looks at her with his brow furrowed, and I can't watch this. I duck into the bedroom and drag my overpriced designer suitcases out of the closet. Three weeks ago, I'd been so proud of how I'd squeezed these out of David Gallagher, but now they're tainted.

When I get home, I'll burn them.

After flipping them on the bed, I pile my clothes inside, not bothering to fold anything. I want out of here as fast as possible. I shut out the voices in the other room, knowing I'll collapse in a heap of tears if I hear them reconciling. All I can picture is Rafe coming into the bedroom to pack up his things and then leaving with Hannah.

I head to the bathroom and swipe all my toiletries into my bag. I grind my palm into my eye socket as a sharp, stabbing pain shoots across my scalp. I pop twice the normal dose of painkillers, hoping to dull the pressure swelling in my skull. I look like a raccoon, which is appropriate because I feel like I'm digging through garbage.

Once I've packed everything up, I drag my suitcases out of the room and stop. Rafe and Hannah are on the balcony. The door is open, but I can't hear what they're saying over the ocean's roar. She's sitting on *my* lounge chair with her hands in her lap while Rafe leans on the railing, his arms crossed over his chest.

I stare at him. His expression is grim, his eyes dark with shadows. The wind tosses his hair in a way that makes my heart ache. He's so beautiful, and he was almost mine.

Then he looks over and catches sight of me. His arms drop, and he says something to Hannah before he enters the suite and rushes over.

"Tris, where are you going?"

I swing open the door and drag my luggage into the hall.

"Back to Chicago," I say. "I'm done here."

"I'll be right back," he yells behind him, closing the door so we're standing in the hall. He wraps his hands around my shoulders. "You can't leave."

"Why not?"

"It's our last night here, and you didn't answer me yesterday..." He trails off. "Have you been crying?" He looks so concerned that it takes all my willpower not to crumple against him and seek the safety of his arms.

"Answer you? Rafe, your fucking girlfriend is here."

"She's not my girlfriend, Tris. How many times do I have to tell you?" His frustration is evident for the briefest moment, but then his shoulders drop. "And I keep telling you that, and yet, she keeps calling, and now she's *here*, and of course you have no reason to believe me."

He moves closer, squeezing the space between us. "Tris, you have to believe me now. I didn't invite her here. I'm as shocked as you are. I have no desire to get back together with her. I planned to tell her the whole ugly truth when I got home. We've been friends for years, and I owed her that in person. I want to be with you. I meant everything I said last night. Please don't leave until we can talk about this."

I suck in a deep breath.

I want so badly to trust him, but one person I believed in has already let me down today.

"You asked me not to say goodbye," I say. "But I need to leave right now, and you need to deal with this. If it's over, then be honest and tell her. Don't contact me again until you do. I won't be caught in the middle of this anymore."

He touches my face, his hand cupping my cheek. "I'm so sorry I've put you through this. You've been so patient and understanding. If the roles had been reversed, I would have lost my mind."

His thumb runs along my bottom lip, and I lean into his touch, worried it's the last time I'll ever feel it again. He tips towards me, touching his forehead to mine. I inhale a deep breath, committing his scent to memory.

"I *am* going to deal with this, Tris. I promise."

I don't nod. I don't speak. I just...break.

Rafe pulls away and stares at me. He wraps his arm around my waist as he lifts up my chin. "Tris, I—" He shakes his head. "Never mind. I'll tell you later. When we're back together." Then he kisses me with such tenderness that my heart turns to dust.

He releases me from his hold, and I step away, needing to put some distance between us. I press the button and face the door. It hurts too much to look at him.

When the elevator arrives, I step inside and turn around because I need to see him one more time. Rafe stands with his hands gripping the walls on either side, staring at me while the doors slide closed.

I'm terrified of leaving right now.

Terrified of what will happen when Rafe returns to that suite.

His face disappears, and I tell myself that if I lose him now, he was never mine anyway.

But that only makes me feel worse.

Chapter Twenty-Eight

To: All Staff List <allstafflist@wmc_purcell.com>
From: Trishara Malik <tmalik@wmc_purcell.com>
Subject: Burn it all down

Dear WMC Purcell,

Please consider this letter my formal resignation from the position of senior engineer at WMC, effective immediately. I do so without regret, nor am I leaving to pursue other opportunities. I do not wish you the best in the future, and I don't want to keep in touch to discuss potential opportunities. Lose my number.

You've stolen five years of my life, and I am done.

Today, Paul Stuart propositioned me and said that if I had sex with him, he'd concede to voting for me for the executive training program. Diane Hart witnessed this scene and told me to look the other way. If this is how your executive team behaves, you don't deserve me or any of the loyal, hardworking employees at this company.

For five years, I have endured sexist comments and behavior, as well as countless racial microaggressions. I've continued to look the other way, and that was a mistake.

Today, I will be silent no more.

To that end, I'm attaching the detailed notes I've kept over the years, outlining every incident I've witnessed and experienced in the presence of Rory McGregor. Some of these involve me directly, and some involve others in the Chicago office. I've redacted names and details, but I'm sure those individuals recognize who they are, and I hope they'll come forward if they feel safe doing so.

I'm also attaching every screenshot I've collected from his social media feed of problematic statements, memes, and article shares. I hope WMC will make use of this information. If not, at least everyone will know and understand who he is.

Let this be a reminder to my peers: always keep those receipts.

Finally, WMC needs to start prioritizing diversity within the organization, but it shouldn't be a checkmark to make yourself look good. David Gallagher awarded me this opportunity only when it suited his goals. I hope that someday, WMC engages in a legitimate process to start dismantling the oppressive systems in which it operates, but I'm done waiting around for that to happen.

There is so much more I could say about my time at WMC, but I'll leave it here for now. I hope this is sufficient to make everyone see what this company stands for.

I trust I'll receive a very generous severance.

Good luck and good riddance … and also, fuck off.

Sincerely,
Miss Trishara Malik

Chapter Twenty-Nine

I lie on the couch holding a giant gin and tonic with my head in Molly's lap while she smooths back my hair. It's been three days since I left Hawaii, and I've heard nothing from Rafe. Not a text. Not a phone call. Not an email.

"He's still in Hawaii with Hannah," I repeat for the millionth time. I told him not to contact me until he'd sorted out his mess, so what other reason could there be?

Molly makes a noncommittal sound. She isn't sure what to say anymore, either.

After the first day, she told me not to worry. He needed time to finish with her and then make his way home. But after three days, it's getting harder and harder to believe that he's ever coming back to me.

"Or he saw the email, and he hates me."

This, too, I've said a million times.

Molly snorts. "He doesn't hate you."

"I dive-bombed his dad *and* his cousin."

"Both of whom he hates. And they deserved it."

I hope she's right. But where is he?

My phone buzzes, and I sit up so fast that my head spins. I've maybe had more than one or two of these drinks. I snatch it from the coffee table, hoping it's Rafe, but it's an email from my bank.

I open it to discover a significant sum has been deposited into my account from WMC. I show Molly, and she cackles.

"Blackmail looks good on you, Tris."

I *am* getting rather good at it. I allow myself a small, triumphant smile.

"It's all anyone can talk about," she tells me again, because this is now my favorite story. She told me everyone lost their minds when they showed up to work and read my email. It's the most reckless thing I've ever done, but I regret nothing. It had to be this way, and I hope it makes a difference.

"When's your interview with EnviroTech?" Molly asks.

"Day after tomorrow," I reply. "But what's the point?"

For a brief moment, I wondered if I'd made myself completely unemployable yet again.

But after I staked my career through the heart for the second time, I responded to the email from EnviroTech explaining that I'd reconsidered the interview. I knew it was a long shot, but they replied immediately, saying they'd be delighted to include me in the selection process.

"Trishara Malik, you will not throw your life away over a man."

I rub my eyes and then take a long sip of my gin.

"I know," I moan. "But Molly, I—"

The words stick in my throat, so I drink more, draining the glass.

"I know," she says softly, rubbing my back. I don't know what I would have done without her this week. "Who would've guessed you'd come home with a broken heart over Rafe Gallagher?"

"You're the one who was rooting for us."

"I know—but I thought we'd be celebrating."

A fresh wave of tears tracks down my cheeks. I wipe them away with the sleeve of the oversized sweatshirt that I've been wearing for the past three days. I grimace at the stained cuff. I'm disgusting.

"Maybe you should take a shower and change?" Molly gently suggests. "You can wallow again after. I'll order sushi, and we can watch a movie."

I lift my armpit to sniff myself. "As long as it's something with a lot of blood and killing and people dying."

"You hate movies like that."

"I know, but today, I love them."

She squeezes my hand, and I head for the bathroom.

Once I'm clean, I put on some comfy clothes and tie up my hair in a messy bun. I still look pale and wrung out, but at least I don't smell anymore.

As I enter the living room, a knock sounds at the door.

I walk over, not even bothering to check through the peephole. I'd welcome a serial killer right now. Maybe he'll do me a favor and cut out my heart. I have no use for it anymore.

But when I open the door, every drop of air is expelled from my lungs.

Rafe stands on the other side, leaning on the doorframe with his arms crossed and a large reusable grocery bag dangling from his elbow. He smiles and holds up his phone.

"As I mentioned, we're doing something different today," he says to the screen, stepping into my apartment. "This place belongs to someone who means a lot to me. I want to introduce you all to Tris."

He flips the phone around, and I drop to the floor, covering my head with my arms.

"What the hell, Rafe? I look like a corpse right now," I hiss. I've morphed into a mole person who's emerged squinty and pale in the bright light of day.

He grins and flips the phone back to himself. "Okay, she's being shy right now, but we'll work on that." He looks around and whistles. "Nice apartment. I'm going to need your kitchen."

His gaze sweeps over me as he kicks off his shoes and then drops the bag on my island.

Dumbfounded, I watch as he unpacks various plastic containers and kitchen instruments. He pulls out a black stand with an arm like a bendy snake and sets his phone in the holder. The smile he turns on the camera is so bright it's like a thousand-watt bulb has exploded in my apartment.

Then he smiles at me, and my heart crumbles in my chest.

"Rafe, what are you—"

He holds up a finger and then pops open one of the plastic containers he's pulled from his bag.

"I know this isn't normally how I do it," he tells the camera. "But I've prepared some stuff ahead of time." He pulls out several rounds of golden pastry crust, each disc about an inch deep and a hand span across.

"The pastry is already made, but you all know the recipe for this one."

I pull out my phone and navigate to the live feed, watching as hundreds of comments pop up, tripping over each other.

Dude, you're hot.
What's going on? Who is this?
Marry me.

Take off your shirt, Rafe.

Where do I find the recipe?

I cover my mouth in amusement as he continues to narrate his actions.

He holds up a second container and lifts the lid. "Here we have my signature lemon curd, swirled with a little rose water. It's butter and sugar and eggs and flavoring. I'll share the recipe when I post the photo."

He flashes me another smile, and I'm too stunned to react.

Molly drifts over and plants her elbows on the counter as we exchange a bewildered look.

"Where are your pots?" Rafe asks, and I point to the drawer near the stove.

He retrieves a small saucepan and fills it with sugar from a bag he's brought along. He turns on the stove and returns to the island, picking up a piping bag and holding it up.

"Won't you say hi?" he asks me. "I'd love for everyone to meet you."

He looks so hopeful that I find myself nodding.

With a grin, he flips over the camera so it's pointed at me. His followers get a fleeting glimpse of me trying to pointlessly smooth down my hair before I wave to the camera.

"Say hi, Tris."

"Hi, Tris," I whisper, and Rafe grins before he turns the camera to himself. He peers at the screen for a moment.

"Read the comments," he says, and I pick up my phone to see what his personal peanut gallery has decided.

Omg, she's so pretty.

Rafe, who is that?

Do you looooove her?

Aw, this is so romantic.

Marry ME, not her.

I'm blown away by how connected they all are to this radiant version of Rafe.

Die BITCH.

Um, okay then.

I scroll through the barrage of comments while Molly reads over my shoulder.

Rafe is back at the stove, mixing sugar in the pot. He tests the temperature with a thermometer as he continues explaining his process to the camera.

Watching him like this, so confident, so in love with what he's doing, standing *in my kitchen*, is a massive turn-on. I don't know what's going on, but everything in me softens.

"The sugar needs to be at 338 degrees Fahrenheit for this," Rafe says as he continues to stir. He keeps up a stream of chatter until he's satisfied. He sets up a baking sheet and covers it with a heat-resistant liner before pouring out the sugar in a series of complicated swirls and patterns.

"We'll let these cool for a minute," he says. Then he retrieves a piping bag of lemon curd and dollops some into each of the crusts. "Normally, I'd suggest also cooling these for a bit in the fridge, but we don't have time for that today. You don't mind slightly room-temperature tarts, do you, Tris?"

He looks up at me through thick, dark lashes, and I shake my head. "No," I say, finding my voice. "Of course not."

He returns to what he's doing, swapping out the lemon for a piping bag full of meringue. He adds a swoosh to the top of each tart and then pulls out a tiny kitchen blowtorch.

Molly and I both *ooh* in amazement as he lights it and browns the meringue. He returns to the pan of cooling sugar decorations and then stops, placing both palms flat on the counter.

"Will you come over here?" he asks. "Please?"

I'm too confused to resist. I'm as pliable as a wet cotton ball. Molly gives me a nudge, and I make my way around the island.

Rafe watches me like I'm holding the moon in my hands.

He tops one of the tarts with a sugar-spun heart and then holds it up for me.

"For you," he says. I study his face, searching for some explanation for all of this.

Sure, this is a nice gesture, but it's been three days since I've heard from him.

"What is all this?" I ask, finally gathering my wits. "Why are you doing this?"

He puts the tart down and takes my hands. "I told you I wanted more than a vacation fling, and I meant it. I know you need a little convincing, so here I am, baring my soul and my heart before you and a few thousand witnesses. I want everyone to know how I feel about you, and I want you to know that I'd never betray your trust, no matter what happens.

"Tris, you are the most amazing woman I've ever met. You

challenge me. You understand me in a way no one else ever has. You make me laugh, and you make me feel things I've never felt before. And even if you send me away, it will be worth it because then, at least, I'll have finally told you that I love you."

The air around us crystallizes.

"You do?"

He smiles, stepping closer, wrapping an arm around my waist. "Yes, how can you not see that by now?"

I open my mouth to reply and then remember the camera as I glance at the screen.

"Oop," Rafe says, turning to address his fans. "Thank you for coming along, everyone. I think it's time to shut this down. I'll let you know how it goes. Wish me luck."

The last few comments scroll up the screen.

Good luck, Rafe!
We're rooting for you!
Don't forget the lemon recipe!
Who is that?
Take off your shirt!

When we're alone, I still have no idea what to say.

"Why are you crying?" Rafe asks, wiping away a tear with his thumb.

"It's been three days," I say. "It's been three days. I thought you'd stayed there with Hannah. I thought you hated me for that email I sent. Why didn't you text or call?"

"You told me not to," he says with a frown.

"I know," I say with a sob. "But when have you ever listened to me?"

He grins, wiping another tear from my cheek. "I'm sorry. I wanted everything dealt with before I came to see you. The slate had to be clean. You deserved that. I'm so sorry for everything I put you through. I should have been more honest with both Hannah and myself months ago. When I left Chicago, it didn't occur to me that I'd hurt you instead by not doing so. Never in my wildest dreams did I think we'd end up where we did.

"Tris, it's always been you. You said I never smiled, but that was because it was easier to keep you at a distance when it seemed like you wanted nothing to do with me. I moved on when it was clear you weren't interested, but a few months ago, I wondered if maybe there was still a chance. I *knew* you had to have felt that spark the day we met.

"Then we ended up on the retreat together, and there was the thing with the room, and it felt like fate was telling me it was finally time."

I've been rendered speechless as he continues.

"As for your email—Tris, I'm so fucking proud of you. That took so much courage. That place has never ever deserved you."

I exhale a sharp breath. "I trashed your dad in front of the entire company."

The corner of his mouth lifts with a smile. "He'll get over it. He can be a dick, but he's also surprisingly open to admitting when he's been wrong. Honestly, I think he kind of respected the way you stood up to him."

"And Rory? Won't family gatherings be super awkward if I'm there?"

At that, Rafe's expression hardens. "Rory has already been told that if he comes within a hundred feet of you ever again, I won't be held responsible for my actions."

I sniff, my tears still falling. "You're such a caveman."

"You love it."

I huff out a laugh, covering my mouth. "What about your mom? Isn't she upset about Hannah?"

He takes my hand and laces his fingers through mine. "I told my mom I met someone who makes me happier than anyone has ever made me. Someone who's become everything to me."

"And?" I whisper.

"And she can't wait to meet you."

That right there is the moment I splinter. All of my fears and worries dissipate, turning into the past. Rafe has proven that I can trust him. He makes me feel safe, and...he is *so* worth it.

But Rafe isn't done with his revelations yet.

He pauses and takes a deep breath as if the next part costs a piece of himself.

"And I quit WMC. I told my father I was done, and this was never what I wanted. At first, I'd planned to do it for you, but you beat me to it."

"I didn't want you to quit for me," I say.

"I know. In the end, I did it for me. Your courage gave me the guts to do so."

My nose is running from crying, and I wipe it with the sleeve of my sweater.

If he still loves me like this, then I don't think he's going anywhere.

"I'm so proud of you, too," I whisper.

He pulls me in closer, a finger trailing my jaw. "Tris, I love you. I want to be with you if you'll have me."

He looks so hopeful and beautiful. His eyes are pools of melted amber reflecting in sunlight. He is everything I wanted and didn't know was right in front of me all along.

"I love you too," I say. "Of course I'll have you."

He wraps me in his arms and kisses me hard. Then, he touches his forehead to mine. "I promise never to let you down again."

It's then I remember. "Uh, Molly." She's watching us with an enormous smile, her elbows on the counter and face cradled in her hands. "I think you can go now."

"Right," she says, blinking. "Of course."

She gathers up her purse and scurries over, wrapping us both in a hug. "Welcome to the family, Rafe. It was a long time coming."

"I look forward to getting to know you better, Molly."

They exchange a grin, and my heart explodes in a hailstorm of candy hearts.

When we're alone, Rafe steps back and carefully rolls up the cuffs of his black dress shirt. "I'm sorry I can't take you to my lair right now. The drive is way too long, and I need you right this very minute. Unless you want to eat the tarts first?"

He gives me that evil smirk I fell in love with, and it turns my knees to jelly.

"What about your followers? Won't they wonder how I responded?"

"Really? You don't mind?"

"Take a picture and tell them," I say.

I'm warming to the idea of mild social media fame. He draws me next to him, wrapping an arm around my shoulders. With his lips pressed to my temple, he snaps a photo of us while I grin at the screen. This smile is a permanent fixture now, like the address above the front door.

He taps on the screen and posts the picture, showing it to me.

The caption reads: **She loves me too.**

His notifications are already blowing up with like after like as the comments roll in.

> Congrats!
> I knew she would!
> Does this mean we're over?
> Why doesn't he ever take off his shirt?

"It's time for me to ravish you," he says, bending down and slinging me over his shoulder. I scream in delight as he heads down the hall.

"Where's your bed?" he asks, opening doors before finding my room. He drops me onto the field of my fluffy duvet and then crawls over me.

"Naked. Now," he says, pulling at my leggings and shirt.

"You're so verbose as a villain," I tease. He snarls as he catches the waistband of my underwear in his teeth.

"Don't make me tie you up," he replies, tugging the fabric down my thighs.

"I might be okay with that."

He scans the room with a distraught expression as if wishing he had brought some rope.

"Next time," he promises as he drops his weight on me. "When I take you to my actual lair."

Then we're kissing as we continue undressing until we're both bare.

"I've missed this so much. I was so scared I'd never get to do this again," he says, his mouth trailing over every inch of my skin.

"I was too," I say. "I thought—"

He cuts me off with a bruising kiss. "Never. I told you I'd come for you. I'm sorry it took so long, but it was all so messy. I promise I'll always come for you. Believe me when I say that."

"I do," I say, gasping as we become teeth and nails and searching mouths and frantic fingers digging into muscle and flesh until our breath is ragged and our bodies are flushed.

When we're finished, Rafe retrieves the lemon tarts from the kitchen, and we share all three in bed. (By share, I mean I eat two and a half.)

"This might be better than sex," I say, licking my fork and then the entire plate with the flat of my tongue.

He narrows his eyes. "I'm not sure if I should be flattered or insulted by that."

I laugh and then crawl over and straddle his hips. He cups the back of my neck, and we kiss again.

"Either way, I'm keeping you both forever," I say softly when I pull away.

Then he smiles, and this one is cumulative.

It's smile upon smile, exponentially growing and expanding with every single one he ever held back.

It's years of smiles that we both owe one another.

And it's then I know that *this* one—this smile is only and forever just for me.

Epilogue

One year later

It's a blustery winter day when I step into The Dessert Wolf and inhale the scent of sugar and icing. Large windows look out on Michigan Avenue, and crisp rows of shiny white tiles cover the floor and walls. A large glass case runs almost the length of the room, filled with rows and rows of colorful pastries and cakes, each one a work of art.

Rafe stands behind the counter, bent over a sketchbook, wearing a white coat with an asymmetrical line of buttons and a monogrammed *W* on the breast. After leaving WMC, he used some of the money from his social media accounts to rent and renovate this space to finally follow his dream. It was a ton of work, but he was determined, and now the linen-covered tables are full every day, and a line forms outside the door every morning.

I watch him for a moment, his pencil flying. He needs a haircut, and a dark curl has fallen over his forehead, just the way I love it. He looks up, and when he sees me, he smiles. It still catches me off guard in the best possible way every single time.

I meet him at the end of the counter, where I lean over for a kiss.

"How did it go?" he asks.

"We got the job," I reply. "Stole it right out from under WMC."

His smile grows even wider. "That's fantastic. I'm so proud of you."

"And"—I step back and tug on the lapels of my suit jacket—"you're looking at the brand-new VP of operations at EnviroTech."

"Yes!" Rafe says, pumping his fist. He lifts the counter flap and comes to the other side, wrapping his arms around me and swinging me off the ground. "I knew you'd get it."

He places me back on the floor, and I tuck that errant lock of hair back.

"How did things go with your dad?" I ask.

David had planned to visit Rafe's shop for the first time today. Their relationship has been strained since Rafe left WMC, but they're attempting to reconcile while Rafe's mom acts as a go-between. She told him how much she regretted being the reason he refused to stand up to David and is doing everything to make it up to him.

Rafe nods, his mouth crooking into a tentative smile. "Good. He seemed a little impressed, I think. We're having lunch next week. We have a long way to go, but it's a start."

"That's wonderful. I'm so happy to hear that." He kisses me again and I stare up at him, feeling more content than I have any right to be.

I peer over his shoulder at the sketchbook lying on the counter. "Do I finally get to see?"

He turns to grab it and holds it against his chest.

"You sure you're ready?"

"Yes! I can't believe you made me wait this long."

Finally, he flips it around to reveal an elaborate multitiered cake. Our wedding cake. Rafe proposed three months ago during a weekend getaway. Of course I said yes, and I've been floating on cloud nine ever since. My parents adore him and are so proud of all my new accomplishments. They come to the shop every week to load up on goodies and insist on paying no matter how often Rafe tells them it isn't necessary. I called them on my way here to share the news about my promotion, and they've invited us for a celebratory dinner tomorrow night.

I reach out to trace his drawing as my eyes well with tears.

"It's incredible," I whisper, and Rafe beams at me.

"I'm also trying out two new flavors for it," he adds. He puts down the book and picks up two small plates topped with thick slices of cake. "Tell me what you think."

He leads me towards the small private table he always keeps reserved in the corner. After putting the cake down, he hands me a fork.

At that moment, a squeal draws our attention to the doorway as Lan and Gabrielle enter the shop.

"You made it!" I scream, running over to wrap them in a hug. It's been a year since we've seen each other, not since the night on the yacht, though we've been in contact almost daily.

Lan was awarded one of the spots in the training program, and she's just accepted a job as the new director of sales here in Chicago. Gabrielle is moving to be with her in a few weeks, and I'm so excited we'll all be living in the same city.

"How was the flight?" I ask as we settle down at the table.

"It was fine," Gabrielle says. "I have news."

"What?" I ask as I hand her a fork.

"WMC has been making big strides in the areas of diversity and inclusion, and they've asked me to head the task force on BIPOC and queer recruitment and workplace policy."

I blink, clearing another blur of tears from my eyes. "That's amazing. I'm so happy for you and for everyone at WMC."

"None of it would have happened without you," Gabrielle says.

"I'm so glad they're trying." I truly mean it. My only hope for WMC is that they've learned from their mistakes. Rory was fired because of my email, and Rafe has heard through the family grapevine that he's been having trouble finding a new job and had to move back in with his parents. I could pretend to feel bad about that, but I really don't.

We also haven't seen Hannah since Hawaii, but Rafe's mom says she's met someone new and has moved on.

"So, tell us everything about the wedding plans," Lan says.

I begin rattling off details to their adoring looks.

"Of course, Rafe is making the cake."

His hands are braced on the back of my chair, and he nods at the two slices of cake on the table. "Tell me which one you like better. One is key lime and basil, and the other is mango chocolate."

Lan and Gabrielle immediately dig in.

"I'm not sure how to choose," Gabrielle says. "Can't you have both?"

"These are incredible," Lan agrees, going in for another bite.

"Are they here yet?" Molly shouts as she bursts into the shop a minute later.

She's heard everything about Lan and Gabrielle, and I couldn't wait for them all to meet. The three of them crash into a gigantic hug, squealing like they're old friends.

Rafe bends down and speaks in my ear. "Come help me get the rest of the stuff I prepared for you."

"I'll be right back," I say as Molly slides into her seat, talking a thousand miles a minute.

I follow Rafe to the counter, where he opens a fridge, pulls out several decadent desserts along with a bottle of Champagne, and sets them on the counter.

"Have I ever told you how good you look in this fancy white coat?" I ask, adjusting his collar and leaning against him.

"Only every single day." I grin and press my mouth to his. "Have I ever told you how hot you look in these skirts?"

"You might have mentioned it."

Molly, Lan, and Gabrielle are chattering so loud that everyone looks their way.

"I'm sorry if we clear out your shop," I say, but he's watching them with a serene expression. He shakes his head and gives me his crooked smile.

"I think people like them," he muses.

"I like them too. It's going to be so great having them here."

"Are you happy?" he asks.

"Of course I'm happy. I've never been happier. I have a job I love, your shop is a hit, and I get to marry my favorite villain in a few months. Are you happy, Rafe?"

He smiles and touches his forehead to mine. "Of course I am, Tris." Then he winks. "With you, I'm always a million out of ten."

Want more Rafe?

Read the "wedding night" from his POV
when you sign up for my newsletter at
nishajtuli.com.

Acknowledgments

Here we are at the end of yet another book. Thank you to everyone who came over from my fantasy books and took a chance on a new kind of story from me. And thank you to every new reader who found me through *Not Safe for Work*.

I'm forever grateful to every person who picks up one of my books.

Thank you to my editor, Madeleine Colavita, for picking up *NSFW* and embracing Tris and Rafe's story. You and I have been through so much together in the past year, and I'm forever grateful I found a home with you.

To Dana Cuadrado and Estelle Hallick—you are the best publicity team a girl could ask for. Thank you for all the incredible opportunities I've had over the past year.

To the entire team at Forever, thank you for all your support, my career, and my stories.

To my agent, Lauren, thank you for being my partner in everything.

Thank you to jessdraws for this stunning cover. They both look exactly how I pictured them in my head.

Thank you to my writing friends who keep me grounded and

are the best hype team ever: Shaylin, Daniela, Elayna, Keshe, Neely, Melissa, Emily, and Kate.

And finally, to my family—my husband, Matt, and my kids, who are always the greatest light in my life.